Lynx/Atilla Duet
A Dixie Reapers Bad Boys Romance
Harley Wylde

Lynx/Atilla Duet
A Dixie Reapers Bad Boys Romance
Harley Wylde

ISBN: 978-160521875-5

Publisher:
Changeling Press LLC
315 N. Centre St.
Martinsburg, WV 25404
ChangelingPress.com

Printed in the U.S.A.

Editor: Crystal Esau
Cover Artist: Bryan Keller

The individual stories in this anthology have been previously released in E-Book format.

Table of Contents

Lynx (Savage Raptors MC 1)
A Dixie Reapers Bad Boy Romance
Harley Wylde

Meredith -- I screwed up. Big time. My dad and his club asked me to leave. I know it wasn't supposed to be forever, but how can I return until I feel I've made something of myself? I thought I was on the right path, going from hot mess to mature adult. Then I did something stupid. Now I don't know what to do. Lynx has been amazing, and as much as I want to throw myself into his arms, I refuse to make the same mistakes over and over. This time, I need to figure it out on my own.

Lynx -- When I heard she was coming to our club, I thought she'd be a spoiled brat. Instead, I not only see the chip on her shoulder, but the wounded look in her eyes. Somehow, I ended up being the one man she runs from. The more I get to know her, the more I want from her. Meredith is very different from what I'd imagined. When she's in trouble and needs help, I'm only too happy to step in. Only one way I know to fix everything -- make her mine!

Prologue

Meredith

The words *I've fucked up* played in my mind on repeat these days. Hell, they'd been repeating for a long while now. Ever since my adopted father decided I'd caused too much trouble. In hindsight, I'd been a bitch and a half. I didn't know why I'd acted so spoiled, or like I had every right to a man who didn't even want me. To say I felt embarrassed was an understatement. But getting kicked out was the worst part of all.

No, actually the absolute worst part was getting Hot Shot involved, and undermining Badger. I'd nearly torn my dad's club apart, all because I was jealous and wanted Doolittle for myself. I'd been acting like a child. The moment Doolittle said he didn't think of me that way, I should have backed off. It had taken him losing the woman he loved to make me see reason.

Everyone thought I'd been acting out because of my dad's health issues. While it had been a hard blow, it hadn't been the reason I'd chased after Doolittle. I'd had a crush on him since the first time we met. Sadly, I hadn't been able to let go, even when I'd known I should have. No one realized I obsessed over the man. They'd thought it was cute, the way I chased after him. I had a problem... several. I needed to figure out how to handle everything and live a normal life. Or as normal as it got when your dad was part of a motorcycle club.

As for Dad... He'd never be completely well, but thanks to diet, exercise, and some medication, he wouldn't be kicking the bucket anytime soon. Or so I'd been told. I'd met with Dad once, unbeknownst to everyone at the Devil's Fury. He'd taken a "ride" and just happened to end up near New Orleans around the time I was leaving and heading to Texas. I'd bounced from club to club while I figured my shit out. Or attempted to.

Right now, I was on my way to Oklahoma to stay with the Savage Raptors. Even though I was due there tomorrow morning, I'd decided to pull off the road and rest for a bit. Or more accurately, I wanted to have a few drinks. I might not be twenty-one yet, but I had my ways of getting what I wanted -- they were called breasts. I had a rather spectacular pair, and I'd learned men went a little stupid when I put the girls on display.

I leaned on the hood of the guy's Camaro, making sure I nearly spilled out of my tank top. Flashing him a smile, I batted my eyes. I nearly had him ready to do anything I wanted. I'd been flirting for the last five minutes, and I could see him wavering.

If my family saw me right now, they'd be horrified. I may have called Minnie a whore, but I was the one acting the part. Some days I felt like I was coming apart at the seams.

I was lost. Drowning. My dad didn't need to see me like this. It would only add to his stress and wouldn't be good for his health. Everyone back home probably thought I was being a bitch by staying away for so long. I'd already extended my trip twice. I couldn't bring myself to tell anyone about my struggles.

Which was why I kept doing stupid shit like this. I didn't know anything about this guy. He could be a serial killer. So, why was I doing this?

Desperation. I didn't know how else to numb myself, or feel like I was in control of -- anything. The control I'd gain from this was only an illusion. I knew it well enough, and yet, here I was.

"You know what would make this conversation even better?" I asked, digging the hole even deeper. Would I ever find my way out?

"What?"

"A motel." I winked. "But we might get awfully thirsty. Want to grab some beer and come to my room? I'm right across the street."

He leered at me, his gaze glued to my breasts. "Yeah. I can do that. What's the room number?"

"109." My heart hammered against my ribs. This was stupid and dangerous. I couldn't keep tempting fate like this.

"You're not going to try and steal the beer and run, are you?" he asked.

"Nope. I'm hoping we'll get to drink them together... and do other things."

"All right." He licked his lips. "I'll be right there."

I stood up and sauntered away, making sure to put some extra sway in my hips. Thank goodness I wasn't a virgin, or I'd have never attempted this. I'd been saving myself for Doolittle. Then I'd been so pissed and heartbroken, I'd jumped the first guy who came along. Since then I'd figured out my body was an excellent way to control the men around me. At least, the ones who didn't know my dad or the Devil's Fury.

Sex and alcohol also made things better for a brief moment. I'd read enough self-help books to know I was struggling to exert control... in all the wrong ways.

If the Savage Raptors were like the other two clubs I'd visited, then they wouldn't let me drink until I turned twenty-one. They also wouldn't touch me. With my luck, they'd keep an eye on me to the point of suffocation, especially since Outlaw was friends with them and also knew a cop in Bryson Corners.

It didn't take long for the guy to show up. He knocked and I opened the door, letting him in. I'd regret this tomorrow. I always did. And yet I welcomed him with a smile... this nameless man I'd forget soon enough.

Just like the others...

Chapter One

Lynx

The girl was a hot mess, and yet I couldn't look away. She'd been here for several weeks already and didn't seem like she planned to move on anytime soon. My club treated her like a princess, for the most part. I wasn't sure they were handling the situation the right way, though. What she needed was a firm hand and some instruction. Instead, she was running wild and heading down a path of destruction. No one here realized what she did at night. No one except me.

Why? Because I'd followed her ass more than once. The second I'd realized she was going to hook up with strangers, putting herself at risk, I'd stepped in. She didn't realize it, and I didn't plan to tell her. Every time her targets got up to take a piss, or she wandered off for a moment, I'd slip in and say a few words. Just enough to send the fuckers running.

I didn't know the entire story behind her visit to our club. Something about causing trouble for one of the Devil's Fury brothers and his woman. Whatever was going on with Meredith seemed to be more involved. Not that anyone asked my opinion. The girl wasn't crying for help -- she was screaming it. I didn't understand why no one could see what was right in front of them.

Even now, she sat at a table outside the clubhouse, sipping on a soda and scrolling through some app on her phone. To others, she'd look bored. I saw the tension in her hands, and the jittery way she bounced her leg. I'd be willing to bet money she was looking for a random hookup. Those were things I saw even while checking out her car.

The front tire on her car kept getting lower, no

matter how many times she'd filled it with air. Which was why I was now checking it for a nail, or anything else that might cause a leak. At least, anything visible. Something told me she'd have to take it in to a shop, and I knew I couldn't fucking trust her around a bunch of mechanics. She'd be screwing one in the bathroom on his break if someone didn't keep an eye on her.

The Meredith the Devil's Fury spoke of previously didn't seem anything like this girl, and yeah, I considered her a girl most days. I knew chronologically she was a full-grown woman, but the way she kept acting out made me want to turn her over my knee and spank her ass like a wayward child. All those curves certainly didn't belong to one, though. Nope. And no matter how hard I'd tried not to notice the shape of her ass, or her large tits, I'd failed miserably. Some nights, they were all I could think about.

She's too fucking young for you.

It wasn't the first time I'd reminded myself of that fact. She'd tried to pass herself off as older, until the Pres asked to see her license. He'd immediately told every last member, officer, and Prospect not to give her a drop of alcohol because she was underage. The Devil's Fury wouldn't have sent her out on her own like this if she wasn't considered a legal adult. Which told me she was somewhere between eighteen and twenty. Since I was in my thirties, it felt like too big of a gap most days. Of course, I knew plenty of guys who'd fallen for younger women. Hell, the entire Devil's Fury had so far, out of those who'd claimed someone.

"Merry, you're going to have to run this to the shop. I think maybe your valve stem has a leak, or it's something I can't easily see." I wiped my hands off with a rag, but the black smears remained on my skin.

She looked up, her brow furrowing. "What did you call me?"

"Merry. Got a problem with it?"

Her cheeks flushed and she slowly shook her head. She stared at me for a moment before standing and shoving her phone into her back pocket. When she got closer, I could smell the citrus scent of her shampoo, and I damn near reached for her. Instead, I took a step back and watched her get into her car. The way she peeled away from the clubhouse and shot through the gates told me she was on her way to cause trouble.

"You going after her?" Spade asked.

I glanced at the VP. The fact he asked me meant he'd been watching, and knew I'd been keeping an eye on Meredith. Did he know why, though?

"Maybe."

He shook his head, a slight smile on his lips. "That one is going to give you a run for your money. She's not as docile as people think."

I snorted. "Who the fuck thinks of her as docile?"

"Most of the club. They only see the good parts of her." He shoved his hands into his pockets. "You're not the only one who followed her a few times. I know what you've been up to, even if she hasn't realized it. Just make sure she doesn't take a bite out of you when she figures it out."

I waved off his concern. "What she needs is a good spanking. No one is doing her any favors by coddling her. You'd think everyone would have figured it out by now. The way she acted with Doolittle should have been a big-ass warning. Instead, they asked her to leave for a while. Not one damn person tried to understand her."

"And you do?" he asked.

"Maybe. Girl is hurting. I don't know what all is going through her mind, and I won't unless she talks to me. Right now, I'm going to make sure she doesn't screw half the mechanics at the shop."

I pulled my keys from my pocket and got on my bike, then headed in the same direction as Meredith. I hadn't recommended a shop for her vehicle, and we had quite a few around town. Bryson Corners was slowly growing, and with it, more and more businesses were popping up. I drove through the streets, checking out each place, until I spotted her car in the lot of Ollie's Oil & More.

Great. She picked the one place that tended to do shoddy work. I had a feeling it had more to do with the guys who worked here than anything else. They were pretty boys who didn't know shit about cars. Not that the women around town cared. It gave them a reason to come drool over the mechanics. She must have heard about the place on one of her trips into town, or had run across one of the mechanics somewhere.

I parked and went inside, spotting Meredith immediately. She'd leaned onto the counter, her shirt tugged down low, and had a big smile plastered on her face as she shamelessly flirted with the asshole behind the counter.

"We'll get your tire patched up in no time," the guy said.

I walked up behind her, reaching over the counter to snatch the keys from the man, and placed my other hand on Meredith's hip. "Won't be necessary."

"Hey!" She tried turning to face me, but I held her in place. "That's my car, and I wanted to bring it here."

"No, you wanted to come in and flash your tits at them. Mission accomplished. Now get your ass into your car and follow me. If these dickheads work on it, it will cost three times as much to fix all the shit they fuck up."

The man's jaw tightened, until his gaze landed on my cut. I watched as he paled and backed up a step, holding up his hands. "Sorry, man. Didn't realize she was Raptors property."

He turned tail and ran, leaving me with a pissed-off Meredith. I leaned in, pressing against her and putting my lips near her ear. "You are two seconds from getting a spanking. Unless you want me to turn your ass red, get in the fucking car and do exactly as I said. Understood?"

I heard her suck in a breath. Felt her tremble. She audibly swallowed and nodded.

"Good girl," I murmured. I put the keys in her hand and made sure she followed me out of the shop. I waited until she was in the car, buckled, and had the engine on before I got on my bike and led her to a respectable shop another mile down the road. I waited until she parked beside me, then helped her from the vehicle and led her inside.

Mack waved when he saw me and I stopped at the counter, waiting for him to finish his call. The moment he hung up, he smiled and held out a hand. I gave it a firm shake.

"Good to see you, Lynx. What can I do for you today?" Mack asked.

"Meredith has a tire that's leaking air. I couldn't see a nail or anything, so I'm not sure where the problem is. Think you can patch it?"

He took the keys and nodded. "I'll get it looked over and let you know what we find. Only the tire?"

I hesitated. She'd been on the road quite a bit since leaving the Devil's Fury. "No. Go ahead and check everything."

Meredith opened her mouth to protest, but I gave her hand a warning squeeze. Something told me she was worried about the cost. I knew she'd been working odd jobs since she'd left home, trying to pay for her own expenses as much as possible. This time, she would have to accept help. I wasn't about to let her ride around in a car that might not be safe.

"Send the bill to me," I said.

"You waiting for the car?" Mack asked.

"No. I'll take her back on my bike and bring her around whenever it's ready. She's not going anywhere today, so keep it overnight if you need to."

I could feel the anger rolling off Meredith and fought not to smile. Yeah, she'd be fun to handle when we left this place. On the upside, if she didn't have wheels, she couldn't come into town.

We got outside and I handed her my helmet. I fitted the chin strap so it wouldn't be loose on her, then got onto the bike. Having been raised around bikers, she swung her leg over the back and settled in against me like a pro. She placed her hands on my waist and I tugged them around to my abdomen.

"We'll grab a bite before we head back," I said. "Hold on tight."

What she needed was some therapy, and the best kind I knew was the open road. I exited the parking lot and headed for the opposite end of town. Once we went through the final light inside the Bryson Corners town limits, I sped up, hitting the two-lane highway at about ten miles over the speed limit. The wind in my hair felt amazing, and as the miles passed, Meredith calmed more and more. Soon, she cuddled against my back, and for the first time since she pulled up to the compound, she didn't seem quite so anxious or scared. I might not be able to see her, other than in my sideview mirror, but I felt the way she'd relaxed into me.

I drove about two towns over before pulling to a stop at a Taco Bueno. I held out my hand so she could get off the bike, then took the helmet from her, hanging it from my handlebar. She seemed hesitant when I reached for her, but finally placed her hand in mine. I led her inside and we ordered before finding a seat.

"Why are you doing all this?" she asked. "Nickname. Fixing my car. Buying me lunch. It's not like we're dating."

"Let me ask you something. Everyone believes you were acting out because you needed time to grow up. Were they right, or is something else going on?"

She tensed and stared intently at the table. "What do you mean?"

"Merry, I've been keeping an eye on you. To everyone at the Savage Raptors, you're just a lost little girl who needs a hand figuring out how to grow up. Well, mostly everyone. There are two people you haven't fooled."

"Who?" she asked.

Ah, so I was right. Did she realize she just confirmed it? Probably not. "Me and the VP. You aren't alone. If you want to talk, I'll listen. Need to ride more? Fine. You can get on the back of my bike anytime you want."

She smiled faintly. "Not sure the women at the clubhouse would like that very much. They watch you, even when you don't realize it."

"The club whores?" I asked. She nodded. "You're royalty, and they're easy pussy. Not sure why you'd let them decide whether or not you ride with me. Put those bitches under your feet, show them their place."

She paled a little. "That didn't go so well last time."

"That's because you fucked up. Minnie wasn't a whore. She was Doolittle's woman. You coveted someone who wasn't yours. This is different."

"I don't think it's a good idea for me to get involved with anyone," she said softly. "I obsessed over Doolittle. Hounded him night and day. It wasn't healthy, and I know that, but... I'm scared it will happen again."

It was the most she'd opened up to anyone, as far as I knew. At least we were getting somewhere. So she'd obsessed over Doolittle, which he'd hated since he wasn't into her in a romantic way. Understandable. The right kind of guy wouldn't be bothered by her behavior. For the most part. Even if Doolittle had wanted her in return, he didn't seem tough enough to give Meredith exactly what she needed. He was too soft. The guy who tamed Merry needed to have a firm hand. *Like me.*

"Let me ask you something. Had you dated much, or ever?" I asked.

"No," she admitted.

"So your first main crush was Doolittle, right?" She nodded in agreement. "Then I think it was a combination of your age and the fact you'd never been interested in someone before. Among other things."

I didn't know her entire story, but what I'd heard and pieced together told me she'd likely been abused in some way. She probably had some mental trauma she needed to work through. If not that, then she had an obsessive personality. Until she figured it out herself, she couldn't very well expect someone to be tolerant of her behavior. Unless that person went in with eyes wide open.

"Other things." She sighed. "You mean the fact I'm completely batshit crazy?"

"Darlin', that's one thing you aren't. Have you met my sister, Ridley? Now, she's batshit crazy, at least if someone threatens her family or her club. Better yet. Jordan, with the Devil's Boneyard."

She smiled faintly. "Yeah. I like both of them. They're strong... not like me."

I reached out and grasped her chin, forcing her to hold my gaze. "You're not a weak woman, Merry. Don't let me ever hear you say that shit again. Understood? You might be feeling lost. You're still young, and I'm sure you've been through a lot. I don't know why you're on such a destructive path, but I don't like it."

"You know." She paused. "Wait. Are you the reason all those men ran off?"

"Yep, and if you keep trying to hook up with strangers, I'll keep getting in the way. You're not allowed to risk yourself. Not on my watch. Do you have any idea how dangerous it is for you to keep doing this shit?"

"It's fine. I take precautions."

"Really? So you get tested regularly for any sexually transmitted diseases? You make sure the man you're letting into your panties isn't going to rape you, sell you, or drug you?"

She didn't respond and I had my answer. No, she didn't do any of those things. First things first, we were going to get her tested. Even though I'd been stopping her behavior since she'd been here, it didn't mean the other clubs had any fucking clue what she'd been up to. How many random men had she fucked since leaving the Devil's Fury? I wasn't sure I wanted to know.

"Why do you do it?" I asked. "Give me a reason if you want me to back off."

"It makes everything stop. For a little while."

All my fears had just come true. Someone had hurt her. Badly. And I didn't think it was Doolittle's rejection. She was using sex with strangers as a way to stop whatever pain she was feeling, and any other unhealthy thoughts running through her mind. It needed to stop.

"When we leave here, I'm going to take you to a clinic. You're going to get tested, since I don't think you've been anywhere near as safe as you think, and then we'll head home. You're coming to my place because we need to talk."

"Is that an order?" she asked.

"Yep. Got a problem with it?"

She slowly shook her head. It was subtle, but I noticed her shoulders relaxed a little, and the tension drained from her. So, she did well with being told what to do, especially if it was in her best interest. Had she been waiting all this time for someone to give a shit and step in?

Whatever was going on, I hoped I could pull her from the darkness. Either that, or join her. As long as I stood by her side, she could hide all she wanted. I'd keep the monsters at bay.

Chapter Two

Meredith

Riding with Lynx had been the first time in forever that I'd felt at peace. Even sex and alcohol weren't substitutes for the open road. Everyone knew Grizzly had adopted me, and I'd spent my teen years at the Devil's Fury. But not many knew my biological father had also been a member of their club. Twister. He'd done some fucked-up shit, and in the end, it had cost him his life.

Either way, it seemed I was a biker's daughter through and through. Nothing could soothe me like being on a motorcycle. I only wished the ride could have lasted longer. On the plus side, Lynx had been called away to deal with something for the club, so the talk he'd wanted to have was put on hold. Indefinitely, I hoped.

He'd called me Merry. No one had done that except Doolittle. It brought up memories I'd sooner forget. When Doolittle said it, I'd felt special, but more in the way a little sister would look up to her brother. With Lynx... I noticed in an entirely different way. He said Merry, and everything inside me lit up in a completely adult way.

I roamed the room I'd been given when I came here. Since the Savage Raptors didn't have families yet, there hadn't been an appropriate place for me to stay. I'd refused to throw someone out of their home, so instead, I'd taken a room at the clubhouse. Of course, once the parties started, their Pres said I had to stay in said room until someone gave me the all clear in the morning.

It wasn't ideal. In fact, if my dad found out, he'd lose his shit. In his mind, I was still his little girl. I might have fucked up, but it didn't mean he loved me any less. The fact I'd been sleeping around would never cross his mind. If he'd thought I'd been acting out before, it was nothing compared to how things had been since I left home.

Out of everyone I'd been around since then, Lynx was the only one who seemed to really see me. Well, he'd said the VP here had a clue about what I'd been up to as well. I hadn't been as sneaky as I'd thought. I didn't understand why Lynx cared. Wasn't I just a messed-up kid to him? Was he trying to save me as a favor to my dad?

He'd somehow known I needed to take a ride today. He'd given me what I needed before I'd even realized it myself. Of course, things would change if he knew what I'd discovered today. Going to the clinic to get tested hadn't been a bad idea. I hadn't exactly been discerning when it came to the men I'd let fuck me, or the ones I'd blown. And I hadn't been as careful as I'd thought. Maybe it was a good thing he'd gotten called out on a job. He'd wanted to take me to his house to talk. I wasn't sure that would be the best thing for me right now.

I pressed a hand to my belly.

You're pregnant. The nurse had kept rambling about prenatal vitamins, seeing my regular physician, and so on. While she'd talked, the first two words had stuck in my head on repeat. A baby. What the hell was I supposed to do with a kid? I'd fucked my life up so bad and still didn't know how I was going to get out of this mess. Now I'd made things even worse.

I paced across the small space again. Back and forth. At this rate, I'd wear out the carpet. Then again, that might not be a bad thing. It probably should be replaced. I was too scared to ask what might be ground

into the fibers. Semen. Blood. Pussy juice. I cringed just
thinking about it, which was why I never walked
around without my shoes on in here.

Someone knocked on the door and I answered.
The moment I yanked it open, a club whore nearly fell
into my room.

"What the hell?" She straightened and sneered at
me. "Why are you in here?"

"Um, it's my room. Why the hell are *you* here?"

"Fucking bitch! I heard there was some woman
staying here. Told the others they had to be wrong. No
way the Savage Raptors would keep someone other
than one of us. How the hell did you bribe your way
into staying here?"

I shoved her back into the hall, following and
shutting the door behind me. Clearly, she hadn't been
around much if she had just heard about me. I didn't
recognize her, but they all looked the same to me. I
knew the men saw them as faceless, nameless holes for
their dicks. It wasn't a secret I was staying here. Of
course, I hadn't been around the club whores either. I'd
stayed in my room, just like I'd been told to do. Or I'd
left before the whores arrived and slipped back to my
room unnoticed.

"First off, call me a bitch again and see what
happens. Second, why I'm here is none of your
business."

She shrieked and took a swing at me. I blocked
her blow and slammed my fist into her face. Lynx had
been right. I was a biker's daughter, and this whore
needed to learn her place. She was beneath me. And
that's exactly where I'd put her.

She fell into the wall, and I hit her again before
kicking her legs out from under her. The moment she
landed on the floor, I put my foot on her stomach and

leaned down.

"You're under a few misconceptions. One, you aren't better than me. In fact, you should be thankful to be in my fucking presence. Two, you mean nothing to these men. You're an object. Something to fuck, like a sex doll, and nothing else. And three, you have no power here. At all. The next time you knock on a door and decide to confront someone, you better make damn sure you're the alpha bitch. I can promise, you aren't. Not in this instance."

I straightened and took my foot off her. When I looked up, I saw Lynx leaning against the wall, a smirk on his lips. He gave me a wink before coming closer.

"She started it," I said, pointing to the whore on the ground.

"Didn't ask. Don't care. You did what you had to do. I'm damn proud of you."

"Are you shitting me?" The whore struggled to stand. "She hit me! You're just going to let her do that?"

I hit her again. "Yeah, he is because I'm a motherfucking princess and you're a piece of trash."

She wailed and collapsed to the floor. I rolled my eyes, and wondered if she thought that would really work. Then I realized the three of us had company. The Pres and VP were both watching.

"Everything good here?" Spade asked.

"Who is she?" the whore asked.

"She's Devil's Fury royalty," Atilla said. "Her daddy is their retired president, so show her some fucking respect. In fact, get the hell out of my clubhouse."

The woman got to her feet and stumbled as she walked away. Spade and Atilla looked from me to Lynx and back again. Spade smiled while Atilla shook his head and left.

"I'm glad to see you figuring out who you are," Spade said. "I'm going to assume Lynx had something to do with it."

I nodded. "Yeah. He said something today, and when that woman came at me, I just... I don't know."

"This isn't a good place for you, Meredith, but you already know that. We didn't have an empty house for you, or an apartment. Your daddy wanted you inside the compound, so that meant we couldn't help you rent a place." Spade crossed his arms. "Since things are complicated, I can't force you to be with anyone. Here or elsewhere. But I think you need to consider some options."

Options? I hadn't really hung out with any of them... except Lynx. Was that what he meant? Or did he think I'd just pick a random Savage Raptor brother to be with for the rest of my life?

"Enough, Spade," Lynx said. "You're going to make her run."

He wasn't wrong. Not because I didn't like Lynx. The opposite. I liked him too much. In fact, I found myself watching him all the time. It was like Doolittle all over again. I was obsessing, and that was a bad thing.

"Get her out of here for now," Spade said. "Get her some food. Dessert. Something. She doesn't need to be around all this shit."

"On it, VP." Lynx reached over to take my hand and led me away from my room and through the main part of the clubhouse. I didn't stop to look around. I meekly went with him. When we got outside, he pointed to his bike. "Get on."

I did as he said, and hoped it wasn't a mistake. Not only because of the baby I'd just learned about, but because Lynx was dangerous for me. He made me want things I couldn't have. I didn't deserve a guy like him. He might be gruff. Even a little scary at times. But just the same, he had a tender side and was a very kind man. Anyone who spent even a short amount of time with him would be able to see it.

Lynx got on in front of me and started the bike up. He rolled it backward out from the line of bikes, then pulled on to the small road that went through the compound. He came to a stop in front of one of the log cabins and cut the engine.

"All this is new. Did you know?" he asked.

"How new?"

"Atilla had all this done within the past year. Originally, we had a building in the middle of town. No fence. Nothing special."

"Why the change?" I asked.

"Found out we had a traitor in our midst. While the other clubs were here, Atilla heard about the setups they had. Once the dust settled, the Pres decided he wanted something similar to the Devil's Fury compound. He saw the Reckless Kings, Dixie Reapers, and several other clubs had something similar and thought we should too."

"Everyone wanted a cabin?" I asked.

"It was simpler for the builders to put in the same house multiple times than to do different designs. They're all completely identical. Three bedrooms. Two bathrooms. The only difference is that some of us enclosed the back decks into sunrooms."

"Were you one of them?"

He nodded. "Yep. Knew I'd want a family someday. Made more sense to close it in. It seemed like something my sister would like, so I thought other women might too. What about you?"

"Sunrooms are nice," I said. "But if every house is the same, what happens if some of your brothers have larger families than others? You're going to try cramming six kids into two rooms?"

His eyes went comically wide. "Six? You want that many kids?"

The smile dropped from my face, and I put a hand to my belly before I really thought about my actions. Lynx noticed the move, and his jaw tensed. He jerked his head toward the house and I followed him inside. Silently, he pointed to the kitchen and I went to sit at the table. After he pulled a bottle of water from the fridge and placed it in front of me, he got a beer for himself and took the seat across from me.

"Seems like we need to have a discussion." He cracked open his beer and took a swallow. "That wild streak catch up to you?"

"It's not your problem, Lynx."

"The fuck it isn't." His eyes narrowed and I could have sworn I heard him grinding his teeth. "What are you going to do, Merry? I'm betting you have no clue who put that baby in your belly. Am I wrong? Do you even know what state you were in at the time? Or was it some random guy while you were on the road between clubs?"

My cheeks burned. I had a feeling it was the man I slept with right before coming to the Savage Raptors, even though I couldn't be one hundred percent certain. I didn't know why he was so upset about this. It wasn't like the baby was his, or that I expected him to take responsibility. This was my mess and I needed to figure it out on my own. I wasn't going to drag someone into my problems again, not like I'd done with Hot Shot.

"I'm right, aren't I? You have no clue who the

father is."

"What does it matter, Lynx? It's not like I'm asking you to take care of us. I'll figure it out."

"How?" He crossed his arms and leaned back in his chair. "You don't currently have a job, except for the random times the diner asks you to step in and pays you under the table for a few hours of work. I'm sure your car needs more than just the tire fixed. No place to live. Unless you plan on going home?"

I shook my head. If I'd thought my dad was disappointed in me before, I could only imagine his reaction now. It might very well cause him to have a heart attack. If that happened, no one at the Devil's Fury would ever forgive me. I'd forever be banned from the only place I'd thought of as home.

"It looks to me like you have very few options right now, Meredith."

Shit. He'd used my full name. He hadn't done that much since calling me Merry earlier. Something told me I wouldn't like what he had to say. But I probably needed to hear it anyway.

"So what do you think my options are?" I asked.

"You can get a job. Save up money and find a place to live. Remain here, or somewhere else, but you can't go home right now. Am I wrong?"

"No. I can't do this to my dad."

He nodded. "The other option is... let someone take responsibility."

"I'm not going to do that. It's not fair. I nearly ruined Hot Shot's life because I dragged him down with me. Being claimed by any of you would be a lifetime commitment. Not just to me, but to a child that isn't even yours."

He tapped his fingers on the table, studying me in silence. When he spoke, it felt like I'd been punched in the gut.

"So Grizzly doesn't love you or think of you as his daughter. Is that what you're saying? You aren't his by blood. By your reasoning, that makes you a burden. Is that how you see it? You think that's how he feels?"

No. I knew my dad loved me. It didn't matter that I wasn't his biological child. Same for my sisters. We were his, and that was that. Was Lynx saying he would feel like my dad did? Assuming he even meant he would be the one to take responsibility. Maybe he had someone else in mind, or was just tossing out possible options.

"Answer me," he said.

"No. My dad doesn't feel like I'm a burden."

"Yet you automatically assume anyone who claims you will be stuck with a woman and kid they don't even like. You must think we're all a bunch of fucking idiots who don't know what we want or need."

"That's not it!" I stood, my chair skidding backward with a loud screech. "Don't you understand? I caused trouble for my dad and his club, at the worst possible time. I nearly cost Doolittle his woman and kid. Hot Shot could have been booted from the club because he sided with me and tried to help. Now I'm pregnant by some random guy I don't even remember. I mean, there was only one on the way here. It's most likely him. Just don't ask me what he looked like, if I ever got his name, or anything else. I'm a walking disaster, Lynx! Who in their right mind would want someone like me?"

I hadn't even realized I was crying until he stood and came around the table. He wiped the tears from my cheeks and pulled me into his arms. And in that moment, I felt safe. Seen. Wanted. I cried until my throat hurt. Lynx lifted me into his arms and carried me to the living room. He settled on the couch with me on his lap, then flipped on the TV. After selecting a comedy, he just held me, running his hand over my hair. He didn't say anything. The silence between us didn't feel awkward.

How did he always know what I needed before I did? The bike ride. Our talk during lunch. Now this?

"I don't know what you've been through during your short life, Merry, and you don't have to tell me. It's clear something haunts you. It drives you to these reckless decisions, and one day it might get you killed. You need help, baby girl. Even the strongest tree can rot from the inside out if it's diseased and doesn't receive treatment. Stop trying to do it all on your own."

"Why do you want to help me?" I asked, feeling pitiful.

"Because I see the woman you're meant to be. You're fierce. Stubborn. A general pain in the ass to those around you, much like my sister tends to be. But you're also kind, gentle, and a sweetheart when you think no one is watching. I was so fucking proud when you put that whore in her place earlier, and I'm damn proud of you right now too."

"I didn't do anything except get knocked up and fall apart."

"Wrong." His hold on me tightened. "Me holding you like this might not seem like much to most people, but the fact you didn't push me away means you're letting me help. That's a big fucking step for you, Merry."

I sagged against him and closed my eyes. "What do you want?"

"I want to keep you safe. To help you grow and

become even stronger. Mostly, I want you to be mine."

"I think it's a mistake," I said. I was certain I'd only end up hurting him or causing problems for the Savage Raptors. It seemed to be my specialty.

"Let me worry about what I can or can't handle. I only need one word from you. A simple yes, and you'll no longer have to figure this shit out on your own. What do you say?"

I took a deep breath and wondered if I could condemn him to what I was certain would be a life of misery. Or was I just selfish enough to agree and suck up all the comfort he wanted to give me?

Chapter Three
Lynx

I could practically hear the gears turning as she contemplated her answer. I could be a total caveman and toss her over my shoulder, tie her to my bed, and not give her a choice in whether or not I claimed her. It would be a mistake. There were women who would accept their fate and go on to have perfectly happy lives. Not my Merry. No. If I tried that with her, I'd lose her. Even if she were here physically, she'd retreat within herself, or try to keep me at a distance. This needed to be her choice.

Would she ever tell me what drove her to be so careless with her life? Any of the men she'd hooked up with could have hurt her, even killed her. Had a specific event pushed to her this point? Or something else? I wondered if she'd ever been checked for any mental illnesses. Probably not the first thing most people considered, but I hadn't exactly led a normal life. My mother and father had tried to sell my sister Ridley into sexual slavery. There'd been times I'd seen our mother spiraling. Something she managed to hide from most people, including my big sister. When I'd gone snooping one time, I'd discovered a bunch of prescriptions in her room.

At the time, I'd been too young to understand. Then my parents were gone, and I'd been shipped off elsewhere. Ridley had her life to live, and taking care of me would have been too much for her. She'd barely been legal back then. Years later, I'd looked up some of those medications to figure out why my mother needed them. Anxiety. Borderline Personality Disorder. And painkillers. A lot of them. I'd wondered if her issues had made it easier for my father to manipulate and control her. She couldn't have been entirely rotten before meeting him. Ridley and I turned out okay, and since we had different fathers, I had to assume our mother had once been a decent person.

Meredith remained silent, and I realized her breathing had evened out. All the crying must have worn her out. I lifted her into my arms and stood, then carried her down the hall to my room. I eased her down onto the bed, removed her shoes, then covered her with a blanket. She looked like an angel when she slept. I smoothed her hair back from her face and leaned down to kiss her on the forehead.

"Rest now," I murmured. There would be time later to hear her answer. Whatever she chose, I needed to get her out of the clubhouse. While I knew my brothers wouldn't do anything to hurt her, the whores were another matter. If one started shit today, there were bound to be others who'd step up and try to intimidate her. What would happen if they caught her on a day when she was ready to self-destruct? Then there was the baby to consider.

I didn't want to betray her by saying anything. If she'd wanted the club to know, she'd have told Atilla or Spade. And yet, if I kept silent, they couldn't properly protect her. They had no idea she could lose her baby. I couldn't believe she'd thought I was a big enough asshole I'd hate a child just because they weren't of my blood. Or rather, she seemed to feel any man wouldn't accept her baby as their own. Since I knew she'd grown up with Grizzly, it couldn't have anything to do with her upbringing.

"You're one big puzzle, sweetheart. A human Rubik's Cube. Maybe one day, I'll get you figured out."

So I wouldn't wake her, I left the room and busied myself in the kitchen. I had no idea if she'd eaten dinner or not. Atilla sent me out on a short run when I'd returned with Merry earlier, and I hadn't seen her until the incident tonight at the clubhouse. Would she be hungry when she woke up?

I rummaged through my fridge and cabinets, trying to figure out what she might like, when the phone rang. I saw Outlaw's name on the screen and answered.

"Hey, man. What's up?"

"Checking in on Meredith," he said. "Her dad didn't hear from her today and he got worried, even though he's trying not to show it. Not sure he realizes several of us know about his daily talks with her."

"Why hide it?"

"Because of how she acted before she left. A lot of people feel betrayed. They believed in her, and on top of that, they didn't want to upset Grizzly, so they tried to push her and Doolittle together. Man, that was some fucked-up shit."

I hadn't heard the entire story. Only bits and pieces. Not my business, in all honesty. Yeah, it had to do with Meredith, so I wanted to ask questions, but I didn't want her to feel like I'd gone behind her back either. Right now, I needed to gain her trust. I thought I was on the right track.

"She's asleep right now."

"And how do you know that?" he asked.

"Because I carried her to my room after she fell asleep on the couch." No point telling him I'd been holding her, or how she'd fallen apart. The goal was for the Devil's Fury to worry less about Meredith. They needed to realize she was doing okay and would be fine without them -- even if it was a big, fat lie. Otherwise, she'd feel trapped. Even now, she'd probably been trying to figure out what she needed to do in order to gain their approval so she could go home.

"Anything I need to know about?" Outlaw asked. "Or your sister?"

"Nope. Just keeping an eye on her." For now. "And even if there was something going on, it would be up to her to tell you. I'm not her father or her keeper, Outlaw."

"Just don't drop any big bombs on Grizzly."

There had to be more going on than anyone was saying. Why did everyone seem so concerned about how he'd react to things? Almost as if they were walking on eggshells around the man. He wasn't their president anymore. Did he have health problems? If that was the case, I could understand why they didn't want it to be common knowledge. The man wouldn't want to seem weak in front of other clubs. Still, he had to be getting up there in years. No one could last forever.

"I don't plan to tell him anything. Whatever gets said it's between him and Meredith. I'm only here to make sure she stays safe."

Outlaw sighed. "Why do I get the feeling you're going to claim her?"

"No idea what you're talking about."

"Uh-huh. You pretty much just confirmed it. Listen, if you decide to keep Meredith as your old lady, do me a favor... bring her home for a visit soon. Grizzly misses the hell out of that girl, even if she doesn't realize it."

"Thought no one wanted her there," I said.

"Tension is still high, but she can't stay gone forever. Besides, we're all as much to blame as she is. If any of us had listened to Doolittle all along, then we could have prevented her from getting so attached."

Attached or obsessed? She didn't seem like the type to chase after a man who didn't want her, unless she'd fixated on him. She'd mentioned something about obsession before, and while I'd considered she might be too clingy for some men, I hadn't worried about it. What if it was more?

Obsession. Reckless behavior. Anger issues. Mood swings.

I had a hunch I might know what was going on with her, but since I didn't have a PhD in psychiatry, I wasn't one hundred percent certain. She needed to meet with a professional. Something told me she wouldn't volunteer for it, though. No, if I wanted someone to observe her, I'd have to be a little sneaky about it.

"I need to make a call. I'll ask Meredith to touch base with Grizzly when she wakes up." Before Outlaw could respond, I hung up and scrolled through the contacts on my phone. I'd helped a woman out about two years ago. She'd had a flat tire on the side of the road, and I'd stopped to change it. She'd given me her card, and we'd kept in touch. Nothing romantic ever happened between us, but I'd found her easy to talk to. Made sense considering her profession.

The phone rang a few times before she picked up. "You've reached Dr. Moira Stern."

"Hey, Moira. It's Lynx. Got a minute?"

She laughed softly. "Never, but for you, I'll make an exception. What's up?"

"I have someone I'd like you to meet. Off the books, if you will. If she knows who you are or what you do, I think she'll run the other way."

She hmm'd. "But you're worried."

"Yeah. Some of her behaviors could be adding up to a much larger issue. I'm not asking for an official diagnosis. I only want to know if I'm on the right track with this, and how you think it would be best to handle it. If she needs help, I want to make sure she gets it."

"Do you finally have a girlfriend, Lynx?"

"Not exactly. Although, I'd make her mine in a heartbeat."

"Even if she does suffer from one or more mental illnesses?" she asked.

"Of course. It's not something she can help. Why do the women in my life seem to think I'm an asshole?"

"There's a story there, but I don't have time to hear it right now. Soon, though. As for your woman, I'll be taking a coffee break at the café near my office tomorrow. If you just happen to run into me there, say around eleven o'clock, then I'd be delighted to meet her."

"Sounds good, Moira. And thanks."

I ended the call and hoped I could convince Meredith to go with me tomorrow. If I could help her figure out why she reacted the way she did, then maybe she could get control over herself and her life.

I went back to the cabinets and pantry, deciding on something simple. I took out some canned veggies, a package of herb and butter rice, then grabbed some pork chops from the fridge. Once I had the oven preheating, I seasoned the chops and set them aside. They were on the thicker side, so I knew they'd need an hour to cook all the way through. No sense starting the side items right away. After I got the chops into the oven, I set a timer for thirty minutes so I wouldn't make the sides too early or too late.

Settling on the couch, I flipped through channels until I found something to watch. Even with one of my favorite movies playing, I couldn't focus on anything other than Meredith. Maybe she wasn't the one obsessing. Perhaps I was.

Just what she needed. A possessive asshole biker.

Then again… it really might be exactly what she needed.

Now I just had to hope she'd agree to be mine. If not, it wouldn't matter. I couldn't force her to stay with me. She was already knocked-up, and not by me. If the baby didn't give her reason enough to be mine, then I didn't know what else to do.

I heard footsteps coming down the hall and gave her a smile as she slowly entered the room, rubbing at her eyes.

"Sleep well?" I asked. I checked my phone. She'd only been asleep about twenty minutes.

"Sorry about that." She plopped down beside me. "I guess I was more worn out than I'd realized."

"I'm not trying to rush you but let me know when you have an answer to my question. I'll have to tell the Pres, and he'll probably call Badger with the news. Make sure we aren't going to cause any issues with the Devil's Fury."

She twisted her fingers together in her lap. "I don't know why you want me. I'm such a mess, Lynx. It worries me that you might wake up one day and wonder what the hell you got yourself into. At the same time, what you're offering sounds amazing. I'm tired. So incredibly tired. Every day feels like I'm swimming upstream against a strong current, and I'm getting nowhere fast."

I put my arm around her and hugged her to me. "I know, sweetheart. Be mine. Let me take on some of your burdens. Help lighten the load. You're going to stress out to the point of either losing the baby, or collapsing. I don't much care for either scenario."

"You really want to claim the baby as yours?" she asked.

"Well, I don't think my club will believe I knocked you up when you first arrived, but I don't plan on telling them any different. As far as anyone else is concerned, the child is mine in every way." I tightened my hold on her. "There's no reason anyone needs to know otherwise. Not the officers in my club. Not your club. This can stay between you and me."

"Spade won't find it odd?" she asked.

"Maybe, but I don't think he'll say anything. He won't care. If I say the baby is mine, that will be good enough for him."

"All right. Then let's do it. I'll be yours."

I turned her to face me and gently tipped up her chin. Slowly, I lowered my lips to hers. It was our first kiss, and she immediately melted into me. Her hands clung to my shoulders, and I felt a tremor run through her body. Despite the fact she'd been sleeping around, her kisses made it clear she didn't have a lot of experience. Didn't matter to me. She was mine.

"The clinic told you today about the baby, didn't they?" I asked.

"Yeah. The STD test they ran gave results at the same time. It came back negative. The doctor asked if I wanted a more in-depth one, but since I didn't have any symptoms, I didn't think it was necessary." She held my gaze. "Unless you want me to do another one?"

I shook my head. "No, if the first time came back negative, then I think you're fine. It's been a few weeks since you were with anyone. You'd most likely have had symptoms by now. I just asked you to get it done to be on the safe side."

"Thank you. For caring. For paying attention and actually seeing me. And just for… everything."

"I still want to know more, but for now, let's just get to know each other better and find our rhythm."

She leaned into me and snuggled close. "Okay."

"And when it's just the two of us, you can call me Wilson. Unless you prefer Lynx. I'm good with either. Whatever makes you most comfortable."

"I think Lynx suits you. Wilson sounds a little too stuffy for a biker."

I smiled. Yeah, it really was. My pretentious parents had given me that name, and I'd hated it ever since I'd realized what sort of monsters they were. I was perfectly fine with her calling me Lynx. I knew my sister still called her old man Venom, even though he'd asked her repeatedly to use his real name. Personally, I thought she did it just to push his buttons.

The timer went off and I stood. "Wait here. I have dinner cooking and need to start the next part. If you don't like the movie that's playing, find something else."

"Should I go get my things?" She pulled her knees up to her chest and wrapped her arms around her legs. "Are we telling your club soon? Am I moving in right away?"

I could hear the anxiety in her voice. Crouching down, I placed my hand on her arm. "What do you want to do, Merry? Want to move in tonight?"

She nodded. I pulled out my phone and shot off a text to Atilla and Spade. *I'm claiming Meredith. And no, I didn't ask permission. Not asking for a vote.*

I showed her the screen before I hit send. Atilla answered almost immediately.

Are you asking for a beating?

I knew he'd do it if he felt it was necessary. But

in this instance, I thought he might be more bark than bite. Only one way to find out.

She's pregnant. You expect me to not claim my woman and kid?

The phone rang right after the message showed as *read*.

"What the fucking shit is this?" Atilla asked.

"Sorry, Pres. Merry's pregnant, and I need to claim her and our baby."

"Motherfucker," he muttered. "You go along, smooth sailing, not causing any issues all this time, and now you drop a fucking bomb in my lap? Fuck you, Lynx."

"If it's any consolation, I asked if this was what she wanted. She agreed to be mine. It's not like I forced her."

"Fine. Then the two of you can explain it to Grizzly. I'll send a text to the club to let them know. If your brothers get pissed they didn't get to vote, you can deal with it."

I smiled. "No problem, Pres. And thanks."

He grumbled a bit more, muttering under his breath. "I'll order a property cut for her. Tell her welcome to the family."

He hung up, and I pocketed my phone. After telling Merry the good news, I kissed her once more before I went to the kitchen to finish making dinner. I had no idea how the call to Grizzly would go, but I knew we needed to get it over with soon. Preferably tonight.

Chapter Four

Meredith

"Your sister is with the Dixie Reapers, isn't she?" I asked.

"Yeah. She's with Venom, and my two nieces are with the Devil's Fury. Farrah is with Demon, and Mariah is with Savage. But I'm sure you know that part already since that's your home. Or was." He folded his arms and leaned against the counter. "Now you're part of the Savage Raptors."

"The Reapers ink their women. Does your club do that?"

He shook his head. "Nope. Then again, you're the first old lady. I guess it all depends on you. Do you want me to ink you as *Property of Lynx*?"

Did I? I'd have a property cut. It wasn't like I needed to have a tattoo saying I belonged to Lynx. And yet, I sort of felt like I did. Need it, that is. I could take the cut off when I was at home, or any other time. A tattoo wasn't so easily removed.

"Can it be done today?" I asked.

"Probably not. I'll have to check with my guy and see. Not sure I want anyone else inking you." He tipped his head to the side and studied me for a moment. "Then again… We should plan a trip back for you to see your dad. It's been a while, right? Don't see why we couldn't take a detour through Alabama so you could meet Ridley as her new sister-in-law. Zipper could ink you."

Sister-in-law? Could he really call me that if we weren't married? Of course, I didn't know if Ridley and Venom had gotten married or not. Some of the bikers did and some didn't. Quite a few just asked the hackers to handle it. What would Lynx do?

The more I thought about it, the more I realized I didn't really care. Since he went by Lynx and not his legal name, it didn't matter what surname people used when they addressed me. I doubted anyone here even knew who Lynx really was. Unless they'd seen his driver's license. Of course, even then, I didn't think they'd dare call him anything other than Lynx.

"I haven't called my dad today," I admitted. "I've called every day. He must be worried."

"It's not too late."

"What do I say?" I asked. "Isn't he going to find it odd that we're suddenly together?"

"Doubtful." Lynx pointed to my phone, which I'd set on the table. "Call him."

I picked up the phone and selected *Dad* in my contacts. As it rang, I put the call on speaker. Now that Lynx and I were officially together, I thought he might want to hear whatever Dad had to say.

My dad answered on the fifth ring. "I got worried when you didn't call sooner."

Guilt hit me hard. "I'm sorry, Dad. I had a lot going on today, but I promise I didn't forget. Is anyone else there right now?"

"No. I have the house all to myself these days. I wish I could figure out this Face thing. Whatever it is."

I smiled. "You need an iPhone to do that. You have an Android. Remember? That's why Adalia used hers the times you've seen me on FaceTime."

He grunted. "Badger and Adalia got me a new one. Since it's with the same carrier, they transferred my number."

"All right. If you want to try FaceTime, I can hang up and call you that way. All you'll have to do is answer."

"I want to see my beautiful girl. I miss you,

Meredith."

My throat grew tight and my eyes stung. "Miss you too, Dad."

I ended the call and tried to pull myself together. Tapping the icon beside his name, I called him back using FaceTime. When he answered, he had the biggest smile on his face, and looked like he'd lost a lot of weight just in the past week.

"There's my girl," he said. He narrowed his eyes, and I realized he was checking out the room behind me. "Where are you?"

"I'm at Lynx's house. He made the best pork chops, Dad. If they're on your approved diet list, you should try them sometime. I think you'd like them."

"Why are you there? Where's Lynx?"

He came around the table and kneeled down beside my chair so my dad could see him. He smiled and gave him a wave.

"Right here, Grizzly."

"That only answered one of my questions," Dad said. "Why is my girl at your house?"

I looked at Lynx and he turned his head to hold my gaze. When I turned back to the phone, my dad looked like he was barely holding it together. Yeah, he'd already figured it out.

"So, my little girl won't be coming home after all," he said, his voice suspiciously husky.

"Actually, I'd like to bring her there to visit. I know it's been a while since you've seen her, Grizzly. In person, that is. I'm sure it hasn't been easy being apart from one of your daughters." Lynx smiled. "We'll swing by the Dixie Reapers on the way there or on the way back. I'd like to introduce her to my family as my old lady."

"Not wife?" Dad asked.

"That's entirely up to her. I will give your daughter whatever she needs, Grizzly. If that's an official wedding and a ring on her finger, then she'll have it. If she's content with a property patch or maybe some ink, then that's what we'll do."

Dad cleared his throat. "It sounds like you know my girl pretty well, so I'm going to assume this wasn't a random decision on your part."

"It wasn't. I've wanted her to be mine for weeks now. When I told her I wanted to claim her, I left it up to her. If she'd said she didn't want a life with me, then I'd have backed off. At no point will I ever force her to do something she doesn't want to do."

My heart warmed at his words and I leaned into him a little. I didn't know why such a sweet man wanted to be with me. I still felt like a wrecking ball, and here he was waiting with his arms open, like he'd catch me no matter what. How could I not want to be with someone like that? My dad was the only other person I'd ever known who was anything like Lynx. Well, and possibly Doolittle. That was probably what attracted me to him in the first place.

"I want to see my girl, but I'm not sure how welcome she'd feel if she came here," Dad said. He focused on me again. "I love you, Meredith, and you know your sisters do too. Same for Badger and Dragon. You have our support. But Doolittle and Minnie... I'm not sure they're ready yet. I'm worried there might be some tension."

"I know, Dad. I figured as much. It's why I've stayed gone longer than originally planned." I didn't blame him for any of it. I'd done all this on my own.

"We'll need a day to plan things out. Maybe two. I know the Reapers and Devil's Fury have a close relationship since my nieces are both there. What would you think about heading to Alabama and we all just meet at Ridley's house?"

My dad smiled. "Think Venom might argue it's *his* house, but I think it's a good idea. I can talk to Farrah and Mariah if you want? I can't ride my bike that far right now."

"Dad, what's wrong?" I asked. "I thought you looked thinner. Is something else going on?"

He waved me off. "I'll be fine. Had a few dizzy spells, and I've lost weight faster than they'd wanted me to. I'm not dead yet, girl. If I can convince either Demon and Farrah or Savage and Mariah to drive to Alabama, maybe I can catch a ride with one of them."

"You and Meredith visit a bit more." Lynx stood but leaned down so Dad could still see him. "I'm going to step out and make a few calls to my family. No rush on ending your chat."

He kissed the top of my head and walked out of the kitchen, leaving me alone with Dad. The moment Lynx left, the smile faded from Dad's face and I knew I'd been right. Something was wrong.

"Tell me," I said. "And don't sugarcoat it."

"The meds and diet aren't enough, Meredith. I've lived a rough life for far too long. I think I'll be joining my sweet May. I've had a good, long life. Not much left for me to do."

"What about the other girls?" I asked, thinking of the two youngest my dad took in a while back.

"Someone already stepped in to take them. Outlaw and Wire worked together to get the girls officially into the system, got all their paperwork to look as legit as possible, and they've been placed with a good family here in town. They won't lose their friends or have to change schools."

I wanted to bawl my eyes out, but I knew that

was the last thing he needed. I fought back my tears and managed to get through the rest of the call. Once I hung up, my hands shaking and body trembling, I started to sob and felt like I might never stop. I didn't know how long he had left, or if this trip might be the last time I ever got to see him. It tore me apart.

Lynx came running and I knew he must have heard me. His boots pounded against the floor as he raced into the room. I'd crumpled over, arms wrapped around myself, trying to hold the pieces together... and I was failing miserably.

"Merry, what's wrong?" He gathered me in his arms and held me close. "Talk to me, sweetheart."

"I think my dad is dying." The words came out broken and felt like they'd been torn from my raw throat. "I'm going to lose him, and I can't even be there with him."

"We'll figure it out. Whatever it takes, I'll make it happen." He ran his hand down my hair. "Farrah and Mariah said they'd make sure he got to the Dixie Reapers compound in three days. Ridley is going make sure there's space for all of us. With all the Reaper kids pairing off with brothers from other clubs, they've put in quite a few duplexes. If you want, we can ask your dad to stay in one with us."

I nodded and held on to him tighter. Lynx might have claimed me, and we'd have a baby sometime in the next nine months, but it felt like I was losing my dad at the same time I'd gained a family. And I didn't know what Farrah and Mariah thought of me. Since they'd been at the Devil's Fury when everything went down with Doolittle and Minnie, they may very well hate my guts. What if they didn't accept me?

Lynx kissed my forehead and helped me stand. Taking my hand, he led me to the master bathroom, where he wet a rag in cool water and dabbed my face before placing it over my eyes. I could tell they were swollen, but his thoughtfulness nearly made me cry again.

"Tomorrow, why don't we go into town for a bit? We can head to a café and get some coffee. Just relax a little. I haven't heard back on your car yet, so we can drop by and check on it. If there's anything you need, we can pick it up while we're out. Sound good?" he asked.

"You're going to spoil me, aren't you?"

"Only if you let me. Something tells me you won't, though. Not all the time at any rate."

"Every now and then might be nice," I admitted. There was a part of me that worried if I let him do too much for me, I'd not only rely on him even more, but my obsession could take over our lives. I needed him to not be so sweet to me all the time. I hadn't been brokenhearted over the fiasco with Doolittle. I'd been upset. Pissed even. But I hadn't been in love with him. If I fell for Lynx, he'd have the power to destroy me.

"Why don't I run a bath for you? You can soak for a bit. I'll run over to the clubhouse and clean out your room. By the time you're done, your things will be here waiting for you to put them away."

"Is there space for my stuff?" I asked.

"There will be." He smiled. "I can clean out a drawer and make room in the closet for now. We can shop for more furniture later so you'll have a set of drawers all to yourself."

"All right. You don't have to run the bath for me, though. I can do it myself."

He nodded and hugged me before stepping out of the bathroom. We hadn't even had sex yet, and I was moving in with him. Would he expect something to happen tonight? No. Lynx didn't seem like the type. At least, not with me. I'd noticed he treated me different from the way he treated everyone else.

Of course, those other women were whores. Maybe that was the only difference. Since I haven't seen him around his sister or nieces, it was hard to say if he was this courteous and understanding with everyone, or if I was special in some way.

I filled the tub with hot water and undressed. I didn't see the point in shutting the bathroom door. Lynx would be seeing all of me soon enough. Perhaps, if he knew I wasn't scared of him, he might make a move. Although, I didn't know why he'd think I would push him away. Not with my history with men.

I sank into the water and leaned back, closing my eyes. He'd been right. This was exactly what I needed. I felt my muscles begin to relax, and my thoughts started to clear a little. Some days, it felt like I had a cyclone blow through my mind. Everything got all jumbled up and tossed about. Like a toddler throwing a tantrum and tossing toys every which way. My thoughts were often like that. My mind would leap from one thing to another, constantly fretting over stuff.

I skimmed my hand over the water. I must have dozed off because the next thing I knew, someone was hauling me out of the tub. Shrieking, I opened my eyes and flailed for a moment, until I realized it was only Lynx.

"What the hell?" I asked.

"Sorry, sweetheart. I spoke with Ridley when I got back from gathering your stuff. She knows you're pregnant and went over some basics with me. Hot water, at least as hot as you probably had it, is a big nope when you're carrying a baby."

My eyes went wide and I placed a hand on my belly. "Do you think I hurt it?"

"Probably not. You can't be more than a month along, right?"

I nodded, hoping he was right. Great. Something else to worry and obsess over. He'd mentioned getting things we needed tomorrow. The first stop we should make was a bookstore, so I could find something about pregnancy. I didn't know a thing about having a baby.

Lynx tipped up my chin after he set me down on the bed. "Hey. It's all right. Let me get a towel and we'll get you dried off and into some pajamas."

I reached up and wrapped my fingers around his wrist. His gaze lowered and skimmed my body before meeting mine again. I saw the hunger there, the *need*, and realized it wasn't one-sided. My nipples pebbled, and I pressed my thighs together.

"Or you could get undressed and join me," I said. My cheeks warmed. I hadn't felt embarrassed when I'd hit on all those other men, so why now? I nearly shook the crazy question from my brain. I already knew why. Because it was Lynx. He wasn't some random guy I'd met in a bar or at a gas station. He mattered.

Shit. I'm so screwed.

Chapter Five

Lynx

The myriad of emotions flitting through her eyes made me hesitate. I didn't know if she was about to use sex as a way to cope with her father's illness, if she thought it was what I wanted, or if she genuinely wanted to be with me right now. My brothers would demand I hand over my man-card if they knew my thoughts right now. Most, if not all, would have already stripped down and been in the bed with her.

Merry wasn't my good-time girl. She was my woman. The one I wanted to be with the rest of my life, start a family and grow old together. I needed to think about the big picture and not just right this second. Would this hurt her, or our relationship, more at a later time?

"I'm going to think you don't want me," she said. She smiled, but I noticed she pulled her hand back. Great. Now I was making her doubt herself.

"I want you. Have for a while."

"Then what's the problem?" she asked.

"Wonderin' if this is something you need right this second, or something you want as a way for us to grow closer. Are you still trying to use sex to gain a moment's reprieve from everything going on inside your head?"

She slumped against the pillows. "Honestly, I don't know. I can tell you that asking you to sleep with me just now was more difficult than hooking up with some random stranger. None of them meant anything to me."

"And I do?" I asked.

"Yeah," she said softly. "You matter to me, Lynx, and I'm so scared of screwing all this up before it's even really started."

I toed off my boots and removed my cut and belt.
I tugged off my shirt and let it fall to the floor.
Kneeling on the bed, I braced my hands on either side
of her. "Then let's talk this through before we go any
further."

My cock was already so damn hard it hurt. I
knew if I unzipped my pants, it would be even more
difficult to pull back if that's what she needed from me
right now. So I remained at least halfway dressed and
fought to control myself.

"Talk?" she asked.

"For starters, what exactly did you get from all
those hookups?"

"A brief moment without chaotic thoughts, pain,
or... feeling uncertain."

I nodded. "All right. Did you let them take
control? Or did you?"

"They usually made me suck them off or bent me
over whatever was handy. None of them bothered to
make me come."

My brow furrowed as I looked down at her.
"Then why the fuck did you sleep with them?"

"When they were fucking me, my mind went
quiet."

Jesus. She needed more help than I'd realized.
She still hadn't told me much about her thoughts and
why she needed to silence them. Did I need to worry
about her trying to harm herself? Despite the
recklessness of sleeping with strange men, it hadn't
occurred to me until now that she might be suicidal. I
didn't think that was it, though.

"Let's see if we can find some ways to quiet your
mind, or give you other things to focus on. And if you
want me to stop, just tell me."

I lowered my head to her neck and kissed the sensitive skin there before working my way lower. My lips closed around her nipple and I flicked it with my tongue. Her body tensed and she gasped. When her nails bit into me, pulling me closer, I took it as a sign to keep going. I'd learned over the years not all women liked someone playing with their nipples. Since Merry's were rather pretty, I was thankful she hadn't shoved me away.

I cupped her breast with my hand and drew back to blow across the hard peak. It puckered even more. I rapidly flicked it with my tongue before sucking it into my mouth. I gave it a tug and lightly scraped it with my teeth.

"Oh, God! Lynx!" One of her hands went to my hair, and she yanked on it. "Don't stop! Please don't!"

Looked like my girl wanted things a little rough. I released her nipple and sat back on my knees. Pinching it between my thumb and finger, I rolled the hard tip. Merry's eyes were closed, her head tipped back. Her cheeks were flushed.

"Does my girl like that?" I asked.

"Yes! It feels so good."

I gave the same treatment to the other side, not stopping until her nipples were swollen and had darkened from the slightly rough way I'd handled them. She'd look stunning tied up and completely at my mercy. With the way she reacted so far, she might very well enjoy it.

"Merry, do you trust me?" I asked.

"Of course, I do."

No hesitation at all. I wondered how many people were on that list of hers, the ones she considered trustworthy. I doubted I was the only one there. As long the others weren't single men, I didn't have a problem with it.

"What do you think about being tied up?" I asked.

"I've never done that before."

"It's not something we have to do. I'd like to, but only if you're open to it." I wasn't about to tell her it wouldn't be my first time. There were some things she didn't need to know.

"Do I still get to tell you to stop if I don't like something?" she asked.

"Always." I leaned over her again and pressed my lips to hers. "I will never do anything to hurt you. Not just physically, but mentally and emotionally. If I do, then I want you to tell me. It's the only way I can make sure I don't make the same mistake."

"Does your club know how sweet you are?" she asked.

"Not exactly."

I wasn't sure it was so much that I was sweet, as she called me, but that I saw more than most people. Which was why I'd been called Lynx. I tended to make observations others overlooked. Native Americans believed the lynx had the gift of seeing or observation, or so Atilla had told me when he'd given me my name.

"I'm willing to try anything once," she said. "Especially if it feels as good as what you were just doing."

"Give me a minute and I'll get you warmed up again." I flashed her a smile as I stood. Going to the closet, I dug around until I found some soft rope. I wrapped it around her wrists, then tied them to the headboard. Once I had her trapped and at my mercy, I stripped out of my jeans and boxers.

Climbing back onto the bed, I decided to pick up where I'd left off. She'd liked me playing with her nipples, so I teased them some more first with my mouth and tongue, then with my fingers. As I pinched and tugged on one, I slid my other hand down between her legs. She was already wet and ready. Parting the lips of her pussy, I rubbed her clit in small circles, keeping my touch light.

It didn't take long before her back bowed and she cried out my name. Her legs trembled and I felt the wetness of her release on my fingers. Thrusting two digits inside her, I pumped them in and out, drawing out her orgasm for as long as I could. She came a second time, and before her pleasure subsided, I flipped her onto her stomach, pulled her up onto her knees, and slid my cock into her slick pussy.

"Lynx! Please!"

She gripped the headboard, her hands still bound, as I fucked her from behind. I reached up to wind her hair around my hand and pulled just enough that she moaned. My hips slapped against her as I took what I wanted while giving her everything she needed. Her pussy tightened on me, and when she came a third time, I knew I wouldn't last.

I took her harder. Faster. Deeper.

My balls drew up, and my jaw went tight as I pumped her full of my cum. I didn't slow until every drop had been drained from me. My breath sawed in and out of my lungs, and I nearly collapsed on top of Merry. Pulling free of her body, I slumped to my side and reached up to untie her.

She cuddled against me, and it only took me a moment to realize she had tears on her cheeks. I wiped them away and held her gaze.

"Did I hurt you?" I asked.

"No. That was exactly what I needed. I think it's what I'd been trying to find, but in all the wrong places."

"That's because you didn't need sex with random men. You needed someone who would take the time to give you pleasure."

She shook her head. "No. I needed someone to take control. Someone I'd feel safe with, even when I was powerless. Because that's how I feel every day."

"Powerless?" I asked, needing her to clarify.

"Yes."

"You're stronger than you realize, Merry. You had power, even before now. If you hadn't, you wouldn't have been able to cause so much trouble with the Devil's Fury. The difference is that now you realize what you did wrong, and you're trying not to make the same mistakes. That's honorable, and it takes a lot of courage to face your fears."

"You'll make sure I don't go down the wrong path again, right? You won't let me fall so far?"

I kissed her soft and slow. "I'll be here to catch you when you fall, Merry, but you won't need me to. Because I'm going to help you get the tools you need to do that for yourself."

"How do I do that?" she asked.

"Sometimes being strong means asking for help. Not just from me, but others. If you'd told your dad or the Devil's Fury about your struggles, do you think things would have ended differently?" No. That wasn't what I wanted to say. This wasn't all on my Merry. Sure, she had to shoulder some of the blame. Her dad's club needed to take responsibility for the rest. "Maybe a better question is why no one bothered to look close enough to ask you what was wrong, or how they could help."

"It's not the first time," she said.

"What's that supposed to mean?" Had they

failed her another time? I seriously wanted to go kick all their asses. And yet, if they hadn't fucked up, she wouldn't be right here now with me. As angry as I was with them, I also owed them.

"Shella," she said. "Another of Grizzly's adopted daughters. They ran her off. It was before I joined the Devil's Fury, but I heard about it. Or rather, overheard someone talking about it. She's with Slash now. The VP went after her."

So he chased after Shella and stopped to ask why she'd been acting out. At least one of them had half a brain. Why hadn't he bothered to use that same sight when it came to Meredith? Or had she acted that way the entire time she'd been with them? I'd try to reserve my judgment until I had all the facts.

"I don't know why things ended differently this time. Perhaps you were meant to be here with me all along. Whatever the case, you can't hide from your dad's club forever. They're your family, Merry."

"Are they?" she asked. "I thought family was supposed to support you, not chase you away when you didn't act the way they wanted you to."

I could tell she was still hurting over what she probably felt was a betrayal. She'd admitted she'd done something wrong, even if I didn't know the entire story. It didn't change the fact they had hurt her.

"They're human, Merry. Same as you and me. They make mistakes. I think, when you're ready, you need to have a talk with them. Help them understand what was going on, and why you acted the way you did. It's not good to let things fester."

She closed her eyes and snuggled even closer to me. It seemed she was finished with the conversation for now. Fine. I didn't want to push her too much too soon. I'd take her for coffee tomorrow, and *accidentally* run into Moira. I hoped she'd be able to shed some light on things, or at least convince Merry to meet her in a more official capacity.

For now, I'd hold her. Make sure she knew how much I wanted to be with her and accepted her. There wasn't much else I could do.

She hooked her leg over mine and slowly slid it up my thigh. When her knee gently nudged my cock and balls, I felt myself harden. I couldn't remember the last time I recovered this fast. Then again, I'd never been turned on so much by a woman before.

"Does this mean you want to go again?" I asked.

She smiled up at me. "I wouldn't say no."

Her lips brushed against mine. The moment they parted, my tongue slid between them. I skimmed the curve of her hip with my hand before rolling us so that she lay under me. Her eyes darkened and her nipples puckered. A feeling of possession filled me as I gazed down at her. This woman was mine.

She spread her thighs wider, and it wasn't an invitation I'd pass up. Pressing my cock against her slick pussy, I eased inside her. Even though she'd said she wasn't sore, I watched her face for any signs of discomfort. All I saw was pure bliss on her features.

Using slow, easy thrusts, I tried to draw the moment out for as long as possible. I felt her tighten around me, and her nails bit into my shoulders.

"Please, Lynx! I need more."

How could I possibly deny her? I pounded into her, taking what I wanted and giving her what she needed. The bed slammed against the wall with every stroke, and it wasn't long before she was coming. The wet heat of her release hit my cock, and my balls drew up. Three more thrusts and I was coming inside her. I didn't stop pumping my hips until every drop of cum had been wrung from me.

Panting, I gazed down at her. I'd never seen a more beautiful sight in my life. I wondered if she knew how much power she had over me. For her, I'd do anything.

Chapter Six

Meredith

I hadn't known what to expect with Lynx last night. He'd given me so much more than I'd ever anticipated. Sure, he'd taken me from behind, but it had been different from before. By the time he'd flipped me over, he'd made me come more than once, and had made everything about *me*. No one had done that before. And since it had only been our first time together, I was certain he'd vary things from time to time. It seemed like the sort of man he was.

I'd woken this morning a little achy, but with a smile on my face. He'd still been lying next to me, and it was my first time sharing a bed with someone overnight. Now, we were on our first outing as a couple. He'd taken my hand when we'd gotten off his bike, and I felt a warmth that was both foreign and exciting to me. He wanted everyone to know I was his.

"I heard from your dad this morning," he said. "He called while you were in the shower. We're going to leave in the morning and drive to the Dixie Reapers compound."

I hadn't thought much about the situation at home, until he'd said that just now. I couldn't remember the last time I'd been able to forget for this long. Possibly never. Since I'd been asked to leave, it had weighed heavily on me at all times. Being with Lynx seemed to be good for me, in many ways.

"On your bike?" I asked.

"No, sweetheart. You're pregnant, and I'm not going to let you ride that far on my motorcycle while you're carrying our kid inside you. I'm also not sure I feel too safe using your car." He gave my hand a squeeze. He'd already told me the list of things wrong with my car. Not that I'd understood any of it. "I'm sure your dad gave that car to you, but how would you feel about trading it in? Or just keeping it for emergencies and getting something newer? We can get it repaired and have it as a backup."

"You don't care if we keep it?" I asked.

"Not at all. We can go buy something new this afternoon. Or at least new-ish. The price of cars has been a bit crazy lately. You either pay out the nose for a vehicle that won't eat you alive in gas fees, or you get a gas-guzzling monster… and even those aren't cheap."

I knew exactly what he meant. It seemed like gas prices had shot up overnight, and while they were slowly falling back into an average range, it wasn't inexpensive to fill up the tank. Although, I didn't know how much traveling we'd be doing after this visit. Just driving around town wouldn't matter too much. It wasn't like I ran all over the place.

"Just don't pick out something too big for me to handle," I said.

He winked and smirked. "I don't know, sweetheart. You seem to handle *big* things just fine."

My cheeks flushed and I smacked his chest. "Behave! We're in public."

I may have scolded him, but secretly, I liked his teasing. It made me feel… normal. Or as close to it as I'd ever felt before. I'd noticed my chaotic thoughts were a little quieter today as well. It seemed like Lynx was what I'd needed all this time. Knowing he saw me, and did his best to understand me, went a long way to making me feel less crazy.

It was finally our turn to order, and I asked for a white mocha while Lynx got plain black coffee. I wrinkled my nose, not understanding how he could drink something so bitter. He paid and I scanned the café for an empty table. It looked busy, and I didn't see a single place where we could sit. Lynx turned around and took my hand again, and I noticed a woman waving at him.

"Um, Lynx. I think she wants your attention." Had they dated? She didn't look like the type who'd fall for a biker. Her blouse didn't have a single wrinkle. The black pencil skirt was both tasteful and conservation. She'd even demurely crossed her ankles and kept her knees together.

"Oh?" He scanned the room and a smile slid across his face when he spotted the woman. "That's Moira. Come on and I'll introduce you."

"Who's Moira?" I asked.

"A friend. I helped her out a while back. She had a flat tire on the side of the road. We've kept in touch and get coffee from time to time." He led me over to the woman and greeted her warmly. "I didn't expect to see you here, Moira."

"Why don't the two of you sit? I'm nearly finished, and there don't seem to be any open tables."

"Thanks. This is Meredith."

I gave her a tight smile. Lynx winked at me again, and I knew he was trying to put me at ease. Maybe he thought my jealousy was cute. It wasn't. It felt awful.

"It's about time you introduced me to your girlfriend," Moira said.

Wait. He'd told her he had a girlfriend? When did he do that? I glanced at him, but Lynx wasn't giving anything away.

"It's nice to meet you," I mumbled.

"Did Lynx tell you how we met?" she asked.

"He said he fixed your flat tire," I said.

"He was such a lifesaver that day. No matter

how many times I tried to pay him, he wouldn't accept anything. So every now and then, I convince him to accept a cup of coffee."

Lynx put his arm along the back of my chair and tugged me closer. Could he feel how anxious I was right now? Could *she*? I didn't want to come across as some jealous bitch, even if it was true. Moira was beautiful, and so well put together. I felt like a trainwreck in comparison. She probably had a good job, her own house or apartment, paid all her bills by herself. In other words, the exact opposite of me. She looked closer to Lynx's age too.

Moira eyed me, and it felt like she saw everything. My insecurity. Anxiety. And the absolute mess I was mentally and emotionally. It made me want to crawl under the table or run as far away as I could.

"The two of you out running errands or do you have special plans today?" she asked, her gaze darting from me to Lynx and back again.

"We're going car shopping," Lynx said. "Need something safe for the baby."

I sucked in a breath. All right. I hadn't realized we'd be telling everyone I was pregnant. He might be friends with this woman, but I'd just met her. Why would he say something like that?

Moira smiled widely. "How exciting! Congratulations. I bet the two of you must be really happy."

Did she really know Lynx? I wouldn't call him excited. Sure, he'd said he'd take responsibility for the two of us, and he planned to call the baby his. It didn't mean he was jumping for joy, though.

"We only recently found out. Still adjusting a bit to the news," he said.

I found myself looking around the café while

twisting my cup on the table. I heard the two of them continue to talk, but I didn't pay attention. It was rude of me to ignore them. I knew it, and yet, I couldn't focus on their conversation. It felt like my throat was getting tight and the walls were closing in on me.

"Meredith." Lynx's hand gripped my thigh. "Hey."

I jolted and looked up at him. "What?"

"Moira's been asking you a question."

My cheeks heated and I glanced her way, finding myself unable to hold her gaze. "Sorry."

"I'm not trying to pry, but I think I can help you," Moira said.

"What do you mean?" I asked.

"Did Lynx tell you anything about me?" I shook my head. "Did you know you would be meeting me today?"

I sucked in a breath. "This wasn't a coincidence?"

"Lynx is concerned, and I think he's right to be. You seem overly anxious. I've also picked up a few other behaviors that I feel should be explored a little more. Would you be willing to come to my office?" She pulled out a business card and slid it across the table. *Dr. Moira Stern, Psychiatrist.*

I shoved my chair back and stood, unable to look at either of them. "You did this on purpose. Everything was set up from the beginning, wasn't it? You lied to me."

My stomach churned, and it felt like a fire had built inside my chest. I knew I needed to get away, as quickly as possible. I nearly ran from the café and hurried down the sidewalk. Pressing a hand against my chest, I worried my heart might pound right through my ribs. It felt like... he'd betrayed me.

Did Lynx think there was something wrong with

me?

Clearly. If he didn't, he wouldn't have tricked me into meeting Moira. He wanted me to see a psychiatrist? I might call myself crazy from time to time, but I didn't like knowing Lynx thought I was too.

"I can't breathe," I mumbled as I staggered over to a bench. I sank onto the wooden seat and leaned over to put my head on my knees. Tears pricked my eyes and I fought to hold them back.

I didn't know what hurt more. The way he'd tricked me into meeting Moira, or the fact he hadn't come after me. Were they still sitting there talking about me? Was she telling him I was all kinds of fucked up? I'd known this was all too good to be true. I should have listened to that little voice, the one telling me to avoid Lynx. I'd worried I'd obsess over him and chase him off. This was worse.

I hadn't done anything to deserve this.

Unable to hold back any longer, I started to sob until it felt like I was breaking apart inside. Every tear was another piece of my heart, and my sanity, falling into the abyss. My stomach cramped, then I felt a sharper pain. A sudden wetness slicked my panties, and I parted my legs, my eyes going wide when I realized I was bleeding.

I tried to stand, but my legs wouldn't hold me. Long legs stopped in front of me, and I looked up to see an officer in uniform. He kneeled down.

"You all right?" he asked.

"No. I... I think something is wrong with my baby." Saying the words made it real. I was having a baby. Or I had been. Something told me I was losing that innocent little life.

"Come on. I'll take you to the hospital. Wanna use my phone to call your family?"

I shook my head. I didn't have anyone to call. After what Lynx had done, I wasn't sure I wanted to see him right now. My dad didn't need the added stress. There wasn't anyone else. Tears slipped down my cheeks again as the officer helped me to his vehicle.

He turned on the sirens and got me to the hospital in record time. As the nurse wheeled me through the doors of the ER, I wondered if I'd ever do anything right. I'd gotten pregnant by accident. Now I was losing my baby. Was I being punished? Did the powers that be know I wasn't going to be a good mother? If I couldn't take care of myself, how could I be responsible for someone else?

Maybe this is for the best.

But if this was the right thing, why did it feel so horrible? I might have been terrified to have a baby, but now that I was losing my little one, I wanted to hold onto them.

So selfish. I was. Even I knew I didn't have what it took to take care of a child. And yet, I didn't want to give up my baby. I couldn't think of another word for myself. Well, maybe not a word, but a phrase. I was still a fuck-up. Would I always be one?

The doubts and worries filled me. I felt myself being pulled down into the darkness once more.

No one wants you.

You ruin everything.

They'll all be better off without you.

Yes. They would… Whenever I was able to leave the hospital, I'd go somewhere else, far from Bryson Corners. And this time, I wouldn't tell anyone where I was going. I'd disappear -- for good.

Chapter Seven

Lynx

It felt like someone had punched me in the gut when I saw the look on Meredith's face and watched her make a hasty exit. I'd wanted to go after her, but Moira stopped me.

"What are you going to say to her?" she asked. "Beg for forgiveness? Tell her it was for her own good? Make up some excuse or try to placate her?"

I opened and shut my mouth, having no fucking clue what to do. I could try all those things, but I didn't know if it would be enough. She'd trusted me. Hell, I wasn't even entirely certain I had all her trust yet, and I'd already tossed it out the window.

Way to go, fucking idiot.

I'd wanted to help. In hindsight, I realized I'd done it the wrong way. Of course, I hadn't thought Moira would throw me under the bus the way she had. I eyed her, wondering what the fuck she was up to.

"Why did you do it?" I asked. "You knew I wanted the two of you to meet, and for it to seem like a coincidence. You agreed to it."

"Did you see her?" Moira asked. "You brought her over without explaining who I was. I'm sure she wondered if we'd slept together, or if I had feelings for you."

"So I should have what? Introduced you as a psychiatrist right off?"

"Sure. You could have told her more than the basic story of how we met. You didn't tell her anything about me, or that we'd never dated. It would have been great if you'd reassured her as to our relationship. Jesus, Lynx. Do you ever use your head?" she asked.

I winced. No. Apparently, when it came to

Meredith, I didn't use my brain one hundred percent of the time. If I had, I'd have known this was a bad fucking idea, and I'd have found another way to bring the subject up with her.

"Go find her, Lynx. Tell her you were trying to help and realize you did it the wrong way. Ask for her forgiveness, or better yet, ask her what she needs. Don't assume you know what's best for her."

I stood and left the café. She'd gone out the door and taken a left, so I followed the same path. When I heard sirens, I hastened my pace, hoping like fuck nothing had happened to her. A police car flew by me as I ran down the sidewalk. I scanned the area along the way and didn't see even a glimpse of Meredith. Where the fuck could she have gone?

An older woman flagged me down. "Are you looking for a young woman by any chance?"

Well, I'd blatantly been searching for something. Maybe it wasn't a stretch for her to assume I was looking for a woman.

"Yes, ma'am. My girlfriend. We had a fight and…" I ran a hand down my face. "I need to tell her I'm sorry, but I can't find her."

She clicked her tongue at me. "That police officer just left with her. I heard him say something about a hospital."

Hospital? What the fuck had happened in the short time we'd been apart? I hurried back to my bike and broke every speed limit between the café and the hospital. I'd fucked up so bad this time. She'd had no one to rely on except me, and I'd done this stupid shit and run her off. If I'd handled things differently, would she have been all right? I'd do whatever it took to get her to forgive me.

I parked and hurried inside. A police officer

stood at the triage desk speaking with a nurse. As much as I didn't care for law enforcement, I needed to know if he'd brought Meredith here. Why was she in the hospital? Had she been hit by a car? Had someone attacked her? Not knowing was the worst part.

"Excuse me. Are you the officer who brought in a young woman?" I asked. "I'm trying to find my girlfriend."

The man scanned me from head to toe. The sneer on his lips told me exactly what he thought of me. I didn't give a shit, as long as he answered my question. He could think I was complete scum, as long as I knew for certain Meredith was here and could find out what happened. I needed her to be okay.

"You the one who made her cry like her entire world had fallen apart?" he asked.

"Yeah. That was me. I admit that I'm an idiot, and I need to apologize to her, but first I need to know if she's okay. Why did you bring her here? Did someone do something to her?"

"Sir, I'm sorry, but until the patient says it's all right to speak with you, we can't divulge any information." The nurse glared at me, then tugged the officer away. "Feel free to sit and wait."

Damnit. I didn't know what to do, so I messaged Wire. If anyone could hack into the hospital records, it would be him.

Need help. Meredith is at St. Mary's Hospital in Bryson Corners. No one will tell me what's going on.

Instead of a text response, I got a phone call. I stepped outside to answer it.

"Wire, can you do it?" I asked when the call connected.

"What the absolute fuck? How can you not know why she's in the hospital?"

Just what I needed. No matter how I spun this, it wouldn't put me in a good light. As long as he helped me right now, I'd deal with the fallout later.

"We had an argument of sorts. She ran off, and by the time I caught up to her, a cop was taking her to the hospital. I have no idea what's going on because neither the officer nor the hospital staff will speak to me."

He growled softly. "Sometimes I really hate the police. Although, I'm sure he thinks he's protecting her from you. I realize he's doing his job, but damn. He probably took one look, saw you were a biker, and wrote you off as the problem."

Wouldn't be the first time. In all honesty, I hadn't led a squeaky-clean life. While I'd never been into anything heavy, as far as illegal shit went, I hadn't exactly been a law-abiding citizen either. With my upbringing, it was a miracle I wasn't the same sort of scum as my father.

"So can you find out what's going on?" I asked.

"Yeah. I'll call you back when I have something. If you get someone to talk to you before then, let me know what they say. Are you going to tell Grizzly? The two of you were supposed to meet him here tomorrow or the day after, right?"

"Shit. I don't want to worry him until I have something to actually share."

"All right. I'll see what I can do on my end," Wire said.

I hung up. My chest fucking hurt. I needed to know she was okay. I went back inside and found the officer near the door, arms folded. *Best to get this over with.*

"You still not going to tell me anything?" I asked.

"Depends. Why was she crying?"

At least he hasn't said an outright *no*. I'd consider this progress. How much should I tell him? I'd keep things simple. Probably the best way to handle it.

"Told you. We had a fight."

He didn't say a word. Just stared me down. I pinched the bridge of my nose and wondered if I should divulge a little more. If I said I worried she might be mentally ill, would they put her under a psychiatric hold? Meredith might really lose her shit then. Looked like he wasn't going to give me much of a choice. I either told him what happened, or he'd continue to withhold information. I didn't have a fucking clue if it was actually legal for him to do that or not, but I wasn't exactly going to go research it right now either.

"She's had a rough time of it lately, and I noticed she tends to do reckless things. I think she's mentally ill. She shows signs of anxiety and does things that could potentially harm her. I asked a friend of mine to observe her and give me an opinion, except Meredith found out the meeting had been orchestrated and she ran off." I leaned against the wall. "I realize I fucked up. I should have told her up front that I was concerned and wanted her to consider getting some help. Instead, I went about it all wrong and now she probably hates me."

"Well, we all do dumb shit when it comes to the women we love," the officer said. "Just ask my wife. I'm surprised that woman hasn't taken a skillet to my head by now. I don't know for certain what's going on, but I can say this much. Your woman started bleedin'. Said she was pregnant."

Shit. Was she having a miscarriage? Had the stress of what happened been too much for her? I felt like the worst asshole on the planet. If she lost the baby because of me... It felt like something was squeezing my lungs so tightly I couldn't breathe. Now she was in there, alone and probably scared. I needed to be with her. She'd been through so much. I didn't know how she'd handle losing the baby.

"That girl of yours don't look to be in a good place," he said. "Hospital won't tell you shit without you bein' her husband. Not unless she tells 'em to say somethin'."

Little late to retract the boyfriend label I'd already given myself. Otherwise, I'd call Wire back and ask him to marry us. Then again, right now he might very well refuse.

"I get it. Hospital rules. I just want to know if she's all right."

"Can't tell you more than I have." He walked off, leaving me alone in my misery.

I paced the ER, and even walked outside for a bit. The minutes ticked by. Then an hour passed. Then two. My phone buzzed and I answered it without even checking the screen.

"This is Lynx."

"It's Wire. Why the hell didn't you say anything about her being pregnant?" he asked.

Now I knew for certain he'd been in her hospital files. There wasn't any other way for him to know she was pregnant. Or had been. I wasn't sure I wanted to hear the answer, but I asked the question anyway. "Did she lose the baby?"

He sighed. "Yeah, man. I'm sorry. Hospital records show they did a D&C, and once the anesthesia wears off, she'll be released. Did you ride there on your bike?"

"Yep." I sat on a nearby bench and stretched out my legs. It felt like time stood still. The baby was gone.

What would this do to Meredith? To *us*? I hated being out here while she was in there facing this nightmare on her own. And it was my own damn fault. "We were supposed to buy a new car today. Something she'd be comfortable driving but would be safe for the baby. Didn't make it past coffee."

"You took her for coffee and she's pregnant?" he asked.

"Uh, what's wrong with that?"

"You fucking moron. She shouldn't have caffeine." I heard him tapping on his keyboard. "I'm accessing funds from one of the trafficking groups I helped take down, and I'm using it to buy a damn car. Someone will deliver it to the hospital, so wait outside for them. Can someone get your bike?"

"I'll call one of my brothers. They'll swing by and get it. You don't have to buy a car. It's not like those are cheap." I also didn't want to feel indebted to him or the Dixie Reapers. Besides, if he hadn't gotten his president's permission, this could end badly for me.

"Well, if Grizzly finds out you knocked up his daughter, then she lost the baby, you'll have to consider it a consolation gift for Meredith... because he's going to bury your ass."

He wasn't telling me anything I hadn't already considered. None of them needed to know I hadn't been the one to actually get her pregnant. If Meredith wanted to tell them, I wouldn't stop her. Otherwise, I planned to remain silent and let them assume whatever the fuck they wanted. My goal was to protect her, even if I'd already fucked that up pretty bad today.

"There's a two-year old Dodge Charger heading your way. Certified preowned, so any major issues should be covered if something comes up. It will all be in the paperwork you'll have to sign when they bring you the keys."

"You put it in my name?" I asked.

"Well, I can't put it in hers since she's in the hospital. There's no way she can sign all those papers right now." Wire lowered his voice, and I wondered if his woman was nearby. "Besides, if it's in your name, it will be harder for her to use it to run. Some part of her will worry that she'll get pulled over and they'll realize her name isn't on the registration. Not to mention you could call it in as stolen."

"Did you do that to your wife? Put her car in your name?"

"Your situation and mine are very different. My woman chased after me. Yours is known for running."

I didn't like the way he'd phrased that. Meredith hadn't been on the run. Not at first. The Devil's Fury essentially threw her out. Sure, they'd said it was only for a short while, but after making her feel so unwelcome, had they really expected she'd just waltz back in like nothing happened? No, she hadn't *run*.

"Not technically," I said. "The Devil's Fury told her to leave. That's not even close to the same thing."

"True enough. Let me know if you need anything else. I'll try to monitor the hospital records from this side, and I'll make sure the fees are covered. I haven't disbursed the funds from that confiscated account yet, or told anyone what's in it. No one will know if fifty grand or so is missing."

"Just don't put your ass on the line for this, okay? I don't need to make waves with your club. My sister lives there, and I'll be pissed if I can't go to the Dixie Reapers compound anymore to visit with her."

"Yeah, yeah. I'll make sure they know you had nothing to do with it." Wire hung up without another word and I shoved my phone into my pocket.

It didn't take long for two cars to pull up at the curb. One of them was a blue Dodge Charger SXT. It looked like Wire had gotten us a good vehicle. I stood and shook hands with the salesman.

"Name's John Turner. You must be Lynx."

I nodded. I noticed the paperwork had my legal name on it, even though the man didn't call me by it. I signed everything I needed to, then listened as he went over the vehicle features. It would be safe for Meredith to drive, and I liked that it had a backup camera, blind spot detection, and a panic alarm. That backup camera would come in handy if my club started growing the way the Dixie Reapers had. Couldn't always see a small kid in a rearview mirror.

John handed me the keys, then got into the other vehicle and drove off, leaving me with a packet of papers and a nearly new car. Only nine thousand miles. I parked the Charger and contacted my VP to ask about having my bike moved, then I went inside to wait for them to release Meredith. Whether she liked it or not, she'd need a ride home, and I intended to be the one to take her. If she didn't like it, then she could yell all she wanted.

Chapter Eight

Meredith

The last thing I expected when the nurse wheeled me out the hospital exit was an unfamiliar blue car waiting for me. The driver's-side door opened and when I realized it was Lynx, I wanted to run away. He came closer and kneeled in front of me. Slowly, he reached for my hand. I forced myself to look him in the eye, and what I saw nearly broke me. Concern. Shame. Affection. How could he be feeling all that?

"I'm sorry," I said in a near whisper.

"No. You've not done anything wrong, Merry. Let's get you home."

The nurse handed him my discharge papers, and the peri bottle they were sending home for me to use. I only half-listened as she went over the basic care instructions. When she finished, Lynx helped me out of the wheelchair and into the car. I didn't know where he'd gotten it. Had he gone out to buy it while I'd been here?

The nurse went back inside as Lynx got into the car. He reached over and cupped my cheek.

"I'm so fucking sorry, Merry. I never meant for you to run out like that."

"I can't do this right now, Lynx." I'd had every intention of walking out of here on my own and disappearing. He'd hurt me. Much more than the Devil's Fury had. Even worse, I'd started to doubt myself again. Why had he done that to me?

He sighed. "All right. Moira told me to stop thinking I know what's best for you and ask what you need. So if you need me to not bring up the subject right now, then I'll wait until you're ready."

Moira. Of course, he'd listen to her. As much as I

tried to convince myself I didn't want to know, I couldn't help but ask.

"The two of you never dated?"

"No. I should have made sure you knew that up front. We really aren't anything more than friends. I wanted the two of you to meet because I thought she could help you."

"So, it really was intentional," I muttered.

I hoped he'd drop it for now. He seemed to understand that's what I needed because he didn't say another word as he pulled away from the hospital and out onto the street. I was still curious where the car had come from. If he'd been so worried about me, why had he taken the time to go buy one?

"This is going to be your car," he said. "It's a gift from Wire, but I don't know if he wants us to tell anyone right now. He had the dealership deliver it while I was waiting at the hospital."

I didn't respond. Although, I was thankful he'd answered my silent question. And I was also happy to hear he hadn't gone shopping while I'd been in the hospital. I didn't know how he'd discovered I was there. The hospital wouldn't have told him anything since I didn't sign papers giving them permission to talk to anyone.

Then again, he'd said Wire sent the car to us. Maybe that's how he knew where I was and what was going on. He'd probably asked the hacker to track me. It wasn't like I could give the hospital a fake name. They'd probably send me a huge bill later. It surprised me no one mentioned anything about a payment while I'd been there.

Lynx drove through the gates at the compound and went straight home. I waited after he parked. He came around to help me from the car and kept his arm around my waist as we went into the house. I eased down onto the couch.

"Wait here and I'll get a few things for you. I haven't had a chance to read the papers, but the nurse said you'd be tired today. You can relax in here and watch TV."

He hurried off and returned a minute or two later with a pillow and blanket. He removed my shoes for me, and helped me get comfortable, before handing me the remote. The scrubs the hospital had given me were more comfortable than I'd thought, so I wasn't in a hurry to change.

We needed to talk. When he went to leave the room, I reached for his hand to stop him. Lynx paused, then kneeled down beside the couch. He didn't say a word, only waited patiently for me to gather my thoughts. This was the man I'd come to know and care about. So why had he done things so differently earlier?

"Earlier, it felt like you'd betrayed me. I didn't know anything about Moira. My anxiety was through the roof the entire time we sat with her, then to discover you'd set it all up from the beginning..."

"I know. It was too much." He kissed the back of my hand. "I'm sorry, Merry. I thought I was doing the right thing. I've been worried about you, and with Moira being a psychiatrist, I'd hoped if she got a chance to observe you then she could let me know if my fears were unfounded."

"She gave me her card. Guess that means I'm a basket case."

He shook his head. "No. You might need help figuring things out, and we may even discover it's something that requires medication, but it doesn't make you a crazy person. I didn't intend to make you feel like one either. I'd thought it would be less stressful if you didn't know what she did for a living."

I snorted. That one had backfired on him in a big way. It did show me one thing, though. He'd had good intentions, like always when it came to me. He knew I'd been struggling, and I'd even admitted to myself I might need help. It was hard to hold onto my anger. Lynx had been the only person to really stop and look, to find out why I acted the way I did and accept me.

"You haven't asked about the baby," I said.

"I heard you had a miscarriage. Honestly, I wasn't sure if I should say anything. I know the baby wasn't planned, but it doesn't make the loss hurt any less. You had to have been scared. I should have been with you."

Yes, you should have. "There's no reason for you to be stuck with me now."

His eyes darkened and his jaw went tight. "What the fuck did you just say?"

"I'm not pregnant anymore. You don't have to take care of me."

He closed his eyes and released my hand. "I'm going to walk out for a few minutes so I won't say something I shouldn't. But know that your words right now really piss me off."

I blinked as he walked out of the room, and then he left the house entirely, slamming the front door shut. Part of me had assumed he'd be happy to have his freedom back. When he'd said he would claim me, he couldn't have known how bad things would be. He hadn't tried to make me his until he'd found out I was pregnant. I'd thought he would be glad to be rid of a nuisance like me.

The door opened and he came back inside, shutting it quietly this time. He came straight for me, sitting on the floor beside the couch.

"Are you under the misconception I only wanted you because of the baby?" he asked.

"You didn't say anything about claiming me until I told you I was pregnant. Why would anyone want to be with someone like me?"

"Someone like you," he muttered. "I knew you had some self-esteem issues, amongst other things, but to hear you say that… Merry, I'm with you because you're the only woman I've ever wanted to make mine. This isn't a casual thing for me. You aren't a fling, or some club whore I'll want to shake off in a few days."

"But I'm…"

He placed a finger over my lips to silence me. "What you are is incredible. You're beautiful, sweet, sexy as hell. Let me ask you something. You've dragged out your exile for far longer than originally planned. Why?"

"Because I'm not good enough yet."

"Says who? Your dad clearly wanted you home by now. Why do you feel like you have to prove anything? Did you stay away because you didn't want them to not accept you when you went back? Were you only worried about yourself?"

"No," I admitted. "It would be a strain on Dad if the club still hated me for what I'd done. I thought if I could mature a little more, show I could take care of myself, then maybe they'd not be so angry when I went back."

"So you did all this for your dad." He reached up to tuck my hair behind my ear. "You have a big heart, Merry. I think you acted the way you did because of a mental illness. It's nothing to be ashamed of. If you need to talk to someone, or need medication, then it doesn't change who you are. It doesn't make you less capable. What's the difference in taking medication for anxiety, depression, or any other mental health issue compared to say... your dad's blood pressure or heart pills?"

I didn't have an answer for him. I'd never considered it that way, but he was right. If I had something wrong with me and needed to take prescriptions in order to be okay, then it wasn't different. Not everyone would see it that way, though, and I knew it. Some would make fun of me, or say it was just an excuse.

"You're safe here, Merry. This compound is your home now. No one is going to disparage you, or make you feel like less than you are." He pressed his forehead to mine. "You're *safe*."

The emphasis the second time really made it hit home. He'd done everything in his power to give me a place where I could be myself. Made me his old lady, opened up his home to me, accepted me as I was, and offered to get me the help I needed. So why had I been so intent on running from him?

"When I was at the hospital, I'd thought you'd be better off if I ran away. Actually, I thought everyone would prefer it if I disappeared forever."

"No." He gripped my chin and forced me to hold his gaze. "I will *never* be better off without you. And if you're having those thoughts, then I'm scared shitless right now. Will you please meet with someone? I don't care if it's Moira or someone else. I'll make the arrangements as long as you'll go."

"I don't know how I feel about Moira."

He nodded. "Fine. I'll check around for someone else. I'm going to call your dad and my sister to let them know we'll be delayed a few days. You can't ride that far right now."

He walked out again, this time pulling his phone from his pocket. I turned on the TV and tried to focus on one of my favorite shows. I understood why he was so worried. I knew the thoughts I had weren't normal. He was right when he said I needed help. What would it feel like to not doubt myself all the time? Or try to mask the pain by getting myself into crazy situations, like sleeping with random strangers? I couldn't even fathom such a thing. I'd been like this for as long as I could remember. Even though I hadn't slept around when I'd been at the Devil's Fury, I'd fixated on Doolittle to the point of obsession. Once that was gone, I'd thrown my inhibitions out the window and done whatever I thought would feel good long enough to numb the sensations and chaotic thoughts.

I spent the rest of the day trying not to let the darkness suck me under. Instead, I watched TV, ate the snacks Lynx brought me, and tried to think of positive things. Like belonging to a man who clearly cared about me a great deal. He might not have said he loved me, but I was now certain he was with me for the right reasons.

Even if I couldn't go back to the Devil's Fury, I'd have a new family here with Lynx. The Savage Raptors had all been nice to me. Not a single one had said anything bad. When Lynx wanted to claim me, they hadn't seemed to balk at the thought of me being part of their family. At least, it hadn't been dragged out forever. If they'd opposed the idea, then I wouldn't be in his house right now.

"Do you feel like sitting at the table to eat something?" Lynx asked. "The papers said you might have an upset stomach, so I made chicken with rice, and I held back on the seasoning for your portion."

"I think I'd like to eat in the kitchen."

He helped me up and kept hold of my waist as I went to the table. I didn't feel like I'd fall or anything, but he seemed concerned. How could I have ever thought this man would do anything with the intent to harm me? I should have known he'd been an idiot and not meant to hurt my feelings.

Lynx pulled out my chair and I gingerly sat down. I felt a bit achy, and I'd been cramping. Although, I hadn't thought to change the pad they'd given me at the hospital. The nurse mentioned it was important to keep it fresh to avoid infection. The problem was that I didn't usually use them.

"I need something from the store," I said.

"Whatever it is, I can get it or ask a Prospect to pick it up."

My cheeks warmed. "It's, um... pads. I need them until the bleeding stops. They said to change them often, so I'll probably need a big package."

He took out his phone and downloaded the app for the grocery store, then passed it over to me. "Order whatever you want or need. I'll see if they offer delivery for today. If not, I'll get someone to pick up the order."

While I took bites of my dinner, which was better than I'd feared, I ordered the items I thought I'd need. Not only pads, but some yogurt and wheat bread as well. As much as I hoped I would be able to eat regularly by tomorrow, I wanted to be prepared. Toast and yogurt were both on my approved foods list.

Lynx took the phone back, paid for the order, then put the device away.

"They'll drop it at the gates within the hour. I chose the express option so you wouldn't have to wait long."

"Thank you. You said you were calling my dad

earlier. What did you tell him?"

He paused mid-bite. "I had to tell him about the baby, and the miscarriage. He was understandably worried. He's on standby until I give the all-clear for meeting in Alabama. My sister also said for me to take care of you and just head that way whenever you're comfortable and feel up to it."

"How far is it?" I asked.

"It's a really long drive. Full day on the road. I think we should break it up. Travel about five or six hours, then get a hotel room for the night. If you need me to break it up more, that's not a problem. We can take as long to get there as we need to."

He was being so sweet and understanding. I wasn't sure where my alpha biker had gone, but I had to admit I liked this side of him too. It turned me on when he got a little bossy. The kinder side of him made me melt. No, I definitely couldn't stay angry at him. Besides, it hadn't entirely been his fault. I should have spoken up instead of running off the way I had. Neither of us were without blame.

"I could be ready to go in as little as two days, or it could be a week or more. They said everyone heals at a different pace," I said.

"I talked to Atilla. He's not sending me on any jobs or asking me to do anything around the compound for right now." He reached over to place his hand on top of mine. "I'll be here to help with whatever you need. If you want space, just tell me, and I'll take a short walk outside or busy myself elsewhere in the house."

"I wish I wasn't the only old lady here." I studied him. "How exactly is it that I became one so easily?"

"No one here has an issue with you, Merry. They knew I wanted you for my own, and there wasn't a reason to deny my claim."

I could think of one. My dad. Unless he'd known he'd be able to win over Grizzly. No, I didn't think that was it. More like he hadn't cared if my dad liked it or not because his only concern had been *me*.

"When you're done, you can wash up if you'd like. The pads should be here by then. No reason we can't call it a night a little early."

"You're coming to bed with me?"

He nodded. "I'll hold you and we can talk, read, watch something… whatever you want."

Sleep actually sounded nice. I hadn't realized I was tired until now. I'd take a nice warm shower, put my pajamas on, and get some rest. Lynx could join me if he wanted to, as long as he didn't care if I was awake or not.

We finished our meal, and that's exactly what I did. I was asleep within a few minutes of crawling into bed.

Chapter Nine

Lynx
One Week Later

It had taken Meredith about five days before she felt comfortable leaving for Alabama, and while we'd stopped overnight along the way, we were finally at the Dixie Reapers compound. My sister met us at the gates and showed us to our temporary quarters. Even though I'd said Grizzly could stay with us, he hadn't made a decision last I'd heard, so walking in the door and seeing him lounging in a chair took me by surprise. Not only me. Meredith tensed behind me, her hand gripping the bottom of my cut.

"Decided to stay with us after all?" I asked.

"I want as much time with my girl as I can get." He stood and came closer. I hadn't seen him in a long while, and the man had aged quite a bit. I didn't think it was all to do with how old he was either. His medical issues had taken a toll on him. "Meredith?"

She peeked from behind me. I watched as tears gathered in her eyes. The moment her dad opened his arms, she darted around me and went straight to him. He wrapped her up in a big hug, and the relief on his face was rather telling. Clearly, he hadn't known what sort of reception she'd give him.

"Why don't I put our things in our room, then I'll head out with Ridley for a bit. The two of you can sit here and talk," I said.

"I wanted to meet your family." Meredith pulled free from her dad. "I know I'm not exactly a stranger to any of them, but it's different now."

"You will, Merry, but I think you and Grizzly need some time together first. I'm sure he knows the way to Venom's house. I'll leave the keys to the

Charger here. I think it would be best for the two of you to drive over."

Ridley cleared her throat and gave Meredith a bright smile. "I've heard quite a bit about you from both my daughters and my brother."

Meredith winced. "I can imagine what Mariah and Farrah had to say."

Ridley shrugged. "I make my own decisions. What I can tell you is that my brother seems happier than ever before. His opinion is the only one you should be concerned with."

Meredith nodded and leaned against Grizzly. The big man held her close, and I saw the look of gratitude in his eyes when we locked gazes. He gave me a slight nod, and I carried the bags to the empty bedroom. Ridley was waiting outside for me when I got back to the front door. I kissed Meredith and left, knowing she needed this time with her dad, even if she wouldn't admit it.

"So, my nieces have been running their mouths," I said.

"When do they not?" Ridley rolled her eyes. "I thought you were crazy when you said you wanted them to bring Grizzly down. Their entire families piled into their vehicles. I'm surprised the big guy could find a spot to sit."

"Wait, so the kids are at your place too?" I stopped mid-step. I didn't mind seeing Farrah and Mariah, even Venom would be a welcome sight. But the children... We'd just lost our baby. How would Meredith react?

"I asked Lyssa and Darian to wrangle them for a little while. You didn't even ask about Dawson. He's all grown-up now."

"I keep in touch with him. Unlike my nieces, he

knows how to reach out now and then. Or how to answer a damn phone call."

Ridley snickered. "They know how to answer. They choose not to most of the time. Probably worried we'll want something."

"How's your other half enjoying his retirement?"

"I think he likes it. He still gets together on a regular basis with Torch and the others. The lot of them play cards and gossip like old ladies. The rest of the time, he's with us at home. Probably why Dawson wanted to move out."

I wasn't going to disillusion my sister. If she wanted to believe that was Dawson's reason, then I'd let her. Since I spoke with the kid somewhat often, I knew the real score. He came from two generations of bikers and didn't have the slightest inclination to join a club. Not the Dixie Reapers, or any other one. In fact, he'd been dating a girl in town. Something told me my sister and Venom still didn't know.

My sister had walked over to the apartments, so we headed back to her place on foot. When I got there, I saw Farrah and Mariah out front, looking as if they wanted to ambush someone. The fierce expressions on their faces didn't bode well for my Merry.

"Look who it is. Trouble One and Trouble Two," I said. "Have you made both your men go gray yet?"

"You're not funny, Uncle Lynx," Mariah said. "You know I wouldn't do something so cruel to Savage."

"Since Demon decided to shave his head a few months ago, and keeps doing it, I wouldn't know what color his hair is these days," Farrah said.

"Maybe he's hiding the fact you're aging him." I smirked and Ridley smacked my arm. "Now, why the hell are you two out here with those looks on your faces?"

"Did you really claim that stupid bitch?" Farrah asked.

The smile fell from my face. I stopped in my tracks and fought for control. If anyone other than my niece had said such a thing, I'd have knocked them on their ass. I counted to ten. Then twenty. By the time I reached forty, I knew there was no way to cool my temper right now.

"Ridley..."

She nodded and stepped forward. "You just said something incredibly disrespectful about your uncle's woman. And at my house, no less. If you didn't come here with an open mind, then fucking leave, Farrah."

"Daddy won't let you throw me out," she said.

"Really? Because I recall being the one to give you some cash when he did exactly that. He told you to pack your shit and leave because you were causing too much trouble. Now here you are doing it all over again."

My sister folded her arms and stared her oldest down. Farrah's posture relaxed, and she sighed before giving a slight nod. The door behind her opened and Demon stepped out. His eyebrow went up as he looked from Ridley to Farrah.

"What did I tell you?" he asked.

"To behave," she mumbled.

"What did I say would happen if you didn't?"

Her cheeks went crimson, and I was certain whatever her answer, it would be something neither Ridley nor I wanted to hear. She hurried into the house and Demon lingered. He pointed inside and Mariah ran after her sister. Looked like he had the two of them well in hand. So, why had everyone let Meredith run wild, then condemned her for it? I had so many questions.

"You really claiming Meredith?" he asked.

"Already did. She's coming by in a little bit. I told her to spend time with Grizzly first. Thought they could use the one-on-one right now," I said.

"Probably. He's missed the hell out of her. No one back home can understand why. Girl was more trouble than either of those two," he said, tipping his head toward the house.

"Can I ask you something?" He motioned for me to continue. "You seem to do just fine with Farrah. I'm guessing Savage doesn't have an issue with Mariah. So why is it a club, who clearly knows how to handle strong, opinionated women, let Meredith fall so far? No, what I really want to know is why you then blamed her for it."

Ridley let out a long whistle. "Okay. This conversation is going to require coffee. Possibly spiked with something."

We went into the house and everyone gathered in the kitchen. I noticed the table wasn't the same as before. In fact, the kitchen looked larger too. Had they done some renovations since I'd been here last? With both Farrah and Mariah having kids, it made sense. Even if they lived in a different state, I knew the girls came home to visit now and then. Dawson would eventually settle down and have a family too.

We each took a seat while Ridley brewed a large pot of coffee. I hoped she planned to make a second one. No one said a word until we each had a cup in our hands, except Mariah. She shook her head when Ridley tried to hand her one.

"I can't. I'm pregnant," she said.

Ridley set the cup down hard, her lips forming a thin line. "Why the hell are you just telling me now?

Does your daddy know?"

Mariah shook her head. "I'm only two months. We were going to wait and tell everyone after I'd made it through the first trimester. I didn't plan on being here so soon."

"Do me a favor and don't tell Merry," I said.

"Merry?" Demon's brow furrowed. "Is that what you call Meredith?"

Farrah snorted. "Wow. Doolittle called her that. If you ask me, it's the wrong name. There's not a damn thing *merry* about her."

I took a swallow of my coffee, letting it scorch my throat. It was either that, or reach across the table and throttle my niece. Demon must have known my exact thoughts because he reached over and squeezed the back of Farrah's neck, hard enough she winced.

"What I'm going to tell you doesn't leave this room. Meredith will tell the Devil's Fury, and Grizzly, if and when she's ready. But I think it might be the only way to get my niece to stop running her fucking mouth." I glared at Farrah. "None of you stopped to consider *why* she acted the way she did. You just thought she was being a bitch, or immature."

"We were in the wrong too," Demon said. "None of us tried to stop her. We thought Doolittle would be good for her, and she seemed crazy about him, so... I guess we all hoped the two would end up together."

"Crazy," I mumbled. "Don't use that word around her either."

"What's going on?" Ridley asked, putting her hand on my shoulder. "Is there something wrong with Meredith?"

"She has an appointment with a psychiatrist next week. I noticed she has a tendency toward reckless behavior. She admitted to obsessing over Doolittle, and she worried the same would happen with me. I told her she could obsess all she wanted." I sighed and took another swallow of coffee. "I think she's got some problems that she can't solve on her own. Ridley, I never told you, but our mom had mental health issues. Found the pills for it one day. I don't think she was always a rotten human being. There's not a doubt in my mind that my father took advantage of her and twisted her to fit his needs. She probably just saw a rich man and thought it would be a good way to take care of you."

Ridley pulled out a chair and sat down hard. It looked like I'd hit her right between the eyes. If things hadn't come to this, I would have taken that secret to my grave. Perhaps I shouldn't have. If Mom had been sick like that, then it was possible Ridley or I could end up with it later, or pass the gene to our children. Which made me eye my nieces.

"You realize that if Meredith *is* mentally ill, you've condemned her for something entirely out of her control. It would be like ridiculing someone with autism or giving an amputee a hard time. Neither of which you'd ever do, right?"

Farrah slumped in her seat, and even Mariah looked ashamed of herself. Not my intention, but I did need them to stop and think before they spoke. One wrong word and Meredith would start spiraling again. She'd been so tense and anxious over seeing these two. Although, I also knew my nieces were rather talented at showing people what they wanted to see. I had no idea if they were genuinely remorseful.

"Tell us about Meredith," Demon said.

"Do you know why the trip was delayed?" I asked.

"Mom said the two of you couldn't make it here

any sooner." Mariah frowned. "We thought you had club business or something."

"Meredith was in the hospital. She had a miscarriage." I scanned the faces around the table. "Yeah, we were going to have a baby. I need her to remain as calm as possible during this trip. She insisted on coming, but I'm not convinced she's fully recovered yet. It's also why I hoped the kids wouldn't be here. I don't know how she'd handle seeing them right now."

"Jesus," Demon muttered. "Did Grizzly know?"

I shook my head. "I told him after we got home from the hospital. She'd wanted to share the news in person. I could tell she was scared, but I think she was a little excited too. I know I was."

Having kids with Meredith seemed like a dream come true. Unless we were both going to pass on fucked-up genetics. Maybe it would be better if we didn't have any. We could always adopt.

"Is she talking to Grizzly about all this now?" Mariah asked. "Can he handle it?"

"I don't know the answer to either question." I leaned back in my chair. "What I need to know is if you can be supportive of Meredith, or if you're going to treat her like the enemy. Because if it's the latter, I'm going to have to ask you to leave when she comes over. You're my family and I love you, but I have to think of what's best for her right now."

"I can be good," Mariah said. "I wish things had happened differently back then. Oh, God. When Doolittle finds out…"

Farrah winced. "That won't be pretty. He took care of her for so long. I know he felt betrayed not only by her but the club as well when we all tried to run Minnie off. If he finds out Meredith acted that way because she was sick, he's going to want to kick his own ass."

"We'll deal with that later." Demon cocked his head. "If I'm not mistaken, I believe Meredith and Grizzly are here. Venom too. Hell, it sounds like a damn herd of buffalo out there."

The front door opened. "Where is everyone?"

Ridley smiled. "In the kitchen, Venom."

He came in with not only Grizzly and Meredith on his heels, but Rocky and Mara as well. The way Mara had looped her arm through Meredith's made my tension ease quite a bit. It looked like she'd made a friend here already. Good. I wanted her to have all the support she'd ever need. Being the only woman back home wouldn't be easy, especially since she hadn't had time to make friends in town.

"Brought a few extra people," Venom said. Ridley stood and he took her seat, then tugged her down onto his lap. Demon patted his legs and Farrah did the same, freeing up a chair for someone. I held out my hand for Meredith.

"And where's an old fart like me supposed to sit?" Grizzly asked.

Mariah jumped up and ran out of the room, returning a moment later with a rolling computer chair. Although, it had so much padding it looked more comfortable than my damn living room furniture.

"Right here," Mariah said. "Best chair in the house."

Grizzly grunted as he sat, and Mariah reclaimed her seat. I also didn't miss the look she shot Meredith, and I didn't like it. Not even a little. I'd noticed Savage was absent and I wondered if he'd decided to stay with the kids. Or did he dislike Meredith so much he couldn't stand to be in the same room with her? The thought was unsettling.

"So, who's ready to apologize to my daughter?" Grizzly asked, giving Demon, Farrah, and Mariah a glare.

"We're sorry," Mariah said. I could hear the lack of sincerity in her voice, and I was certain Grizzly could too. "We should have been more supportive and…"

I hugged Meredith, tugging her closer against my chest. "I told them about your appointment next week, and about your hospital stay. I hadn't planned to say anything to you, but I don't want there to be secrets between us."

"Thanks," she murmured. "So you forgive me for acting out now that you know there was likely a reason?"

Mariah's cheeks flushed. "Um, well…"

"If the three of us being here makes you uncomfortable, we'll leave so you can spend time with Venom and Ridley," Demon said. "It's not our intention to make you feel ill at ease."

Meredith sighed. "It's fine. You can stay. It's not like this is my house anyway. I can't exactly run you off."

Ridley waved a hand. "By all means. Chase them off if that's what you need to do. Besides, Venom already threw Farrah out once, and I damn near did it already today. She should be used to it by now."

Farrah stuck her tongue out at Ridley and Demon smacked her on the thigh. Pretty damn hard by the sound of it. It certainly got her attention, and she immediately became more obedient. *Interesting.*

Chapter Ten

Meredith

"Do you need anything?" Ridley asked. "I don't just mean right this second, but in general?"

Her kindness threw me off a little. I'd walked in the door expecting open hostility. Well, maybe not from Ridley. She'd never given me a reason to think she wouldn't like me. Her daughters, on the other hand, had most likely been badmouthing me up to this point. It's pretty much what the entire Devil's Fury had done. Even my sisters weren't the same when we spoke.

"I wouldn't mind something to drink, for right now. As to the other, I think I'll be okay. I have Lynx, after all." He gave me a slight squeeze in acknowledgment. "And my dad."

"The Devil's Fury are your family too," Demon said. "I admit we didn't act much like it the last time you saw us. There's plenty of blame to pass around. I'm sorry for whatever part I played. All I can do is ask for your forgiveness, and hope you'll give me another chance to prove I'm worthy of being your family."

I hadn't expected such a thing from Demon. As the Sergeant-at-Arms, he was one of the toughest men in the club. To hear him ask for me to forgive him -- that was *huge*. It wasn't that I disliked anyone at the Devil's Fury. But I also didn't feel welcome there anymore. I'd had a nice talk with my dad. Things between us were back to normal, or as much as it would ever be.

I'd made my peace with him. Since I knew he wouldn't live forever, it was important for us to remain as close as possible. Even if I couldn't go to the Devil's Fury to visit him, I'd continue to call him frequently.

And now that he could use FaceTime, I'd get to see him, even if it wasn't in person.

"Farrah and I will take a walk," Demon said. He forced Farrah to stand, then took her hand and led her from the room. I hated feeling as if I'd chased Ridley's daughter from her home. Mariah squirmed in her seat before standing as well.

"I don't have anything against you, Meredith, but I don't want my presence to make you uncomfortable. I'd love to hear from you sometime. Maybe we can call each other every now and then?"

I nodded, not knowing what else to say. She left, leaving the rest of us sitting in silence. Neither Venom nor Ridley seemed upset by this turn of events. I'd thought they'd be angry I'd made their kids leave. Instead, they were offering me their support. My throat felt tight and my eyes burned with unshed tears.

So far, I'd cried several times since losing the baby. Never *about* the baby, though. Logically, I knew I'd lost my child. Since I'd only recently discovered the pregnancy and hadn't had a chance to really accept the fact I was going to be a mom, it made it feel less real.

"I love my girls," Venom said. "Doesn't mean I always agree with them. I think the two of them leaving right now was the best thing for them to do. This is your first time meeting all of us as part of the family. If they can't behave, then they have no right to sit here with us."

"You aren't angry with me?" I asked.

Venom smiled. "No. If I were, you'd know it. You have my woman's seal of approval. Good enough for me. Besides. Lynx seems to have a good head on his shoulders. He wouldn't have claimed you if you were as rotten as they say."

"Oh, I was pretty bad," I said.

My dad reached over and patted my arm. I knew he was telling me everything was all right. I didn't know if my life would ever be what most considered normal, but at least I knew I had the support of some wonderful people. Lynx. My dad. Now Ridley and Venom. I'd met Rocky and Mara right before coming here, and they were really nice. I'd liked Mara right away.

"I don't have any idea what happened," Mara said. "What I do know is that I'm a pretty good judge of character. I liked you from the start, Meredith. If you're open to it, I'd like to be friends. I know there's an age difference between us, but…"

I waved her off. "Lynx is older than me. My dad always told us age was just a number. I've found women my age tend to cause a lot of drama."

Ridley smiled. "She's not wrong. Welcome to the family, Meredith. If the Savage Raptors give you any trouble, you're welcome here anytime."

Venom growled softly. "Woman, I'm not the VP here anymore. You can't go saying shit like that without discussing it with Savior and Saint at the very least."

"It's the thought that counts," I said. "And I appreciate it. You've made me feel welcome."

"More than my fucking club did," my dad said. "If my other daughters and the grandkids weren't at the Devil's Fury, I'd ask to spend my last days with the Savage Raptors so I could stay close to Meredith."

And now I couldn't hold back the tears. I looked at my dad. *Really* looked. The first moment I'd seen him in person, I'd known he wasn't doing well. It hadn't hit me until now exactly how soon I might lose him.

"Last days?" Rocky asked.

"Heart failure," Dad said. "Not much time left. I haven't told everyone, but last visit to the doctor, they said I had a month or less. It's why I wanted to see Meredith one last time."

I pressed a hand to my mouth to hold back my sobs. Lynx turned me so my face was against his chest, and he ran his hand up and down my back. I'd only recently gotten my dad back, and I was going to lose him for good this time. It didn't seem fair.

"You've been with your other family all this time, right?" Mara asked.

"I have. They've known my days were numbered, but I haven't told them the latest. If I had, they'd have done everything they could to keep me home. Then I'd have missed out on seeing Meredith again. I needed to hug my daughter and hold her in my arms one more time."

"Damn, Grizzly." Venom shook his head. "This is all kinds of fucked-up. You can't go with Meredith without feeling like you chose her over the others. And she can't go with you because your club still has their heads up their asses."

"Exactly."

"I won't be fully healed for four to six weeks," I said. I felt Lynx tense and realized I hadn't told him the entire truth. I'd only said no sex for that long. It should have been in the hospital papers, but maybe it hadn't been. I hadn't bothered to read them. "When we leave here, I need to go home. I have an appointment next week, and I'll need to find a doctor in town so I can have a follow-up from my D&C."

"If you'd told me…" Lynx trailed off, but I knew what he was going to say. If I'd said I wouldn't be fully healed until possibly six weeks, he'd have kept me home. Then I'd have lost the chance to ever see my dad again.

"I needed this," I said. "I'm sorry I didn't tell you everything."

"I'm not sure this trip gave either of you the closure you needed," Rocky said. "I, for one, vote that you can stay as long as you want. I know the plan was only for a few days, but maybe you could stay until you have to return for your appointment."

"We won't be imposing?" Lynx asked.

"Not at all," Venom assured us. "If Demon, Savage, and their families can't stay that long, then someone here will make sure Grizzly gets back home."

"What do you say?" Grizzly asked, looking at Lynx. "Can you and my girl stay here a while longer?"

I leaned into Lynx. "Can we call and change my appointment? I know it's important, but so is this."

Ridley cleared her throat. "Actually, if you don't mind seeing someone different, the club knows a good psychiatrist. He helped treat Janessa and Kalani when Tex found them. His name is Dr. Sykes."

"Would you mind calling him?" Lynx asked. "If he can meet with Merry while we're here, then I'll call Atilla and ask about extending our stay."

"The apartment has one of those stacking washers and dryers," Venom said. "You'll be able to wash clothes if you didn't bring enough. Plus, there are plenty of stores nearby."

"You don't need to run this by your club officers?" Lynx asked.

Venom shook his head. "They know what's going on and why the lot of you are here. I have no doubt they'll be fine with a longer visit. If they have an issue with it, I'll take the heat for it."

Ridley huffed. "Like they'd dare say anything to you. Everyone knows you stepped down voluntarily.

It's not like anyone wanted you to leave your position as VP."

"So, are we in agreement?" Grizzly asked. "We'll stay longer?"

I nodded. Even if Lynx hadn't wanted to stay, I'd have fought to have more time with my dad. Knowing I could meet with a doctor while I was here just made everything better. If the Dixie Reapers trusted the man, then so would I. The fact he'd treated their women before meant I wouldn't have to be so secretive about being part of a club. Or rather, having partially grown up in one. It wasn't something easy to explain, and I knew only giving half-truths wouldn't be helpful.

"I'll call Dr. Sykes tonight and see when he's free," Ridley said.

"I'll let the officers know about the change of plans." Venom smiled. "It will be nice having more time with you, Meredith. I hope you'll stop by often while you're here."

"If Mariah is here, why didn't Savage come to the house with her?" I asked.

Everyone went silent, which was answer enough. The fact he hadn't come with her tonight told me plenty. He still didn't like me, and probably hadn't wanted to see me. It drove home the fact that once Dad was gone, I wouldn't have a single ally with the Devil's Fury. Demon might have apologized, but he wouldn't be able to sway the opinions of the entire club. I no longer felt welcome there. Sad how the Dixie Reapers had been so welcoming, yet the people I'd lived with didn't want anything to do with me.

"I'm going to ask them to return home without me," Grizzly said. "I'll call Adalia and Badger when I leave here. They won't be happy with my decision, but they'll have no choice but to deal with it."

"Are you sure, Dad?" I asked.

He nodded. "I've let the Devil's Fury keep the two of us apart long enough. Not anymore."

My heart warmed at his words. But I also knew if he died before he got back home, I'd never forgive myself for robbing my sisters and their children of getting to tell him bye. At the same time, I wanted to be selfish and spend his last days with him.

"Love you, Daddy," I said.

He stood slowly and leaned down to kiss the top of my head. "Love you too, girl. I'm going to head back to the apartment. I'll make my calls on the way. You stay here longer."

"You're welcome to keep sharing the apartment with us," Lynx said. "Even when the others leave."

He shook his head. "I appreciate the gesture, but I'll move to one of the empty ones. The two of you still need time to bond, and Meredith is healing. She'll want some quiet time to herself sometimes."

"Whatever you think is best," Lynx said.

I wanted to tell my dad to stay with us, except he was right. I would want some time alone to process my thoughts and feelings, and I knew I needed time alone with Lynx. I wasn't the only one who'd lost the baby. He'd been so ready to accept the child. This had to be hard on him too.

"Well, if everyone is going to stick around for a bit, why don't we order pizza or something?" Ridley asked.

My stomach had been iffy that first night, but pizza sounded pretty damn good right now. I nodded my agreement and made myself comfortable in one of the now empty chairs. Lynx hadn't uttered a single complaint about me sitting on him, but I wasn't exactly light. I had to be putting his legs to sleep.

I'd lost my family with the Devil's Fury, but it seemed like I'd gained so much more. For the first time in forever, I felt accepted. Wanted, even. Until now, Lynx was the only one who'd made me feel this way since the day I left the Devil's Fury. Now I had so many more people in my corner. It felt really amazing.

Chapter Eleven

Lynx

I was proud of Meredith and pissed as fuck at my two nieces. I'd nearly bitten my tongue off in an attempt not to make too many waves, but I was done. While Meredith got to know Rocky, Mara, Ridley, and Venom a little better, I decided to take a step outside. My sister eyed me, and I knew she had some idea as to what I was about to do. I only hoped I didn't piss off Grizzly, since technically my nieces were now part of his club. It was one thing for him to be upset with the Devil's Fury and another for me to say something. However, the way he'd decided to stick around for Meredith made me think he'd be giving me his support in this matter.

I banged my fist on the doors of the two apartments where my nieces were staying with their families. Demon opened the door, took one look at my face and held up a hand as he backed into the unit. Then he shoved Farrah outside and shut the door. I even heard the lock click, which made me smile. Savage and Mariah both came to the door at their place.

"I have some things I need to discuss with my nieces. You're welcome to listen, but if you try to get in the way, I have no problem introducing my fist to your jaw."

Savage tipped his chin up a little, then gave a nod and stepped outside with Mariah. I didn't hear or see the kids anywhere, so I figured they must be visiting with the smaller Reaper children somewhere in the compound. Good. I didn't need them to hear any of this.

"I appreciate that y'all came all this way to bring

Grizzly so he could see Meredith one more time. It's too bad you didn't come with an open mind. Instead, you arrived believing you knew everything about her, had already condemned her, and are unwilling to move past what happened." I looked from Farrah to Mariah. "You said you were sorry. I'm not sure I believe you. Over the years, you've learned to say whatever you thought would get you out of the hot seat when it came to your parents. So that's what you did today. You said you were sorry, in the hopes your parents wouldn't think poorly of you."

"Aren't you going a little far?" Savage asked. "You don't know what happened. You weren't there."

"You're right. I wasn't, but I sure wish I'd fucking been there. Want to know why?" I asked.

He shrugged. "Does it matter?"

"He tried to tell us she's mentally ill and that's why she acted the way she did," Farrah said. "It's an excuse and nothing more. She needs to own up to what she did. Do you realize she nearly destroyed Doolittle's life? She drove Minnie away, and he nearly lost her."

"So you've never done anything you were ashamed of? Never said or did something you shouldn't have?" I folded my arm. "Or for instance, never pushed your dad so far he threw you out of the house?"

Farrah winced and Mariah tried to hide behind Savage. Yeah, I'd heard all about her bullshit too and how Venom handed her to Savage practically gift-wrapped to keep her from fucking up her life. These two acted like they were perfect little princesses.

"I got news for the both of you. Your shit stinks like everyone else's and neither of you are perfect. Far fucking from it! Until the two of you can pull your heads from your asses, I don't want anything to do with you. Don't call me. You sure the fuck better not ask me for help with anything. As of now, Meredith is your aunt."

"She's younger than us!" Mariah said.

"And? What's your point? How many years is there between you and Savage? Or between Farrah and Demon? Remind me again..."

That shut her up. Even Savage looked a little embarrassed by her comment. She seemed to have forgotten Darian was younger than Ridley. Yeah, my sister's dad had claimed a woman younger than his kid. Now the two women were best friends.

"Grizzly needs this time with Meredith, and I'm glad he's getting a chance to be with her before it's too late. I only wish the Devil's Fury would admit they fucked up. Y'all were the only family she had. When you turned your backs on her, it left her without anyone to rely on. You sent her out into the world, where she floundered and made even bigger stupid decisions than before. It's a damn miracle she didn't fucking die. Not one damn person along the way stopped to wonder *why*. What made her act like that? Was she seeking attention? Did she think she was better than everyone else? Or was it a cry for help that every fucking person in her life ignored?"

"What do you want from us?" Savage asked.

"Nothing. Only for the lot of you to forget you ever knew Meredith, until you're ready to accept her. In all honesty, I think she's washed her hands of you. By the time you realize what you've done, it will be too late. She'll refuse to have anything to do with any of you. Can't say that I blame her."

"You don't want to hear from us?" Farrah asked. "You're really going to turn your back on your blood family for that woman?"

"Yeah, Farrah. I am. You see, you have Demon, Mariah, your parents, and the entire Devil's Fury. In fact, you have every Dixie Reaper willing to do anything for you. You have one of the biggest families in the world. Meredith? She only has me, and now she has the Savage Raptors, and we're admittedly a lot smaller than either the Reapers or the Fury. Hell, you two also have the Devil's Boneyard since Darian's dad is with them."

I wanted to scream. To hit something. Or someone. How the hell had Venom and my sister raised these girls to be so damn selfish and narrow-minded? I didn't remember them being like this. I heard a door open and looked over my shoulder. Grizzly stepped out and came closer, looking worn the fuck out. I felt like an asshole because he'd likely heard everything, and I'd only added to his burden.

"Sorry, Grizzly. I should have taken this elsewhere," I said.

"No. You're not doing anything wrong. You're standing up for my little girl. These three are being assholes, pure and simple. I only wish I'd been stronger to rein all this in when it first started. I'm fucking tired, Lynx. I can't get any damn peace. At home, no one will talk about Meredith. If I bring her up, the tension in the room goes up by about a thousand percent." He sighed. "Savage, I need you and Demon to take your families home. I've already spoken to Adalia and Badger. I'll call Shella and Lilian tonight."

"I wish you didn't have to choose which daughter to spend time with," I said. "But I'm grateful you're taking the time to be with Meredith right now. She needed this. Well, maybe not the bullshit these three brought along with you."

"Shouldn't you have more respect right now?" Savage asked. "At least our women were born into the Dixie Reapers. You're not on your own turf."

I heard a whistle behind me and turned to see both Savior and Saint heading our way. Neither man looked happy. I wasn't sure if I'd pissed them off, or if Savage's comment just now had done it.

Savior looked at Farrah and Mariah. "You two finished causing trouble? If so, pack your shit."

Farrah gasped. "Are you throwing us out? This is our home!"

Saint shook his head. "Nope. This *was* your home. You live with the Devil's Fury now. It's time you went back. Lynx got permission to be here, and he hasn't caused any problems. In fact, I like the way he's standing up for his woman. Even heard him apologize to Grizzly. He didn't have to do that. He's not the one being a pain in the ass."

"We'll head out in the morning," Savage said.

"I'd prefer you leave now." Savior crossed his arms. "Think all of the Dixie Reapers would for that matter. Stop at a motel on the way home if you need to, but I want you gone."

Demon stepped outside with two bags in his hands. "I'll load up our vehicle and be gone with Farrah and Rebel within the next half hour. Sorry my wife doesn't know how to keep her mouth shut. We'll work on it."

Farrah silently fumed, but I had no doubt Demon would eventually get through to her. Probably not in a way she'd like, either. He didn't take any of her shit, and that's exactly the sort of man she needed.

"Fine. I'll go get the kids. Mariah can pack our things and we'll leave tonight as well," Savage said. "I don't understand why everyone is taking Meredith's side."

"We aren't," Savior said. "We're taking the *right* side. If Grizzly doesn't have an issue with her, then we don't. She's family now, since Lynx is Ridley's brother."

"Anyone bothered to ask Doolittle and Minnie what they think?" I asked.

"I did," Grizzly said. "Want me to call them back? Maybe everyone needs to hear what they have to say."

"I think if anyone needs to hear it, it's Meredith. Unless it's something that will upset her," I said.

He shook his head. "It won't. When she comes home, we'll call them back and I'll put it on speaker. Minnie feels pretty bad right now. She assumed we'd all spoiled Meredith too much. Knowing she needed help and everyone turned their backs on Meredith... Well, Minnie feels partly responsible, even if she isn't. Doolittle didn't like knowing he'd failed her either."

"Thanks, Grizzly. If she knows not everyone at the Devil's Fury hates her, it might help her heal a little." I hoped so at any rate.

"Farrah and Mariah will be welcome to return when Meredith and Lynx aren't here," Savior said. "But you need permission first. No dropping in unannounced. In the past, we've overlooked it when you did that. Not anymore. If you're grown enough to run a woman out of her own club, then it's time you start acting like an adult and follow *all* the fucking rules."

Mariah went into the apartment, supposedly to pack. Savage left to get the kids, and Demon practically shoved Farrah into their vehicle. Once we were alone, Savior sighed and relaxed.

"Sorry you had to deal with that," he said. "If I'd

known they were going to be little shits, I'd have told them not to come. Since they were from the Dixie Reapers and have family here, we thought they'd be the best choice for this trip."

"It's fine. They're my family. I'd hoped they could behave themselves, and maybe give Meredith a chance. Guess I expected too much." I ran a hand through my hair. "I didn't mean to bring so much drama to your club."

"There's always something. Especially whenever teen girls or young women are involved."

"I'm telling your daughter you said that," Saint said.

"Please don't fucking do that," Savior said. "Ares is already a handful."

"Meredith still with Ridley?" Grizzly asked.

"They were ordering pizza. Want to come back and join us?" I asked.

He nodded. "Yeah, I'll walk with you."

"Why don't we take the Charger? Meredith is probably going to be tired by the time we come back." She probably would be, but that wasn't the only reason I suggested the car. The man looked like he might fall over between here and there. I didn't know how he was still upright.

"Sounds good."

I went inside and grabbed the car keys. I'd left them before so Meredith could drive to Ridley's. Instead, she and Grizzly had walked there. I wanted to spank her ass. Not only did she not have any business running around so much, but she should have forced her dad into the damn car one way or another. The man looked like he was knocking on heaven's door.

By the time we got back to Ridley's, the pizza was there, and everyone seemed to be having a great time. I sat beside Meredith again, and Grizzly reclaimed the cushy leather chair.

"Everything okay?" Ridley asked.

"Is that your way of wondering whether or not your bratty children are gone? If so, then yes. They're both heading out tonight. Dawson not stopping by?" I asked.

"I told him we'd ordered pizza and that you wanted him to meet Meredith. He's supposed to come visit." She sighed. "I wish he'd stayed at the compound. I don't know why he's so dead set against following in his daddy's footsteps."

I knew. I wasn't going to tell her, though. It might break her heart. Her little boy was up to far more than she realized. Although, if Wire was still tracking all the Reaper kids, then he had to know what was going on. I wasn't sure why he hadn't said anything yet. Maybe he and Dawson had an understanding of some sort.

A car pulled up outside and I had a feeling it was my nephew. When he entered the house, I couldn't help but smile. Kid looked good. Clean-shaven. Hair trimmed neatly. He'd worn a navy polo with jeans and sneakers. Hell, looking at him, no one would know he was a biker's kid.

"Good to see you, Dawson," I said, standing to give him a hug.

He hugged me back, then kneeled down beside Meredith. "You must be my new aunt. Welcome to the family."

"Dawson is Ridley's youngest," I said. "Which makes him close to your age."

Dawson laughed a little and gave Meredith a gentle hug. I was glad he was so welcoming toward her, and I could tell it pleased her. At least one of

Ridley's kids wasn't being an asshole.

"Go get a folding chair," Venom said. "Find a spot to sit and grab some pizza."

Dawson did exactly that, and we spent the next hour eating and having a great time. I liked seeing Meredith so carefree and happy. She fit in with these people, and it made me wish we had more women back home. I wondered what it would take to get another brother or two to decide to settle down. Probably a fucking miracle.

This was exactly what Meredith needed. Hell, I needed it too, even if I hadn't realized it. When people talked about family, this is what I pictured. Not the chaos we'd had earlier. For the sake of Meredith and Grizzly, I hoped the rest of our visit remained this peaceful.

* * *

Meredith

"I had a nice time visiting with everyone," I said as we rode back to the apartment. I'd immediately climbed in the back seat, giving the passenger seat to Dad, which he'd tried to refuse. In the end, I'd won with the argument I had shorter legs.

"I'm sorry about Farrah and Mariah," Lynx said. "They'll eventually come around. And if not, then you won't have to see them again."

"I don't want to keep you from your family," I said.

"You aren't." He reached back to place his hand on my knee. "I had a few words with them. They know exactly how displeased I am with their behavior."

My dad cleared his throat. "There's a call I need to make, and I want you to listen."

I didn't know who he'd be calling that would

require my presence, but I wasn't going to refuse his request. We got to the apartment and went inside. After a short bathroom break, I sat in the living room while Dad made his call. When I heard Doolittle's voice on the other end, my heart nearly stopped. What was he doing?

"Doolittle, it's Grizzly. I have Meredith and Lynx here, and you're on speaker. I think she needs to know you aren't angry with her."

"I'm here too," Minnie said. "And, Meredith, I'm not upset with you over what happened. Not anymore."

"I think I owe you an apology," Doolittle said. "You followed me everywhere, and I called myself your friend. Not once did I stop to consider your behavior might be caused by something else. It didn't occur to me you needed help and didn't know how to ask for it."

Were they being serious? I looked at my dad and realized he'd told them. They now knew everything I'd confided in him, and if I knew Doolittle as well as I thought I did, then he was feeling guilty. He was such a sweet man.

"I'm sorry for trying to keep you two apart," I said. "I didn't love you the way Minnie did. It wasn't until things had gone too far that I'd realized I was obsessed with you. I'd fixated and didn't know how to break free of it."

"Are you getting help now?" Minnie asked.

"I will be. Ridley said the Dixie Reapers know a good psychiatrist. She set it up so the man will come here to meet with me. We're actually having our first session tomorrow." I swallowed hard. "I'm a bit scared, but I know I need help. I can't keep going down the dark path I've been on."

"If you ever come back to the Devil's Fury, you're welcome in our home," Doolittle said.

"I'm going to talk to the old ladies and try to get them to see reason," Minnie said. "If Doolittle and I don't have an issue with you coming here, then there's no reason they should."

"I can't tell you how much I appreciate that." I heaved a big sigh. "But... I don't think I'll ever go back. My home is with Lynx now, and the Dixie Reapers have been very welcoming. I'm comfortable here and with the Savage Raptors. After everything that's happened, I don't think I'll ever feel that way about the Devil's Fury. I can't."

"I understand. I'm sorry to hear you say that," Doolittle said. "If you ever need anything, please don't hesitate to reach out to us."

I smiled a little. "When I want a pet, I'll be sure to call you. I know you'll find the best one for me, and it will need love as much as I do."

I took Lynx's hand and left the room, letting my dad wrap up the call. Lynx pulled me into his arms when we reached the bedroom, and I let him hold me. Talking to Doolittle and Minnie had helped. Being held by Lynx was even better, though.

"Want a shower?" Lynx asked.

"Yeah, I think I do."

"Wait here and I'll go warm the water. I think your dad plans to move into the unit next door since Farrah and Demon are gone. You both need some quiet time. As much as you've missed each other, I know it's an emotional time, and that can be draining too."

I hesitated only for a minute. "Lynx, there's something I need to tell you."

"What?"

"I love you." I held his gaze. "I know it's too

soon, and things have moved entirely too fast with us. Even though I worried I'd become obsessed with you like I did with Doolittle, I can tell things are different this time. I don't want to even think of living a single day without you. You make me happier than I've ever been."

"Even when I fuck up?" he asked with a grin.

"Well, maybe I'm not happy *then*, but I still love you."

"I love you too. I think I fell for you the moment I saw you." He kissed me before he walked out of the room. I heard the front door shut and knew my dad had left. Creeping down the hall to the bathroom, I found Lynx testing the water temperature with his hand.

"Why don't we shower together?" I asked.

"Thought you needed four to six weeks to heal."

I nodded. "I do. Doesn't mean we can't shower together. We just can't have sex."

But I could give him a blowjob.

"Your dad just left," he said. "So we have the place to ourselves."

"Then what are you waiting for?"

He removed his cut, then pulled his shirt over his head. I admired his chest and inked arms as he toed off his boots and unfastened his belt. By the time he'd stripped, I hadn't taken off a single piece of clothing. I'd been too busy drooling over my sexy biker. I quickly undressed and got into the shower with Lynx.

He soaped my skin, being gentler than ever before. After he finished cleaning me, I washed him as well. The moment my hand closed around his cock, it jerked against my palm.

"Easy, Merry."

"The doctor said I can't have sex. It doesn't mean

I can't do other things." I looked up at him. "I want to make you feel good, Lynx. You did that for me, remember?"

"Merry, you don't have to do this. I'm not with you because I want sex all the time. You need to heal, sweetheart."

I nodded. "And I will. But I really want to do this, Lynx."

"All right." He leaned back against the wall, and I rinsed the soap from his cock. Gingerly going down to my knees, I cupped his balls and licked his shaft. "Jesus. You're going to fucking kill me."

I grinned before sucking him into my mouth. I loved his taste. The feel of him against my tongue. When he groaned and threaded his fingers through my hair, a little thrill ran through me.

"That's it, Merry. Don't fucking stop. Feels so good."

He pumped his hips, his cock sliding to the back of my throat. I nearly gagged and forced myself to relax. When I swallowed, his body shuddered. I did it again, and Lynx lost control.

His hold on my hair tightened, and he fucked my mouth with long, deep strokes. I could barely breathe and fought not to panic. His movements became jerky and his cock swelled right before he filled my mouth with his cum. The hot stickiness coated my tongue, and I swallowed as much as I could, but the rest trickled from the corners of my mouth.

Lynx panted for breath as he pulled free and helped me to my feet. He washed my face and kissed me.

"You're so fucking incredible," he murmured. "You aren't hurting, are you?"

I shook my head. My scalp was a little tender,

but that was all. I knew he'd been asking about the cramps and bleeding. Those weren't any worse than before. I washed again, fearing I might get an infection if I didn't stay clean. Then I got out and dried off.

Lynx carried me to the bedroom and eased me down onto the bed. He took clean pajamas from the suitcase, as well as a pair of panties and a pad. He handed everything to me, and I got dressed while he pulled on a pair of boxers. The rest of the night he held me in his arms, and I eventually fell asleep.

Chapter Twelve

Meredith

Meeting Dr. Sykes hadn't been as scary as I'd feared. He'd been kind, and didn't seem the least bit judgmental, no matter what I said. He'd made notes as I spoke, asked questions to guide me, but not once did he make me feel like I was losing my mind.

"Well, I don't want to give a diagnosis after one visit," Dr. Sykes said. "But I believe you have bipolar disorder. I can give you some literature on it, and you can see if that seems to fit how you feel and react to things. I do want to meet another two times before I give an official diagnosis, or prescribe anything. In the meantime, I'm going to leave you some homework."

"Homework?" I asked.

"I want you to keep a journal. Write down your thoughts and feelings each day. If something big happens, record it and try to analyze your emotions both then and later. I also want you to fill out a graph." He pulled a piece of paper from his briefcase and handed it to me. "The line is what most people consider *normal*. Think of it as neutral emotions. If you're depressed, then you'll record it below the line. If you're feeling manic, then it goes above the line. How far above or below will depend on the severity of what you feel at the time."

He went into a brief description of how mania might present, as well as the lesser signs of depression. By the time we'd finished, I thought I had a better grasp on things.

"I think I understand. Thank you, Dr. Sykes."

"I'll return in three days. When you're using the chart, try to label each dot with the date and time. It will help determine how quickly your mood swings happen. I don't think this is depression. There are too many other factors, from what you've told me."

I nodded and looked at the paper in my hand. If this is what I needed to do, then I'd do it. Maybe I'd finally not feel like such a basket case if he could figure out what was wrong with me. If I needed medication, then I'd take it.

"You're welcome to call me before our next appointment. Don't bottle things up, and don't wait until it's too late. I'm here if you need me, and it looks like you have a good support system at home."

I thanked him again and saw him out. Lynx and my dad were next door. After Dr. Sykes left, I went to get them. The session was better than I'd thought, and for once, I felt like I had hope of living a normal life.

Now if only I could find a way to make my dad live forever...

"You good?" Lynx asked.

"Better than. He's coming back in three days. We'll still be here, right?"

Lynx nodded. "We'll stay as long as we need to. You'll need a follow-up for the D&C. Um, I don't know if Ridley told you, but Dr. Sykes is gay. His partner, Dr. Myron, treats most of the ladies here at the Dixie Reapers. I can make an appointment with him if you'd like."

"Yes, please. I need to know I'm healing okay, and don't have to worry about getting an infection. When we go home, I want to feel healthy again. In all ways."

Lynx kissed my temple and put his arm around my waist. "I'll do whatever you need me to."

"Your club okay with you being gone for so long?" Dad asked.

"Atilla knows everything," he said. "I was told to

take all the time I needed and return when Merry was ready. She's our first old lady, so I imagine they'll do whatever they can to make sure she wants to stick around. They know if she leaves, I'll be chasing after her."

I leaned into him. "I'm not going anywhere."

"Wish I could say the same," Dad said.

I noticed he looked paler than before. Releasing Lynx, I went to him. Folding my arms around him, I couldn't stop the tears from falling. I was going to lose my dad, and there wasn't a damn thing I could do about it. It was selfish to keep him here. I wasn't the only one who needed to tell him bye.

"Daddy, I love you. If you need to go home, I understand."

"Home is a relative thing, Meredith. I think you've learned that."

I shook my head. "No, Dad. The Devil's Fury is your home. You need to be there, and when it's your time, you can finally rest beside May. We lost some time together, but I'm grateful I got to see you again. I can't be selfish and keep you here."

I broke down sobbing and couldn't seem to stop. My dad held me, and I felt Lynx behind me. It didn't seem fair. I'd fallen in love with an incredible man, had a new family, and now I was losing my dad. The pain felt unbearable. How would I ever keep going when I knew he wasn't in this world anymore? No more phone calls or being able to see him on FaceTime. One day, I'd reach for the phone and realize he wasn't there anymore. And I had a feeling it was coming sooner than any of us anticipated.

"Love you, Daddy. So very much."

"I love you too, Meredith. I have from the beginning. Even when I'm gone, I'll still be watching over you. As long as you remember me, I'll be with you. When you feel lonely, or miss me, put your hand over your heart and close your eyes -- that's where you'll find me."

Lynx pulled me into his arms and I clung to him.

"Is it time?" Lynx asked.

"Yeah. I think it is." My dad sounded so sad right then. "I have some things to finish back home. I'll get someone to take me back in the morning. Take care of her."

"Always," Lynx promised.

* * *

Lynx
One Week Later

I could tell Meredith wasn't ready to go home, and yet she didn't really want to stay either. She'd met with both Dr. Sykes and Dr. Myron one last time yesterday. They'd put in referrals to doctors back home, to make sure she'd be well taken care of. Dr. Sykes had also officially diagnosed her with bipolar disorder, along with anxiety and a few other things. She wouldn't have an easy path to travel, but she'd eventually be in a good place again. I'd make sure of it.

"Sweetheart, Atilla and the others are anxious for us to get home. I've been gone a while, and there's work for me to do. Plus, you're the club's only old lady. Aren't you ready to figure out what that's going to mean?"

She looked up from the book she'd been reading. "You mean like the things the ladies here do?"

"Yeah. Well, maybe not exactly like it. Our club is exactly that -- ours. As the first old lady, it's up to you to determine what that's going to mean moving forward. You'll set the pace for everyone. When the others find their women, it will be you who helps them settle into life with the club. Think you're up for it?"

"Like Ridley did when Venom claimed her."

My sister had in fact been the Dixie Reapers' first old lady. Something she'd always been proud of, especially since she'd been the daughter of one first.

"Just like Ridley," I said. I knew Meredith idolized my sister. The more she'd gotten to know her, the more Meredith seemed to like my sister. I hoped the two would get to see each other again soon. Ridley had already made her promise to call every week. Same with Mara.

"Okay. When do you want to leave?" she asked.

"How about today? We can tell everyone bye, load up the car, and travel about halfway before we stop for the night."

She looked around the apartment and I knew why she resisted going home. This was the last place she'd spent time with her dad. It didn't matter that Grizzly wasn't coming back here again. By remaining here, she was doing her best to hold on to those last moments with him.

She didn't know that I'd asked him for a favor before he left. I'd made a short recording of him. When I thought it was time, I'd show it to her. I'd already asked Wire to back up a copy for me. It was the one thing I never wanted to lose because I knew how much it would mean to my Merry.

"All right," she agreed. "Let's go home."

It took an hour to pack and load the car and tell everyone bye. I noticed she seemed sad as we pulled through the gates, and I knew I'd either have to bring her back soon, or have my sister come visit. Too bad we weren't a little closer.

When it came time to pull off for the day, she

insisted I keep going. I did make quite a few stops for her to use the bathroom, change her pad, and stretch her legs. And I asked if she was sure she wanted to keep going. So many times, in fact, she'd smacked my arm the last time I'd asked and told me to shut up and drive.

By the time we pulled into the Savage Raptors compound, she'd fallen asleep in the passenger seat. I took us straight home and unloaded the car. She didn't wake up, not even when I lifted her from the car and carried her inside. Atilla and Spade stopped by when they saw we were back.

"She doing okay?" Atilla asked.

"As well as can be expected. Any news so far?"

He shook his head. "Badger said he'd call me the second it happens. But that old man could hold on a while longer. You said he had a month, right?"

"That's what the doctor said, but he looked like he was done. I think knowing Merry was all right was the only loose end he needed to tie up. Now that he's been assured she'll be okay, he probably feels better about leaving everyone behind."

Atilla cleared his throat. "Damn. That's… Shit."

I nodded. Yep. It wasn't going to be easy on anyone when Grizzly left this world, but his daughters would especially mourn his loss. The fact he'd made time to see Meredith meant the world to me. It couldn't have been easy on him.

"Anything you need from us?" Spade asked.

"Whenever I'm out on jobs, could you make sure someone keeps an eye on her. She's finally been diagnosed and has a few prescriptions to take. I'm not sure what it would take to send her spiraling, though. If I'm not here, I want to make sure someone will be around to catch her if she falls."

"We've got it covered," Spade said. "She's one of us now."

"There's a property cut for her. Wasn't sure if she decided to get inked or not," Atilla said.

"I'd wanted Zipper to do it. With the miscarriage, and her overall mental state, he suggested waiting. If she still wants ink, she can get it later. Might be asking for more time away to take her back to the Dixie Reapers in the near future. She really hit it off with Mara and my sister."

"Whatever she needs, we'll make it happen," Atilla said.

"Thanks, Pres. She's had a rough time of it. Hopefully, things will get better now. I know she's going to be heartbroken once Grizzly is gone. She'll need all of us then."

"Why don't we do some sort of dinner at the clubhouse tomorrow?" Spade asked. "We can boot out the club whores, and it will give everyone a chance to get to know Meredith more."

"I think she'd like that."

Speaking of… Meredith stumbled into the room. "Why didn't you wake me up?"

"You needed to rest. Atilla and Spade came to check on you." I motioned to the Pres and VP. She slumped against me and gave them a tired smile.

"Glad to have you home, Meredith," Atilla said. "Whenever you decide what you want to do around here, just let me know. Or if you don't want to do anything, that's fine too."

"But if you're going to beat on another club whore, I want to know in advance so I can watch." Spade winked at her. "That was fucking awesome."

"So the beating of club whores is permitted." She nodded. "All right. Although, as long as they don't touch Lynx or try to put me in my place, I won't have an issue with them. I know they serve a purpose."

"She's different," Atilla said. "Most old ladies would have thrown a fit over there being club whores. Probably a good thing you grew up in this way of life. Although, we aren't quite like the Devil's Fury."

Spade chuckled. "Yeah, for one we don't have our heads up our asses. Their loss is our gain. If they hadn't made you leave, you and Lynx might not have met. At least, not this soon."

I held Merry tighter. "We were destined to be together. Call me a sap or what-the-fuck-ever, but I believe she was meant to be mine."

Atilla shook his head but had a smile on his face. He was right. This club *was* different, and in a good way. There might be ideas we could pull from the Dixie Reapers, Devil's Fury, or even the Hades Abyss to improve the compound, but at the end of the day, we'd follow our own path. This club had given Meredith a chance from the very beginning. From what I understood, so did the club down in New Orleans. I hoped that wouldn't ever change. I didn't want us to become the sort of men who didn't take the time to figure out the truth before pointing fingers at people. Or in the most likely case, running them off or burying them.

"You up for a big dinner at the clubhouse tomorrow?" I asked. "The club wants to officially meet you as my old lady."

"Sounds good." She smiled up at me. "Think one day I might get another title too?"

"Wife?" Spade asked. "Shit. He hasn't fixed that yet?"

He wasn't wrong. I'd intended to speak to Wire about it. I knew he could hack into the appropriate offices to create a marriage license for us. He'd done it for others in the past. At the time, I'd been more concerned with everything Merry was going through.

"Haven't had a chance to discuss it yet. I wasn't sure if that's something you'd want. And if it is, do you want an actual wedding?"

She shook her head. "Not necessary. Just do what everyone else has."

"I'll text Wire in a little bit. He'll probably have it done before morning."

"In that case, we'll celebrate you not only having an old lady but a wife." Spade grinned. "Good to have the both of you home. Get some rest. Plan on being at the clubhouse by five o'clock tomorrow. If we wrap up by seven, then anyone who wants a good time can let the club whores back in."

The Pres and VP left, and I helped Merry unpack. It was definitely good to be home.

* * *

When they'd said a dinner at the clubhouse, I hadn't quite expected something so fancy. Spade had personally hung white Christmas lights around the room. Someone put tablecloths on all the tables. The bar had been scrubbed down and was now laden with trays of food. Wings. Macaroni. Mashed potatoes. Chopped brisket. They'd even brought in a cake that said *Welcome Home* and some pies. I knew none of these bastards had made this stuff, but it was the thought that counted.

"Time to officially introduce you to everyone," I said, taking Merry's hand. "Guys, as you know, I claimed Meredith. We're also married as of this morning. Why don't you each come up and say hi now that she's part of our club?"

Atilla and Spade came first, each giving her a

hug. The Sergeant-at-Arms was next. Thankfully, her dad was a large man, so General didn't startle her. Our Treasurer, Maui, and Secretary, Knuckles, came up next. After that, she met the patched members of the club, and our only two Prospects -- Ben and Lucas.

"The two Prospects are the closest to your age," I said. "But they're still older than you."

"I don't care about that."

I led her over to a table and fixed her a plate before joining her. I noticed the Pres already sat down beside her. Good. If everyone saw how much he accepted her, then there wouldn't ever be a question of her belonging here. If my club tried to pull the same shit as the Devil's Fury, I'd go on a fucking rampage.

"You settling in okay?" Maui asked, taking the other open spot.

"Everyone here has been great." Merry smiled at him. "I feel right at home."

"Good. You ever need anything and can't find Lynx, I'll be happy to help."

"Same goes for any man in this club," Atilla said.

"Only thing that would make it better would be having another woman around," Merry said.

Atilla held up a hand. "Nope. I have no intention of settling down. I'm too old for that shit. I'm in my sixties and too set in my ways."

"I'm pretty sure Scratch, Cinder, and several others settled down when they were close to your age. Never say never," Merry said.

"Bite your tongue, girl! Last thing I need is a woman in my house." Atilla took a swallow of beer. "But feel free to set up the younger ones. Maybe someone can tame them a little."

"Challenge accepted!"

Was it just me or did my wife seem a little too

happy about it? Shit. *Wife.* I wanted to smile every time I even thought the word. When I'd heard she was coming here, I never expected she'd bewitch me. Merry had me firmly under her spell, and there wasn't anything I wouldn't do for her. I loved her more than my next breath.

Whatever the future had in store for us, I knew we'd get through it. She'd had a rough start, and I didn't think it would be smooth sailing from this point forward, but I'd make sure to always catch her when she fell. We hadn't discussed kids. If she didn't want to have any, then we wouldn't. Even if she did want them but was too scared to get pregnant again, we'd adopt. I'd fill her every need and every desire, no matter what it took. She was my entire world.

Maui leaned in. "You got a good one. Hold onto her."

I nodded, having no intention of ever letting her go. If she ran, I'd follow. And I damn well dared anyone to try and take her from me because I'd put them six feet under. There wasn't anything I wouldn't do for her. I'd even die for her.

"Love you," I murmured in her ear.

She kissed me softly. "Love you too."

I'd finally figured out what true happiness was… and it was all thanks to the woman at my side.

Epilogue

Meredith

My hand shook as I hung up the phone. I hadn't expected anyone from the Devil's Fury to call me anytime soon. When I saw Badger's name light up on my phone, I'd known. Before I even said *hello*, I knew exactly why he was calling.

Dad was gone.

The tears streaked my cheeks, and I couldn't bring myself to move or speak. Even breathing hurt. My heart was breaking, and while I knew he was no longer in pain, it didn't ease my suffering.

"I love you, Daddy. I hope you're at peace now," I murmured once I found my voice.

Lynx came up behind me and wrapped his arms around my waist. He kissed the top of my head and just held me as I cried. I'd known it was coming. The day he told me bye at the Dixie Reapers, I'd known I'd never see him again.

It didn't make this any easier.

Nothing would have.

"He loved you, Merry. So much. Cry as much as you need to, then we'll go out and do something for Grizzly."

"Like what?" I asked.

"Whatever you want. If he had a favorite food, we'll go eat it and you can tell me your favorite memories of him. Did he like a particular movie? We can watch it. However you want to celebrate his life, that's what we'll do."

"Okay. He'd like that. A celebration of life instead of me bawling my eyes out because he's gone."

"Take your time, sweetheart." He held me tighter. "Get all the tears out. It's okay to mourn his loss. This world won't be the same without him. There are a lot of people who will miss him. Even me."

I might miss Dad, but I had Lynx and the Savage Raptors. In a way, I owed my new life to my dad. If he hadn't told me to leave for a little while, I would never have come to Oklahoma. Lynx seemed to think we'd have still met at some point. Whether we would have or not, it wouldn't have been the same.

Thank you, Daddy. For everything.

* * *

May

Watching Grizzly struggle had been the hardest thing I'd done. Well, aside from leaving him in the first place. I'd had no choice. The cancer had eaten away at me until I couldn't hold on any longer. I'd kept watch over the years, trying to protect him from afar.

Seeing his girls surround him in his final hours was bittersweet. Especially since I knew one was missing. That girl was something else. She'd let him go, knowing it would be the last time she'd see him. Even though her sisters had been awful, she'd not wanted to deny them the closure of saying goodbye. I hoped only wonderful things came her way. If any of them was deserving, it was her.

Grizzly cracked his eyes open and reached out a hand to our oldest, Adalia.

"Need you to promise me something. Forgive Meredith. Forgive yourself. She's your sister, and she needs you." He struggled to take a breath. "One day, I want all my girls to be able to sit in the same room together again. Take care of each other."

Adalia sniffled and nodded. "I will, Dad. I'll make sure it happens."

"You gave me a wonderful life," Lilian said.

"You were patient. Supportive. If anyone deserves the titles of *Best Dad*, it's you."

"I agree," Shella said. "I'm sorry I was such a pain. I love you, Dad."

"The club will be in good hands," Badger said. "So will your daughters and grandchildren. You can rest now."

Grizzly smiled and closed his eyes, breathing his last. The family surrounding him cried as if their hearts would never mend. I knew, in time, they'd smile when they remembered him. Much the way he and Adalia had done when I'd left.

I smiled and reached out my hand. It felt like I'd been waiting forever for him. John looked the same as he had when we'd first met. Seeing the much younger version of him filled my heart with warmth. Even I looked the same as I had back then. Heaven was a rather incredible place, and now I got to share it with my one and only love.

"It took you long enough," I said.

"Had some things to take care of." He smiled. "Adalia has her own family now. Turned the Devil's Fury over to Badger. And I raised a few more girls. Knew it's what you'd want me to do."

I nodded. "You're right. They needed you, but now it's time for you to have what *you* need."

He pulled me into his arms. "I do. Only thing I ever needed was you, May."

I took one last peek at those around Grizzly's bed. Each of his daughters were wrapped in the arms of the men they loved. Even the one miles away would have the support of someone who loved her.

That's your legacy, John. You did so good. "I'm proud of you," I said.

"For what?"

"Staying when they needed you to. I know it wasn't easy. You wanted to follow me when it was my time to go."

He nodded. "I did. You were my entire world, May. Always had been. Always *will* be."

"I love you, John, more than anything."

For the first time in far too long, he kissed me...

and I finally found peace.

Atilla (Savage Raptors MC 2)
A Dixie Reapers Bad Boys Romance
Harley Wylde

Solena -- At the age of fifteen, my parents forced me to give my baby up for adoption. I never got to see his little face or hold him. All these years later, it still hurts -- so much that one night I decide to dull the pain with alcohol and sex. There's only one man I want, but the President of the Savage Raptors MC might be more than I can handle. I've had a crush on him for a while now. He says he can only offer one night. I want more. I want it all.

Atilla -- Lost my woman seventeen years ago. Thought I'd lost my daughter too... until she showed up on my doorstep. Now I have a pregnant teen living with me, and a woman who wants more than I'm able to give her. Solena is far too young for me. Hell, she's barely older than my daughter. So why is keeping my distance so damn difficult? Is it really okay to fall in love again?

Prologue

Atilla
Three Months Ago

I couldn't believe Lynx had settled down. And not with just anyone. Nope, he'd gone and claimed one of Grizzly's adopted kids. It would have given us a tie to the Devil's Fury, if Meredith hadn't been the black sheep. For her sake, I hoped she could mend things with her sisters. I could only imagine how hard it was on her, living so far from home and no longer having a support system. She had us, but I knew it wasn't the same.

Of course, now that she and Lynx were together, she wanted everyone to get a happy ending. She'd talked about the rest of us pairing off. I knew it was because she didn't enjoy being the only woman here. It had to be lonely for her. The only other females were the club whores, and she wasn't exactly going to hang out with them.

When she'd asked me about finding someone, I'd lied and told her I was too damn old and set in my ways. Said if I hadn't found the woman meant to be mine in all this time, then she wasn't out there. Except... I had found her. A long-ass time ago.

Rebecca had taken my breath away the first time I saw her. She'd been so full of life. It wasn't any wonder I'd fallen for her ass over teakettle. One smile and she'd had me wrapped around her finger. A kind word and I'd been hooked. We'd had the best summer of our lives, and I'd hoped for more. Then she'd told me the news... she was moving away.

She'd been younger than me by quite a bit. It hadn't stopped me from adoring her. I'd have married her. Well, maybe not. She hadn't been made for club life, and it had been the only thing holding me back. It's why no one knew about her. I'd kept that part of my life separate and for good reason.

Even though we'd been apart, we'd kept in touch. Letters. Phone calls.

The day I received a picture of a sonogram in the mail, my heart had nearly stopped. Rebecca was pregnant -- and the baby was mine. I'd been scared and excited at the same time. I hadn't known how things would work out, but I knew I had to have her by my side. We'd discussed her moving back here, and I'd been ready to do anything to make it happen.

It had taken longer than planned, and before I could bring her home, the doctor had put her on bed rest. Something wasn't going quite right with the pregnancy, and my sweet Rebecca was ready to do anything to keep our baby safe and healthy. Nothing else mattered to her. We'd still talked on the phone, and she'd given me every update on the baby. It was a girl, and we'd named her Casey.

I took a shot of vodka, then another. It was the anniversary of Rebecca's death, and it always hit me hard. Hit by a drunk driver before our child could even be born, I'd lost them both. Normally, I'd go to the cemetery to pay my respects. She may have never returned to Bryson Corners, but her family had her buried about an hour down the highway in their family plot. It always bothered me that Rebecca's family didn't give our daughter a proper burial. I didn't know what happened to her body, and since we weren't married, no one would tell me a damn thing.

"Everything okay?" Spade asked as he settled on the stool beside me.

"Do I fucking look like I'm okay?"

He shook his head. "Not even a little. Get like

this every year about this time. Can't figure it the fuck out, though."

"Some secrets are my own." I hoped he'd leave it at that. If I'd kept her here, would we have had a happy life together? Could she have handled being part of this club? I wasn't sure, but at least little Casey would have been alive. She'd be a teenager now.

Since losing my family, I'd never once been tempted to settle down. Watching Lynx fall in love had been bittersweet. I was happy for the two of them, but days like this it made me miss my woman even more. I had no idea if things would have worked out between us, but our kid would have tied us together, and I'd have done anything for my daughter whether her mom and I were still together.

The clubhouse doors opened, and Rebel popped his head inside. "Um, Pres. Might want to come out here a minute."

What the fuck was happening now? I stood and walked over to the door, yanking it all the way open. Nothing could have prepared me for the sight in front of me. If I hadn't known Rebecca was dead and gone, I'd have thought her teenage self was standing on my steps.

"Are you Atilla?" the girl asked.

"Yeah. Do I know you?"

She shook her head and pushed her hair behind her ear. When she shoved her jacket aside to pull something from her pocket, I saw the swell of her stomach. Kid didn't look old enough to be out of high school and she was pregnant? Well, as long as she wouldn't say it was mine. No fucking way I'd have touched someone so young, not even dead-ass drunk. Didn't matter if she looked like my sweet Rebecca.

"You knew my mom." She came up the steps

and handed me a picture. Rebecca. My throat grew tight and then her words registered.

"What?"

"My name is Casey," she whispered. "And I think you're my dad."

Holy. Fucking. Shit. It was like the earth tipped under my feet, and if I hadn't locked my knees, I'd have gone down hard. Casey. It was the name we were going to give our baby. And this girl claimed Rebecca was her mom. Was the reason there hadn't been a tiny grave because the child didn't die? My mind was reeling.

Everything hit me at once, like a freight train. With so many eyes on us, and my pregnant daughter standing in front of me, I knew I needed to keep my shit together. I could freak the fuck out when I was alone.

"I think we have a lot to discuss," I said. "Not here. You can follow me to my house."

She gave a nod and went to her car. The back seat looked crammed full of shit, and I wondered if she was here for more than dropping the *daddy* bomb on me. Where had she been all this time? Who had raised her? Why did she wait until now to find me? I had so many fucking questions. I could only hope she had the answers.

I also wanted to strangle Rebecca's family. I didn't know for certain if they'd been the ones to keep Casey from me, but I couldn't think of anyone else who would have. They'd known Casey was mine. Rebecca and I hadn't kept it from them. Discovering I had a kid after all this time… I was both excited to meet her and pissed as fuck at the people who'd kept us apart.

I got on my bike and rode slowly, making sure Casey could keep up. My house wasn't far. I pulled into the driveway and killed the engine, then waited for her to exit her vehicle. She checked out the house and scanned the surrounding area. Not once did she ask me anything. Casey meekly followed me into the house, and I pointed to the kitchen.

"Let's sit in there. Want something to eat or drink?" I asked.

"Water would be good."

She took a seat at the table while I got a cold bottle of water from the fridge and set it down in front of her. I took out a beer for myself, thinking I'd need it for whatever discussion we were about to have. I studied her face and saw parts of Rebecca, but that wasn't all.

"I have your eyes," she said.

I nodded. Yep. That she did. Her hair color was closer to mine as well, but the rest was all her mom. I couldn't take my eyes off her. It amazed me I had a daughter. Of course, whoever had kept her from me deserved a sound beating. As much as I wanted to blame Rebecca's parents, I wouldn't until I knew for certain they were the ones who'd lied and said my daughter was dead.

"I guess you have questions," she said. "I don't blame you. I had a lot over the years myself."

"Where'd you grow up?" I asked.

"My grandparents took me in when I was born. They raised me until I was seven. That's when my grandfather died, and my grandmother had to move into a home. She'd started showing signs of Alzheimer's. After that, I lived with my aunt and uncle."

I leaned forward and braced my arms on the table. "What aunt and uncle? Your mom was an only child."

Her brow furrowed and her nose scrunched a little, just like Rebecca's used to do. "I didn't know Mom was an only child. I've always known them as Aunt Su and Uncle Mark. They lived down the street and were always coming over."

"How did you find out about me?" I asked because I seriously doubted her grandparents had told her a damn thing about me. They'd never thought I was good enough for their precious daughter. Didn't matter she'd been in her late twenties when we got together. It wasn't like she was a teenager.

"Mom's diary. When we were cleaning out the house to sell it, I ran across it in a box up in the attic. I didn't tell anyone I had it, and I read it in secret. I was so young I didn't really understand a lot." She took a swallow of her water. "About two years ago, I pulled it out and read it again."

"You're what? Seventeen?" I asked.

"As of today, in fact." She gave me a tired smile. "You haven't asked about the baby. *My* baby."

"Noticed it. Figured you'd say something if you wanted to."

"Well, that's different from what I'm used to. I refused to sign the baby over to someone else, so Aunt Su and Uncle Mark threw me out. I loaded my stuff in my car and thought this might be a good time to meet my father. Not that I'm expecting you to take care of me or anything. I'll figure things out on my own."

I snorted and shook my head. "Stubborn. I'm afraid you get that from me. And hell no, I'm not letting you figure this shit out by yourself. While I might have thought you died with your mother all those years ago, it doesn't change the fact you're mine, Casey."

Tears gathered in her eyes, and she pressed her

lips together. My heart ached. How the fuck had those people treated her all this time? She'd been so certain I would turn her away. Had they told her I was some sort of monster? Maybe said I hadn't wanted her? We'd lost so much time.

"Thanks... Dad."

Hearing her call me that healed a piece of my broken heart. She was exactly what I'd needed all this time. Our family might never be whole, but as long as we had each other, then we'd be able to weather the storms.

"Come on. I'll show you to your room." I stood and held out my hand for her. Whatever it took, I'd make this work. I also planned to find the little shit who got her pregnant. She hadn't said he wouldn't take responsibility, but why else would she have shown up on my doorstep? Not to mention, she wouldn't tell me who'd knocked her up. Once I found him, the fucker was going to learn a very painful lesson. No one screwed with my baby girl and got away with it.

Chapter One

Solena
Present Day

I didn't know why I was here. This wasn't my scene. The music was too loud, the women too wild, and the smoke nearly choked me. So why the hell hadn't I turned around and gone home? The man at the end of the bar was the only reason I hadn't run for the hills.

I'd seen him around town. In fact, he often came to the café where his daughter worked. The pregnant teen was working on her GED and waiting tables. I'd once been in her shoes, so I could sympathize. Except, I didn't get to keep my baby. I'd been fifteen when my boyfriend didn't take no for an answer. The result had been a little boy. One I'd never even gotten to hold. My parents had told the doctor to take him away before I even got a good look, and I had no idea where he was now.

I'd tried to find out, but I had had no luck. The place my parents supposedly used for the adoption had never existed. My stomach churned every time I thought about it. What had happened to my little boy? Was he okay? Did a loving family get him? Today he was especially on my mind, since it was his birthday. Which was the second reason I'd come here. I'd wanted a distraction so I wouldn't think about him. Obviously, it wasn't working.

I took a swallow of the cocktail I'd ordered and tried to get the courage to speak to the President of the Savage Raptors. He'd always seemed nice when he'd stopped by to visit Casey. We'd exchanged a few words here and there. Every time I got close to him, my heart raced, and I fought the urge to reach out my hand and touch him. Something about him called to me. I'd never been the type to go for bad boys or rough men. Atilla looked like both, and yet, I'd seen how gentle he was with Casey. Perhaps it was that side of him I yearned for.

More than once, I'd gone to sleep hugging my pillow, wondering what it would be like to have Atilla lying next to me. I didn't know what I found so fascinating about him. I knew people would say he was too old for me. Their opinions didn't matter. I'd never been so drawn to someone before, and I found him to be the sexiest man in town. Possibly in the entire world.

"You going to keep staring at him or go make a move?" someone asked from beside me. I startled and glanced in the man's direction. *Spade* was on his leather cut, along with *Vice President*.

"Was I being that obvious?" I asked. Should I wipe my chin? Had I been drooling over the man? Wouldn't be the first time. One of my co-workers once threw a napkin at me after Atilla left the café. I'd literally been salivating over him like a dog after a bone.

"Oh, yeah. I'm sure you've seen him wave off every woman who approached so far. I have a feeling he won't turn you away. You're different from the other women here. I can't quite figure out *why* you came to a party at the clubhouse. You don't seem like the sort to do this kind of thing."

"I'm not. It's my first time doing anything like this, and I'm extremely nervous."

Spade smiled faintly. "You came for him, didn't you?"

I nodded. I couldn't deny it. The alcohol in my system hadn't been enough to give me the courage to go up to him. I wasn't sure anything could help me. What was I expecting from this, anyway? I wasn't the one-night-stand type, and I didn't think the man had come here to find a girlfriend. When I'd thought about getting a drink and possibly getting closer to Atilla, my brain hadn't gone as far as the next step.

I yearned to speak with him. Get closer to him. If he kissed me, I might die from both pleasure and a shock to my system. In all this time, I'd never desired anyone. With Atilla, I found myself watching him whenever he was nearby, and wanting nothing more than to cuddle up to him. I couldn't help but think if a man like him were part of my life, things would be different. It wouldn't change my financial issues, but having someone to lean on, to give me their support and a little affection would have meant the world to me. Not just anyone… *him*. It had to be Atilla or no one.

Truth be told, I hadn't slept with anyone since that one time. Then again, I didn't consider what my boyfriend had done to me to be considered sex. He'd raped me. I knew it. He knew it. Everyone else thought I'd given consent, then changed my mind after the fact and made a fuss over nothing. Even my parents hadn't believed me.

"Maybe I should just leave," I said.

"Or you could follow me." He snatched up my glass, and I hurried after him, keeping an eye on the open beverage. I knew nothing about these men, or what they were capable of. He wouldn't put something in it, would he? I chased him down, only to come to a halt next to Atilla. Spade set my glass on the bar beside Atilla's beer, then motioned to the empty stool. "Sit. Talk. But stop staring at him like a creeper."

My cheeks warmed, and I wanted the floor to

open up and swallow me. Atilla's lips kicked up on one corner and I saw the amusement in his eyes. I sat down and took another swallow of my drink. Then drained the glass. Atilla motioned to the guy behind the bar and before I knew it, I had a fresh drink sitting in front of me.

"You're Solena, right?" he asked.

He remembered my name? It pleased me more than it should have. It wasn't like he said I was special or anything. Just because he knew who I was didn't mean anything. For all I knew, he remembered every person he ever met.

"Yeah. I work with Casey at the café." *Way to state the obvious, idiot.*

"So, why did you come here?" Atilla asked.

"To see you." I winced. I hadn't meant to blurt it out. It seemed the alcohol was affecting me more than I'd realized.

"That right?" He grinned. "And what were you hoping to gain from it?"

"I don't know," I admitted.

He eyed me up and down. "Well, you're showing off more than you usually do, but you're still overdressed for a place like this."

I looked around the room and noticed most of the women were naked already. And the things they were doing... I quickly turned my head. It felt like my face was on fire, and I knew I could never be like those women. Not that I condemned them for being so free. It just wasn't something I could ever do. I had stretch marks from my pregnancy, and a little extra around the middle. I'd be too embarrassed to strip naked in front of everyone.

"Come on. I'm getting a fucking headache. Grab your drink." Atilla stood, picking up his beer.

I picked my cocktail up and followed him toward the back of the building. He entered a door at the end of the hall and flipped on the lights. It looked like a boardroom. Well, a rustic version of one. The wood table looked sturdy. He pulled out one of the leather chairs and motioned for me to sit.

"Is it okay for me to set my glass down?" I asked.

He snorted. "Not going to hurt anything."

With the door closed, it was far quieter than it had been in the main room. The fact we were alone made butterflies riot in my stomach. I didn't know why he'd brought me in here. Did he expect something?

"Thanks for being so nice to Casey," he said. "She talks about you quite a bit."

"She's a good kid." He chuckled and leaned back in his seat. "What? Why is that funny?"

"You calling her a kid. You look about two seconds older than my daughter," he said.

"I'm twenty-three, and while I know that probably makes me young enough to be your daughter, my life hasn't been all sunshine and roses. Some days I feel more like a little old lady." I motioned to the other room. "All that is so far beyond what I'd ever consider doing. I meant what I said. I came here for you."

He shook his head. "Honey, I'm far too old for you to be looking my way."

"You're what? Maybe fifty?" I asked.

"I'm in my sixties," he said. "Biggest age gap I've ever had in a relationship was with Casey's mom. She was in her late twenties and I'd been nearly fifty. Twenty years was bad enough. Forty? You must be fucking crazy."

I took another swallow of my drink and

contemplated his words. I knew people wouldn't look favorably on a relationship between us. They'd put all the blame on him, not considering for a moment I'd been the one to chase after him. The man was a silver fox. Who cared how old he was? He was kind, had a gentle touch, and I found him to be rather sexy.

I wanted to tell him what happened to me. Talk about the son I never got to meet. But would he even care? It wasn't like we were friends. Acquaintances at best. I didn't want to go home, where I'd do nothing more than sink deeper and deeper into a depression. It happened every year on this day.

"I came here tonight to forget," I said. "Today is a bad day for me. I thought you might understand, since Casey said the two of you hadn't met until recently. Sorry if I was too presumptuous."

His lips twitched. "Presumptuous. Big word."

I shrugged. I might work in a café, but it didn't mean I was stupid. After my parents gave my baby away, my grades had dropped to the point I barely graduated high school. College hadn't been in the cards. In fact, by the time I was Casey's age, I'd had myself emancipated and moved out on my own. I'd been working at the café all this time. It might not be a glamorous job, but the manager had given me a chance when no one else would. For that, they had my loyalty.

"So, what exactly were you hoping to gain from tonight?" he asked. "Because a quick release is one thing. Forever? That's not something I can offer anyone. Pretty sure my heart died the same time Rebecca did. I have nothing to offer anyone."

Right. And even if he did, it wouldn't be with someone my age. He'd made that clear already. Could I do a one-night stand? It would ease my pain right at this moment, but what about tomorrow? Something told me being intimate with this man would only make me want him more.

I finished my drink and stared at the empty glass. I knew Casey lived with her dad, which meant he probably wouldn't take me to his house. Did he want to go to mine? Or... I thought about the women in the other room. He didn't want us to go back out there, did he?

"You're hesitating, which means this isn't what you really want," he said.

"I don't think I can put on a show like those other women," I admitted.

"Can't take you home with me, honey. Casey is sleeping in the room next to mine."

"I know."

"Come on. We can use an empty room down the hall. Unless you've decided you want to leave?"

I stood and followed him from the room. He opened the second door we came to, and I saw a small bedroom with an attached bathroom. After I cleared the doorway, he shut us in and locked the door. At least I wouldn't have to worry about someone barging in. It set me at ease a little.

He shrugged out of his cut and set it on the dresser. I fiddled with the hem of my dress before lifting it over my head. Standing before him in nothing more than my heels, bra, and panties, I felt self-conscious. Wrapping my arms around my waist, I tried to hide my imperfections.

"When you said this wasn't your scene..." He paused. "You didn't mean you're a virgin, did you?"

"No. I'm not a virgin."

He nodded. "You still sure you want to do this? I'm okay with getting another drink and just talking, or listening, if there's something you need to get off your chest."

I couldn't pass up this opportunity. For one, I hoped he could help me feel more normal. Not having sex since getting pregnant at fifteen made me feel like a freak. I'd also lost two boyfriends because of my inability to have sex with someone. I needed to get over it.

"I'm sure I want this. I want *you*," I corrected.

"Come here, pretty girl."

I stepped closer, and he cupped the back of my head with one hand while placing the other on my waist. He tugged me against his body and lowered his lips to mine. Holy hell, the man could kiss! My legs trembled and I couldn't catch my breath. It felt like I'd fall if he released me.

Atilla slid his hand from my hip up my back and I felt him pop the clasp on my bra. He pulled away long enough to remove the garment, then stared at my breasts like a starving man. He cupped one, giving it a light squeeze before stroking the nipple. I gasped and arched into his touch, feeling pleasure zinging straight from the hardened peak to my clit. I'd never realized such a thing was possible. Sure, I'd read romances where the woman came multiple times. I'd thought it was pure fantasy. Now I had to wonder.

"You like that?" he asked.

I nodded mutely. He lifted me and placed me on my back on the bed. Kneeling on the floor, he removed my shoes, then slid my panties down my thighs and let them drop to the floor. Atilla dragged his hands up my calves to my knees and spread me open.

"When's the last time a man made you come?" he asked.

"Never," I admitted.

"Then I guess we better change that."

He stood and toed off his boots, then removed his shirt. He unfastened his pants but left them on as he placed a knee on either side of my hips. Looking up at him, I felt so tiny. Atilla seemed larger than life. For an older man, he'd kept in shape. I reached up and placed my hand on his chest, feeling his strength.

"If I do something you don't like, tell me. Otherwise, I might not pick up on the hint you aren't enjoying yourself. I know some women fake it, thinking that's what a man wants. It's not."

"All right." I licked my lips. "So far, I like what you've been doing."

He winked and leaned down, taking my nipple into his mouth. He sucked on it long and hard, making my toes curl and my heart race. I'd never known it would feel this incredible. He switched sides, and I felt my pussy grow slick. I'd be so embarrassed if he made me come just from this alone, but I was close. I could feel something building inside me, this burning need.

"Please, Atilla. More."

He placed his hand between my legs and stroked my pussy. His fingers teased me, brushing over my clit several times. Even that slight amount of stimulation, plus his lips on my breast, was enough to make me come. I cried out, my body tensing as pleasure flooded me.

"That's one," he said.

One? One what? I didn't understand what he meant until he eased a finger inside me and pressed the heel of his hand against my clit. I bucked against him, still sensitive from my orgasm. He worked my pussy like a pro, making me feel crazy. I wanted to latch on and never let him go. I came twice more and yearned for more.

He leaned down and kissed me. "Next time you

come, it's going to be on my cock."

Atilla took out his wallet and pulled out a condom. I wasn't sure how I felt about him keeping one with him. Did he do this sort of thing often? The night I'd gone to the clubhouse, he'd been alone and brushed off every woman who approached. I'd thought maybe he was different from the others. How many of those women had he been with? My concern must have shown on my face. He leaned down, getting close enough I could feel his breath on my lips.

"Hey. I'm clean, okay? Haven't been with anyone in a while and got tested after the last time. At my age, I don't need sex all the damn time like those youngsters out there."

"All right." If he said so, then I'd believe him. Maybe I didn't have a reason to, but he also hadn't proven himself to be untrustworthy. My gut said he was an honorable man.

He stood and shoved his pants and underwear off. The sight of his cock made my breath catch. It wasn't overly long or thick, but to me, it looked perfect. I'd never thought a man's dick would be attractive. My cheeks warmed as I watched him roll the condom on.

He spread my legs wider and settled between them. I felt the head of his cock press against me, and the burn as he stretched me. He slid in slowly, taking his time. Reaching up, I held onto him.

"You okay?" he asked.

"I'm good. Just… need you to move or something."

He smiled faintly and reached between us to play with my clit. By the time he was thrusting into me with long, deep strokes, I knew I was close to coming again. His strokes became erratic, and I felt the heat of his cum, even through the latex. He strummed my clit faster, and I screamed his name as I came again. Panting for breath, I looked up at him and wondered if he'd just ruined me for any other man.

Atilla reached down to hold the condom as he pulled out. He removed it, then carried it into the bathroom. I heard the sink running, and he came back with a warm, wet rag. He used it to clean me up before kissing me softly.

He got back onto the bed and pulled me against his chest, holding me as he ran his hand up and down my back. Tears pricked my eyes, but I refused to cry. Why did he have to be so wonderful? It hurt knowing I couldn't keep him.

At least I'd have this one night to remember for the rest of my life.

Chapter Two

Atilla

What the hell had I been thinking? It was one thing to have a clubhouse quickie with one of the sluts who came to party. Sleeping with Solena had been something else entirely, which was why I'd held her afterward. I didn't know what pain she'd been trying to chase away, and maybe I should have asked, but I hoped I'd given her what she needed. Although, I wasn't sure why I couldn't get her off my mind.

I hadn't formed an attachment to a woman since Rebecca, and I didn't plan to start now. Getting mixed up with a sweet young thing like Solena was all kinds of wrong. I knew it, and yet I'd done it anyway. I wondered what trauma she'd been repressing last night with alcohol and sex. She'd said she wasn't a virgin, but she'd still been as tight as one. Made me think she didn't sleep around. I'd thought she just didn't party. Perhaps it was more than that.

"Morning, Dad," Casey said as she wandered into the kitchen, still looking half asleep. I got up and poured her a glass of juice before making her some toast. I'd already learned she couldn't handle more than that first thing. Anything else made her throw up.

"Morning. You sleep okay?" I asked, noting the dark circles under her eyes.

"Not really."

I held out my hand, and she gave me her phone. If I didn't have so much shit going on here, and a daughter who was going to pop at any moment, I'd have hauled my ass out of town to have a little chat with dear Aunt Su and Uncle Mark. I scrolled through the texts they'd sent her last night, getting more pissed off by the minute.

"Did these fuckers seriously call you a whore and demand you give your baby up?" I asked.

"Yeah. Said they had everything set for a private adoption."

"You haven't lived with them for months. What the fuck are they thinking?" I asked.

"They know I'm due now. Although, why they care about my baby is a mystery. Like you said, I don't live with them anymore. Other than getting bombarded with their texts, I haven't spoken with them since I left."

I finished making her toast, handed it off to her, then poured myself another cup of coffee. At my age, I should cut back on caffeine, but you only got to enjoy life once. Of course, I now had two reasons to stick around for a while. I not only had my daughter back, but a grandbaby on the way.

"Anything else you need for the nursery?" I asked.

"Dad, you've done enough. She'll have a bed, changing table, clothes, diapers, and any other necessities. Thanks to your club, she also has a baby seat and stroller."

I kissed her on top of the head before I sat. "Can't help but worry. I have a lot of years to make up for."

"It's not your fault. They lied and let you think I'd died with Mom. Since they never said much about you, I don't know why they did that. If you'd been part of my life, then things might have turned out differently."

"True, but would you really change anything if it meant your daughter wouldn't exist?" I asked.

"No." She didn't even hesitate. "Her dad might be an asshole cheater, but I love my daughter."

"Good girl." I smiled. "Your mom would be

really proud of you."

"One day I'll have a place of my own and will take care of my daughter without needing anyone's help," she said.

"Well, for now, keep saving your money."

She nibbled on her toast and sighed. I knew what she was about to ask. It was the same thing every day. I wish I had better news for her.

"Do you think Meredith will want to go shopping with me?" she asked.

"Casey, you know it's hard on her. She lost her baby. I promise she's not keeping her distance because she doesn't like you. Seeing you ready to give birth is painful for her. Lynx has her in therapy, and she's improving. Just give her a little more time."

Casey nodded. I knew she understood, even if she didn't like it. My girl was smart, and more mature than most girls her age. Which made me think about Solena again. She'd said she was twenty-three, and yet, I'd never thought she acted like someone in their early twenties. What the hell had the woman been through?

And now I was thinking about her again.

"You have plans for today?" Casey asked.

"Not really. Why? Need help with something?"

She shook her head. "Thought maybe you could stop by the café and have lunch. I should be able to take my fifteen-minute break then, so I could sit with you for a little bit."

"You should take time off. It's getting so close to your due date."

"I don't want to risk losing my job, Dad. Besides, when it's not busy, the manager gives me tasks I can do sitting down, like stuffing the napkin holders or refilling the salt and pepper shakers."

"Just don't overdo it."

"I won't." She stood and carried her dishes to the sink. "I need to shower and study a little before I go to work."

"Why don't you let me drive you? What if you go into labor while you're on the road between here and work?" I asked.

"Fine, but I think you're worrying too much."

I winked. "That's my job. Soon as that baby gets here, you'll understand."

Casey rolled her eyes and walked out of the kitchen. I finished my coffee and read the news on my phone. Since Casey had left hers behind, I unlocked it and read through the messages from Su and Mark again. What were these fuckers up to?

Sure, I got it on some level. They must have felt like Casey's parents since they took her in after her grandparents were gone. But they'd thrown her out, and she hadn't lived with them for the last three months. What did it matter to them if she kept her baby or not? If I didn't know better, it was almost like...

"Son of a bitch," I muttered. They wouldn't have, would they?

I called Outlaw, hoping he could find some information for me, or at least ask one of his hacker friends to do it. I knew he wasn't able to do as much as he once could. Not since some asshole nearly crushed his hands.

"What's up, Atilla?" he asked the moment the call connected.

"I'm hoping like fuck I'm wrong, but I need you to look into some people for me. They lived down the street from my daughter's grandparents and took her in. I just know them as Aunt Su and Uncle Mark. Casey never gave me their last name. I know they aren't her actual aunt and uncle."

"And I'm looking into them because why?" he asked.

"They're pushing for Casey to give the baby up for adoption. Since she hasn't lived there for about three months, and they have no claim on the child, it made me wonder what was in it for them."

"Shit," he muttered. "All right. Text me any info you have, like an address, phone number, or something, and I'll narrow things down a bit. I'll most likely hand this off to Wire and Lavender once I have more details. I hope you're wrong, though."

"Me too, brother. Me too."

As soon as the call ended, I sent them the last known address I had for Rebecca's parents, as well as their names and the number they texted from. I didn't know if he'd be able to find Su and Mark or not, but I hoped so. I didn't like the fact they were messaging Casey. In fact, I needed to get her a new phone with a number those assholes didn't have. She didn't enjoy speaking to them, so there was no reason she couldn't cut them out of her life.

I got up and stuck my head in Casey's room, catching her attention. "I'm going to head out for a bit. I'll be back before you go to work."

"All right. If I need anything, I'll find Spade," she said.

"Just don't go to the clubhouse. If he's not at his house, then look for Rebel or one of the Prospects."

"Got it, Dad. I'll be fine."

I went to my room to get my cut, as well as my wallet and keys. I got on my bike and headed for the front gate. Ben waved as I went through, and I drove to the nearest phone store. Once I had a new one, along with a new number, for Casey, I picked out a sturdy case for it and paid for everything. I'd brought her old one with me, and they were able to transfer everything to the new device.

I stored it in the saddlebag on my bike and scanned the street. I felt someone's eyes on me. It wasn't an unusual occurrence. People around town noticed the men in my club. The curvy woman trying to hide behind a potted tree caught my attention. I nearly smiled when I realized it was Solena. What was she doing? Did she really think I couldn't see her?

Clearly, she didn't want my attention, so I didn't wave or call out to her. Instead, I got on my bike and drove home. When I walked in the door, I found my daughter frantically tearing apart the house.

"Whoa! What's missing?" I asked.

"My phone. I know I had it in the kitchen with you. Now I can't find it."

I winced. "Sorry. That's my fault. I took it with me."

I pulled out both phones and handed her the new one first. Her brow furrowed as she checked it over, then I gave her the old one.

"Why do I have two?" she asked.

"New phone and new number. Everything should have transferred. Once you've checked the new one to make sure there isn't anything missing, I'm going to have the old one wiped and send it somewhere to be refurbished." I folded my arms. "I don't want to chance those fuckers having a way to track your every move."

I knew I should tell her my concerns about Su and Mark, but I didn't want her to worry. The stress would be bad for the baby. Right now, she just needed to get her GED, have a healthy baby, and get her life on track. I'd give her whatever support she needed in the meantime. With some luck, Outlaw could tell me I'd been completely wrong about the assholes who wanted to hand my grandbaby over to someone else. My gut was telling me that wasn't the case.

"What time do you go to work today?" I asked, glancing at my watch.

"In about…" Her eyes went wide and her jaw dropped. Right about that time, I noticed a puddle at her feet.

"Shit. Hold tight. I'll get your bag." And something to put down on the seat of the SUV. After I picked up her hospital bag, I snatched a trash bag from the pantry and a towel from the laundry room. I shoved the bag into the back seat, tucked the trash bag and towel into the seat, and helped my daughter to the vehicle.

I paused only long enough to text Spade. *Casey's in labor*.

I didn't wait to see if he'd respond. Instead, I got behind the wheel and backed down the driveway. The Prospect at the gate barely got it open before I was barreling through it. Thankfully, St. Mary's wasn't very far.

"How far apart are your contractions?" I asked.

She stared at me blankly. "What?"

"Are you feeling any pain? Maybe it feels like cramps, or does your lower back hurt?" I tried to think of things I'd heard about over the years. Since I hadn't been through this before, it was all new to me.

"Oh. Well, I get a sharp pain across my stomach, but it's not anything I can't handle. I didn't want to whine about it."

I tried to process her words and just shook my head. If there was ever a time to bitch and moan, this was it. I pulled up to the ER and helped her from the car. A nurse came out with a wheelchair.

"We've been expecting you. A Mr. Spade called," she said.

Looked like my VP had gotten my text. Good. I handed my daughter off to her and parked the SUV before hurrying inside. It looked like I'd be meeting my granddaughter soon. I couldn't wait.

Since we'd pre-registered, there wasn't much to be done. I double-checked with the front desk to make sure they had my credit card on file, as well as the insurance I'd purchased for Casey. Once that was done, all I could do was sit and wait. My ass barely hit the chair before the same nurse came over to me.

"Your daughter is asking for you," she said. "Usually the baby's father would be the one to go back with her, or perhaps her mother, but she said neither is in the picture."

"Her mom is dead, and the baby's father..." I shrugged. I wasn't about to go down that road right now. I'd left the little punk alone so far, only because it's what Casey wanted. The moment she changed her mind, I'd be teaching the little fucker a lesson he'd never forget.

"Come on. I'll walk you through everything. I'm sure a few things have changed since your daughter was born."

No way was I going to admit I hadn't been there for her birth. It hadn't been my choice. I followed the nurse and washed up before pulling on sterile scrubs. Once I was ready, she led me into the delivery room, where my daughter looked far too chill for someone about to give birth.

"You doing okay, Casey?" I asked.

She held out her hand. "I'm good. Ready to meet your granddaughter?"

"Yep."

I wrapped my fingers around hers, thinking she'd likely break my hand once it came time to push the baby out. Fuck if that little kid didn't pop out almost immediately. The doctor told her to push three times, and we had a baby.

"Congratulations! We'll get your little girl cleaned up, and then you can visit with her."

I focused on Casey's face while they delivered the afterbirth and got her cleaned up. By the time they handed the baby to her, she looked ready to take a nap.

"Is this normal?" I asked the nurse in a low voice, not wanting Casey to hear me. "It just seemed too easy."

The nurse shook her head. "Not the least bit normal. It happens from time to time, but first babies usually take longer to deliver. Your daughter had to have been in labor for hours, if not for the last few days. She never said anything?"

"Not one word."

"That one is a trooper." The nurse patted my shoulder. "You've raised a good one."

I liked how she said nothing about Casey being only seventeen and now a mom. No one had made her feel bad for having a kid when she was still one herself. Everyone we'd met during this process had been supportive, and always had a smile on their faces.

"Dad," Casey called out.

"What is it?" I went back over and looked down at the pink wrapped bundle in her arms. My granddaughter was a beauty with thick, dark hair. It curled a bit on the ends. I reached out my hand and she curled her little fingers around my pinky. And just like that, the little girl owned me heart and soul.

"I want to name her after Mom. I thought we

could call her Becca for short," she said. "Rebecca Ivy Cutler."

That had been the first thing we'd done when my daughter showed up. I'd had a paternity test done to prove she was mine, then we'd had her last name changed. Thanks to a local judge, I'd also become her official guardian. Which meant no one was going to take my daughter from me.

"I think your mom would have really liked that," I said. I leaned down to kiss Casey on the forehead, then did the same to little Becca.

My family was expanding, and I couldn't have been happier. I knew having a baby in the house would mean sleepless nights. Didn't matter. Little Becca could scream or cry as much as she wanted. I only wished I could have done all this with my own child. I hope Rebecca's parents were rotting in hell for what they'd done.

Chapter Three

Solena

I'd hidden from him. Why? I wanted to smack my head against the wall. The second I saw him across the street, I'd panicked. When I'd slept with him, I'd known I'd see him around town, and at the café. If I couldn't handle keeping things casual, I shouldn't have taken off my damn clothes. Besides, it hadn't really solved anything. I still missed my son and worried about him. The only thing I'd gained was a memorable night, my crush skyrocketing into severe lust territory, and a slight hangover this morning.

I felt like an idiot.

"Hey, Solena. Can you cover Casey's shift today?" Dave asked.

Was something wrong? I wiped my hands on a rag and nodded. "Of course."

"Thanks. I'll get coverage for the rest of her shifts that are already on the schedule. I just didn't have anything planned for today," he said. "She went into labor this morning. Someone from the club called when she was on her way to the hospital."

It must have happened after I saw Atilla. There was no way that overprotective Papa Bear had been out shopping while his daughter was in labor. I'd heard she was having a little girl. I hoped everything went okay. My fingers itched to grab my phone and check on her. We worked together and nothing more. She might find it odd if I sent her a text. We'd exchanged numbers the first week she started working, in case anything came up. Of course, I didn't blame her for not reaching out when she went into labor. I still remembered the pain of giving birth to my son.

I envied her a little. She had someone supportive

who was letting her keep her baby. Maybe if my parents hadn't been complete assholes, I'd have been able to keep my son. They'd nearly thrown me out of the house when I told them I was having a baby. Instead, they'd shown the community how much they cared about me by "helping" me stay in school and get the prenatal care I needed. Then they'd given my baby away without my consent. Since I'd only been fifteen, I hadn't had a say in the matter. If I'd been emancipated, then I'd have kept my son. Maybe it was something I should have attempted, but there weren't too many places that would hire someone who was only fifteen.

Instead, I'd let my parents force me to sign away my rights. I'd given them control over the fate of my child, and I'd paid the price for it every day since. They'd made me feel like I didn't have a choice in the matter. I'd had nowhere to go. They'd said they were going to kick me out if I didn't give up my baby. Why couldn't they have at least let me hold him just once?

"You okay?" Dave asked.

I realized I'd been staring into space and reminiscing about my child. I gave him a smile and got back to work. As far as managers went, Dave was pretty great. He always made sure we got our breaks, tried to give us the schedule we needed, and was understanding if someone got sick and couldn't make it in. Not a lot of places were so lenient.

"I'm going to take up a donation for Casey. Thought we could give her some cash for whatever baby items she may need. Will you let her regular customers know there's a jar by the register?" Dave asked.

"Sure. I can do that."

Why couldn't I have known Dave back then? I'd felt so alone during my pregnancy. My parents made me feel ashamed, even though I hadn't been at fault. They'd called me names, made sure I knew how disappointed they were, and I'd even lost what few friends I'd had.

You will not wallow in self-pity! Snap out of it!

Last night had been a terrible idea. Would this have hit me as hard if I hadn't handed myself to Atilla on a silver platter? Being with him had been wonderful, and also heartbreaking. I knew he'd never want me the way I wanted him. No, I *needed* him. I'd been a quick release and nothing more. He'd made it clear he couldn't offer me anything. Had asked multiple times if I was sure I wanted to go through with it. Like a fool, I'd said yes.

Part of me regretted it. Only part. I'd had no idea sex could be like that. I felt sore this morning. Even though Atilla's cock wasn't the size of a porn star's, it had felt big to me. Every step I took was a reminder of what we'd done last night. I hoped it was the *only* reminder I'd have. He'd used a condom, but I knew those weren't foolproof. Not having a boyfriend, or planning to have sex anytime soon, meant I wasn't on birth control. Honestly, I'd never used it. It had seemed like an added expense I didn't need.

Sunny, one of my co-workers, came over with a bright smile on her face. "I'm going by the hospital after my shift to take a look at the baby. Want to come?"

My heart ached at the thought. I didn't begrudge Casey her sweet baby, but I wasn't sure I wanted to see her. Not yet anyway. I felt too raw after last night. Between thoughts of my son dragging me down, and knowing I'd never have a shot with the one man I wanted, I wasn't in a good place today.

"I think I'll wait a bit. I'm sure all the Savage

Raptors will visit throughout the day. I don't want to overwhelm her."

"Hmm. I didn't think of that." Sunny shrugged. "Well, I have a little gift for the baby. I can always drop it off and leave it with one of the men if she isn't up for company."

"Did Dave tell you about the donation jar?" I asked.

"Yeah. I think it's a great idea. I bet a lot of customers will shove a few dollars in there, if not more. Casey is such a sweetheart. Everyone loves her."

She wasn't wrong. Even I liked Casey. The girl seemed to always have a positive attitude, no matter what life threw her way. I'd heard a little about the people who'd taken her in. They didn't seem very nice. Then again, they weren't worse than my own parents. The difference was Casey had the courage to walk away. I hadn't done that.

"You sure you're okay?" Sunny asked. "You seem off today."

"I'll be fine. Yesterday was a rough day for me. I guess I'm still in a bit of a fog."

"Well, if you need anything, just give me a shout."

My co-workers were all wonderful. We didn't hang out as friends, but they checked on me if I missed a shift. It was the closest thing I had to a support system. The bell over the door jingled, and I looked up, my heart racing when I saw a few of the Savage Raptors come in. Atilla wasn't among them. Not that it surprised me. He would probably stay at the hospital with Casey until she could go home.

"Who wants to see baby pictures?" one of them asked, waving his phone around.

"I do!" Sunny practically bounced over to them.

"Oh my gosh! She's so cute. What did Casey decide to name her?"

"Becca. After her mom."

And that's when my knees nearly gave out. I gripped the counter hard to remain upright. Atilla had already said there wasn't a future for us. Why did it matter that his daughter named her child Becca? Besides, it wasn't like the big biker picked out the name. It made me wonder if he'd think about his lost love even more now that he not only had Casey living with him, but his granddaughter shared a name with her.

I forced myself to walk over and see the baby pictures. I made all the appropriate remarks, even held a smile, but inside I felt like I was dying a little. Somehow, I made it through the day with no mishaps. I left work and went straight home. It made me feel a little petty, since everyone at the café had talked about going to see Casey and little Becca. I'd been the only one to bow out, aside from those who had to work the dinner shift.

My phone rang with an out-of-state number. One I didn't recognize. I almost didn't answer, but something made me hesitate for a second. I clicked the *accept* button.

"Hello?"

"You don't know me, but my name is Lavender." Hearing a woman's voice set me at ease a little. "I have some information I think you might want."

"Um, I'm sorry, but what's this about?" I asked.

I kicked off my shoes and unfastened my braid, massaging my scalp. If this woman was trying to sell something, she'd dialed the wrong number. I made do. I could pay for my apartment and other necessities. Anything else wasn't going to happen. Not anytime soon.

"You gave birth to a little boy at St. Mary's hospital in Bryson Corners, Oklahoma, eight years ago, correct?" the woman asked.

My breath caught, and my heart nearly stopped. "How do you know about my son?"

"Oh, good. I have the right number. Your name is Solena, right?"

"Yeah. But again, how do you know about my son? Is this some sort of joke? What do you want?" I asked, feeling my panic and anger rise.

"I'm a hacker. You have a motorcycle club in your town. Savage Raptors. My husband and I were looking into something for their President. It ended up being a much bigger problem than anyone expected. I ran across your name and the information for your little boy."

My throat grew tight. "He's alive?"

"Yes. Your parents attended a small rural church, correct?"

"They did. I haven't spoken to them since I moved out. What does that have to do with anything? Are you saying the church facilitated the adoption?"

She snorted. "That's one way of putting it. Anyway, I'll call back when I have more information. Right now, we're still trying to connect all the dots."

"Wait! My son... what's his name?" I needed something. Anything. A tiny crumb of information. After going without my son for so long, this was the most hope I'd had since the day he was born.

"Santiago."

Before I could ask for anything else, the call ended. I stared at the phone in my hand as tears slipped down my cheeks. I had so many questions. What did the church have to do with anything? Why had Atilla asked them to look into something that ended up being tied to my son? And what were the odds?

I'd never believed in coincidences. Only fate. Had it been fate that I'd met Atilla? Was there something bigger at play?

"Santiago," I murmured. Knowing my son's name filled me with joy. Would I be able to meet him one day? He'd be eight now. Attending elementary school. Making friends. Did he like to play catch or chase a soccer ball? What sorts of movies and books did he like?

One little piece of information, and now I had a thirst to learn everything about my little boy. I almost dialed the woman back, but something told me it wouldn't do me any good. If she'd wanted me to know more, she'd have said so. The way she'd been somewhat abrupt and stuck to facts and questions told me she was a professional. A hacker? I knew what that meant, of course. Or at least, I knew what TV told me that entailed.

"What are you looking for, Atilla?" I murmured. I needed to know.

Taking off my sweaty work clothes, I rinsed off in the shower, put my hair up in a messy bun, and threw on some black leggings and a pink tunic-style shirt with black and gray swirls across it. I slipped on my black canvas slides and grabbed my keys before hurrying out the door.

I hadn't planned to go to the hospital to see Casey and the baby, but now I needed to. Or, more accurately, I needed to go see Attila. I didn't know if I could convince him to talk to me or not. But I had to try. This was the closest I'd ever been to locating my little boy and finding out if he'd had a happy life. I couldn't just sit and wait, hoping that the woman -- Lavender -- would call again.

I drove to the hospital and parked near the entrance. It felt like it took forever to reach the maternity ward, and the second I entered the waiting room, I saw a half dozen Savage Raptors. Atilla wasn't among them. However, Spade was there, and he came over right away.

"You here to see the baby?" he asked.

"Um. Yes and no. I want to see little Becca, but I need to ask Atilla something."

He rocked back on his heels. "Sorry, but with the way things went down last night, I don't think it was more than just the one time."

My cheeks warmed. "It's not about that. A woman named Lavender called me. I have some questions I need answered. She mentioned Atilla specifically."

"Right. Okay, then. Wait here and I'll go get him. I'm sure he could use a coffee break, anyway."

Spade walked off, leaving me with the other men in his club. They stared at me before going back to their conversation. Had they heard everything? Probably. Great. That meant even if they hadn't seen me last night, they now knew I'd slept with their President.

Spade returned a few minutes later with Atilla right behind him. The big man didn't seem amused. If anything, I saw a storm brewing in his eyes. Shit. Maybe I should have held off and at least waited until he'd gone home.

"Outside. Now," he said.

I swallowed hard and meekly followed him. I'd thought he literally meant outside, as in the parking lot, but he surprised me by going to the cafeteria. He motioned to the various food items.

"Get something to eat. You look like you're going to pass out." His tone seemed softer than before, and I reached out to grab the first thing I saw -- a turkey sandwich. I also got a bottle of juice and a yogurt cup. Atilla walked over to the hot food area and ordered a burger with fries. He gently placed his hand on my lower back and led me to the cashier, where he paid for our food.

"You don't have to do this," I said.

"Hush, woman. When's the last time you ate?"

I shrugged. I honestly didn't remember. While I'd worked all of my shift and Casey's, it was a bit of a blur. He chose a table against the wall on the far side of the cafeteria, away from the other people. At least it would be quiet, and I wouldn't have to worry about people listening to our conversation.

"Now, you told Spade someone named Lavender called you?" he asked.

"Yes. I'd just gotten home from work when my phone rang. I didn't recognize the number and almost didn't answer. I'm glad I did. She said she was a hacker and was looking into something for you when she ran across information on my son."

He held up a hand. "Wait. What son?"

"That's a long conversation," I said. And one I wasn't sure he deserved to know. He'd made it clear we didn't have a future. Why did he care if I had a son?

"Do I look like I'm going anywhere? Casey and Becca are fine. They can do without me for a short while. Talk to me, Solena."

"Can I ask what she was looking for?"

The way he leaned back in his seat and folded his arms made me feel like I'd done something wrong. Was it bad that I'd asked such a question? It seemed logical to me. A woman I'd never met called me out of the blue, mentioned Atilla's name and said she'd found my son, and I was supposed to what? Sit at home and wait patiently for someone to possibly give me more information?

Not likely.

I stared back, waiting to see what he'd do.

Chapter Four

Atilla

Why the fuck had Lavender called her? And why didn't I know Solena had a kid? We weren't exactly friends, but we'd talked here and there. I didn't remember hearing anything about a child. Most people brought up their kids when they talked to Casey. I didn't know why my daughter's pregnant belly made them think she needed to hear all their stories of when their kid was a baby and stayed up all night.

It wasn't technically club business. After all, I'd called Outlaw, who had called Wire and Lavender, to dig up dirt on Su and Mark. I needed to know why they wanted my grandbaby so badly. Or rather, why they wanted Casey to give up her daughter. If they'd run across something while looking into that couple...

"My daughter was staying with two people she called Aunt Su and Uncle Mark, even though they weren't related. For some reason, they kept texting her, wanting her to give her baby up for adoption. Since she doesn't live with them anymore, I thought it was strange." My name was called, and I went to pick up my order. When I got back, I took a bite of my burger before I continued. "I called a friend who happens to be a hacker. Or he was. He then reached out to Lavender and her husband, to see if they could find anything suspicious on the couple."

Solena paled and tensed. Interesting. Was it their names that brought on that reaction? The part about adoption? She'd mentioned a son, but again, I didn't recall her ever talking about one. Had she given her baby up for adoption? And if so, how long ago? She'd said she was only twenty-three. Was it somewhat recent?

"Solena, you said Lavender called about your son. Talk to me. What's going on?"

The stubborn set of her chin told me plenty. I'd hurt her by being so adamant I'd never settle down. Rebecca had been my one and only. Or so I'd thought. But if that was true, why had I woken up thinking about Solena first thing this morning? Not to mention the mere thought someone might have hurt her, or something nefarious might have happened to her boy, made me want to shelter and protect her. I'd never had that reaction to a woman. Not since Rebecca. Well, I felt that way with Casey, but she was my daughter, so it was different.

I waited to see if she'd talk to me. I wasn't sure how much I should say about what Lavender and Wire were working on. If her boy had gotten mixed up in this somehow, then she had a right to know. And if not… it might not be club business, but it *was* personal. I wasn't sure how much I wanted to let her in. What would Casey think about it? I'd only recently gotten my daughter back. I didn't know if I was ready to risk driving her away by bringing a woman home, especially one closer to her age than mine.

"When I was fifteen, my boyfriend raped me. No one believed me. They said I'd consented and changed my mind later. It's what my boyfriend claimed happened. I don't know why they all took his side." Her eyes darkened and her lower lip trembled. "I got pregnant. I was still fifteen when my son was born. My parents never gave me a chance to hold him or even see his face. He was taken away immediately and put up for adoption."

I fisted my hand on the table, wanting to find the little shit and beat the hell out of him. It didn't matter if he'd only been a kid. He'd been old enough to know right and wrong. The thought of someone hurting her in such an awful way made me see red.

And that's when I knew I was fucked.

It didn't matter if I *wanted* to let her in, because she was already there, worming her way into my heart. I already cared. Wanted to protect her. Hold her and tell her everything would be fine.

Shit.

"Is that what you wanted?" I asked, trying to stay focused.

"No. I wanted my baby, despite everything. My parents didn't give me a choice. My boyfriend must have agreed with them because I remember his signature on the papers they forced me to sign. I've never known what happened to my little boy. Last night..." She looked away.

"What about last night?" I asked.

"It was a bad day for me. That's why I was at your clubhouse drinking. Or part of the reason. My son has been on my mind a lot lately. I've wondered if he's happy. If he's even still alive. What sort of life he's had. Lavender gave me the first hope I've ever had. I even know his name." She smiled a little. "Santiago."

"And Lavender found out about your boy while looking into Su and Mark?" I asked.

"I guess so. She said she'd been working on something for you. The fact they wanted to put Becca up for adoption, and that led to Lavender finding Santiago, makes me think they're part of the organization who took my baby." She pressed her lips together. "She also mentioned something about the church my parents attended when they lived here. Both my family and the church have moved. I don't know where because I cut all ties with my family when I moved out. I just know they put their house up for sale, and I noticed the church was vacant one day when I drove past it. Of course, it could have just shut down entirely and not changed location."

I'd file the information away about the church. Had it really been a church? Or was something deeper going on? How were Solena's parents involved? Instead of putting the puzzle together, I seemed to only end up with more pieces I couldn't fit together.

"Was there anything off about the adoption with your son?" I asked.

"The adoption agency my parents mentioned didn't handle the case. I've never known who put my baby in the hands of complete strangers. It's possible my parents did it themselves. They're awful enough."

"I'm sorry, Solena. It seems we have more in common than I thought. Until Casey showed up at the clubhouse, I'd thought she was dead. I'd received the news her mother, Rebecca, died before she could give birth to our daughter. No one else told me Casey was still alive or had been safely delivered. The anniversary of what I assumed to be *their* death always hit me hard. Oddly enough, that's the same day Casey showed up. On her seventeenth birthday."

"I always thought not knowing was the worst part. Now I know he's alive, and have no idea if he's healthy and happy, if his parents love him, or anything other than his name and he's alive. I think it's even worse."

"Give me a minute. I'm going to finish this burger and fries, then I'll see if Lavender or Wire will give me more info. I know what it's like to need closure. Since she called you, I know you have her number. But you came to me instead of calling her back. Your reasons are your own, and I don't need to know why you did it." I cleared my throat. "And for what it's worth, I'm sorry about what I said last night. It didn't occur to me it might have made you feel like I was using you. I'm a guy. A biker. And admittedly, I can be an asshole. Usually, I'm only an asshole when I need to be one."

She gave me a genuine smile that time, and I considered it a win. I finished my food, threw our trash away, and took her by the hand. The fact it felt so small in mine made my protective urges rise up even more. I didn't know what Lavender had found, or why the fuck she'd call Solena and only give her a small piece of news about her son. She'd better have a damn good reason, because it pissed me the fuck off.

I led Solena out of the hospital and to a small courtyard I'd discovered when I'd taken a walk earlier. We sat on one of the park benches and I pulled out my phone. Even though I didn't speak directly with Wire very often, I had his number. The phone rang three times before he answered.

"Wire speaking," he said as the call connected.

"It's Atilla."

"We're still looking into some things," Wire said. "But we should have news for you soon. Lavender had a bit of luck earlier and it helped her connect a few pieces."

"I'm aware." I tried to keep the irritation from my voice. "Why the fuck did she call Solena and drop that kind of bomb on her?"

I could hear him breathing, but otherwise, the line was silent. I knew the fucker was still there. I gave him another minute, then hung up the phone. Instead of calling him back, I called Outlaw.

"Just got a text from Wire," he said when the call connected.

"Hello to you too," I muttered. "What did the

asshole have to say for himself?"

"He wasn't aware you knew Solena."

I counted to ten. Then twenty. Nope. Still pissed.

"What the fuck does it matter if I know her? Why would Lavender do that to her? She's a mom. Did she stop to think how it would have made her feel if their roles had been reversed? It was a hurtful thing to do, and I don't fucking appreciate it."

Outlaw whistled. "Damn. You have it bad. But noted. I'll have a talk with him. I'm sure Lavender was in the zone and trying to tie things together. She probably didn't stop long enough to consider how her actions would impact Solena."

"I get it. I do, but it doesn't make me any happier."

"They've been sharing information with me as they find things. From what I'm looking at, it seemed like Solena's family handed off her son to their local church. The pastor then placed the child in a home. It's the same pastor who's been in contact with Su and Mark." I heard Outlaw's chair creak as he sighed. "If I had to guess, we're looking at a human trafficking ring. I can only hope the kids are all safe and are actually with loving parents, but after all the horrific things we've seen? I'm struggling a bit to hold on to the faith we'll find them in good health and still alive."

Motherfucker. I couldn't tell Solena that. No way in fucking hell. Lavender apparently told her that Santiago was alive. At least there was some small comfort in that. If the kid was still breathing, then we just needed to get him home to her. The rest would eventually work itself out -- probably with a shit ton of therapy.

"What about Santiago?" I asked. "Did they send you anything on him?"

"Let me check." It took a few minutes of papers shuffling before he found what he was searching for. "Got it. Santiago is... Fuck."

"Not instilling a lot of confidence right now," I said.

"Yeah, sorry. It's just... he's bounced around. A lot. But Atilla... he's in Bryson Corners right now. I'm going to text you everything I can find on his location. You'll need to extract him. Fast."

"Got it."

"And, Atilla? Don't tell the mom what's going on yet. Now isn't the time."

Outlaw ended the call, and I stared at Solena, wondering what the hell I was going to do. Once I had the information from Outlaw, I'd know a little more. Either way, it didn't sound like the kid was in a good place.

"What's going on?" she asked.

How the hell could I look her in the eye and lie to her face? I couldn't. Outlaw said not to tell her anything yet, but I could at least give her a little hope, right? I knew how much she'd missed her boy. If I could get him back for her... I thought over the years I'd had without Casey. I'd have given anything for someone to tell my daughter was alive.

"Well, I don't know for certain yet, but... how would you like to have your son back?" Tears gathered in her eyes, her lips trembled, and then she threw herself into my arms. I held her as she sobbed against my chest, and I knew I'd do whatever it took to bring her kid to her. "It's going to be okay, Solena. I'll get him back for you. Just promise me something."

"Anything," she said.

"Get him whatever help he may need. I have no idea what the kid has been through. Outlaw is going to tell me how to find him, but he said your boy has been bounced around some different homes."

"He's only eight," she said, wiping the tears from her cheeks.

"What do you need for him?" I asked.

"Everything." She smiled. "I never thought I'd get to see him, much less hug him. Now you're telling me he can live with me?"

I nodded. "I'll make sure it happens. Whatever it takes."

"I don't know what size he wears or anything. What if I get something that doesn't fit? Or toys he doesn't like?"

I felt her trembling and knew she was both excited and scared. As much as I wanted to go back up to be with Casey and Becca, I knew they had plenty of people in their corner. Solena didn't seem to have anyone. Who stood beside her during hard times? Who lent a hand when she was floundering?

"Come on. Let's go see the baby, and I'll make sure Spade stays with Casey. Then you and I can go make sure you have the basics for your boy."

"Are you sure?" she asked.

"I'm positive." I stood and held out my hand. She slid her palm against mine. I closed my fingers around hers and led her back into the hospital.

The fact my heart was slamming against my ribs wasn't something I'd admit to anyone. It was like the first time I'd seen Rebecca. Excitement hummed in my veins, and her hand felt incredibly right in mine. I had too much going on and felt like I needed to be in twenty places at once. But knowing my daughter and granddaughter were in good hands gave a small measure of comfort.

I didn't know what would happen with Solena, if

anything. Maybe I'd get her kid back, and I wouldn't see her again unless it was at the café. But I suddenly wondered what it would be like to have more with her. Casey was seventeen, and she was getting her life figured out. She had a kid of her own. One day, she'd move out.

"I know what I said before, but once you have your son back, I'd like to talk some more and maybe re-evaluate things."

"Like what?" she asked.

"Us. I thought I was too old to find someone. I had Rebecca, but she's been gone seventeen years. There will never be a day I don't love her. I guess I always felt like letting someone else in would be the same as me trying to replace her."

She squeezed my hand. "Atilla, I would never presume to take her place. Not in your life or Casey's. Honestly, I'm jealous as hell. She's been gone all this time and still has your love and devotion. I can't even imagine what that's like. When I heard the baby's name, it felt like someone stabbed me in the heart."

"That was Casey's idea," I said. "I didn't name my granddaughter."

"I know. Even if you had, it's petty of me to be upset over something like that. The two of you had a life together. You knew her long before I came into the picture. I was only six years old when she died and gave birth to Casey. And yes, I know the age difference between us freaks you out a little. I can't say it didn't give me pause, but in the end, I don't care what anyone else thinks. We have a right to be happy."

"I know." I stopped her and leaned down to press my lips to hers in a brief kiss. "I can't make a lot of promises right now. Your life is about to change when Santiago comes home, and I'm still figuring out how to be a dad. Now I'm a grandpa too. Let's just take it one day at a time and see where things go. Are you all right with that?"

She smiled up at me. "Yeah. I can live with that."

For all I knew, this would blow up in my face, but for the first time in seventeen years, I'd met a woman who made me want something more. I owed it to myself, and to Rebecca's memory, to see where this went. I knew she wouldn't have wanted me to be alone for the rest of my life. That wasn't the sort of woman she'd been. So I'd honor her by doing whatever it took to be happy.

Chapter Five

Solena

If someone had said I'd be spending the evening running around town with Atilla, then having dinner together, I'd have called them a liar. And yet, here we were. I still didn't know where Santiago would sleep. My apartment was only a one-bedroom unit. It had been plenty big enough for me. Now that I was going to have my son with me, I'd need more room. Except I couldn't afford a bigger place.

"What else do we need to get?" Atilla asked, before taking a bite out of his taco.

"I don't think my apartment can hold anything else."

He paused with the taco halfway to his mouth for another bite. "Do you have room for your kid?"

My cheeks warmed. I dropped my gaze to the table, not wanting to admit I didn't know how I'd take care of him. Since he was old enough to attend school, I could work while he was in class. But what about the rest of the time? I was making do with things the way they were now. Adding the expense of having my son with me, and needing a larger apartment, would be nearly impossible to overcome.

"Solena, what's wrong?"

"I can barely take care of myself. How am I supposed to keep my son alive and give him all the things he needs? You said he might need help. Like a psychiatrist, right? That sounds expensive. What if coming to live with me isn't the best thing for him?" I felt the tears brimming in my eyes, and I fought to hold them back. Had I only been fooling myself? Atilla had purchased nearly everything today. I hadn't even been able to do that much, and there was so much more he'd need once Santiago was home. Clothes and shoes were things I couldn't really purchase until I knew the right sizes. We'd gotten a few shirts and elastic waist pants in two different sizes so he'd at least have something. I knew he'd need a lot more.

"Hey." He reached over and took my hand. "It will be okay, Solena."

"How?" A tear slid down my cheek and I wiped it away. "I can't do this, Atilla. I want to, so much. But…"

"Can you make it work for a few days? Maybe a week?" he asked.

"Why? What's going to change in that short amount of time?"

"Just give me some time. I'll help you figure something out. All right? Don't give up."

I nodded and went back to eating. He was right. I'd wanted this for so long. I couldn't let fear hold me back. There were enough obstacles without creating new ones. For all I knew, my son thought I'd never wanted him. I didn't know how to make him believe it hadn't been my choice to give him up. From what Atilla said, it seemed like Santiago hadn't lived an easy life. I didn't know what to expect. Had they abused him? Or had no one ever wanted him, and that's why he'd been bounced from home to home?

"What about Casey and Becca? Shouldn't you go back to the hospital?"

Atilla waved me off. "It's fine. The club is keeping an eye on her. I have a feeling Rebel and Maui are especially being watchful."

"It doesn't bother you? That they might like her?" I asked.

"Neither will make a move. She's too young and has a lot to sort out. They know it and won't cross a line. The fact they're interested in her means they're invested in her safety, as well as Becca's. I know my club won't let anything happen to them, but those two? They'll be worse than a mother hen watching over her chicks."

"She's seventeen, right?" I asked.

"Yep. Turned seventeen three months ago. Why?"

"Then in less than a year, she's legally an adult. What about then?" I noticed the way his jaw tensed. Yeah, he wasn't as laid back about as he'd made it seem. No matter how much he trusted those men, that was still his little girl. "She's lucky to have you. All of you. Not all girls are loved by their families."

He finished off his food, shoved his plate aside, and leaned forward, bracing his forearms on the table. "Want to talk about it?"

"My parents were... different. Strict. Conservative. When I got pregnant, I thought for sure they'd abandon me. They didn't. However, they did use it to their advantage. They made it seem like they were benevolent, letting me remain at home while they cared for me. Then they forced me to sign away my rights to my child before I even got to see him. They never once showed him to me or let me hold him."

"Your name, and your son's, are Hispanic. But you have green eyes and..."

"I'm super pale?" I smiled. "My mother was a Latina. My dad had red hair and green eyes. His family was Irish. My name is Solena Murphy. It's probably just luck that Santiago has a Latino name."

"Do you speak Spanish?" he asked.

"No. My father didn't approve of my mother teaching it to me, and he made me take French in school. I never met my dad's family. One time, I heard him talking to my mother about them. I think they were rich and didn't approve of him marrying my mom. At least, that's how it sounded."

"Why do you think they didn't love you?" he asked.

"I can't remember ever getting a hug or kiss from either of them. Only criticism. They weren't just strict. It went beyond that. I'm not really sure how to explain it." I took a sip of my drink. "When I graduated high school, I left and never looked back. I couldn't forgive them for what they'd done. I was so wrecked after giving birth to my son my grades suffered. I barely graduated from high school. College wasn't even an option. If I hadn't left on my own, they would have forced me out. A less than perfect daughter didn't have a place in their home."

"I'm sorry to hear that. Every parent should love and cherish their child. I wish like hell I'd known about Casey before now. I'd have loved to have had her with me all these years. I feel like I missed out on a lot."

"I don't know a lot about her situation, or how she was raised, but it's clear how much she loves you. She knows you're there for her, and nothing else matters. When she needed help, she came to find you. The fact you welcomed her was probably a great comfort to her."

He reached over to take my hand. "You've never had anyone, have you?"

I shook my head. I wasn't looking for his sympathy. Soon, I'd have my son back. I wouldn't be alone anymore. No matter what it took, I had to make this work. I'd let my boy down once already. At fifteen, I hadn't felt like I had any other option than to go along with my parents' wishes, especially since Santiago's father had signed the forms. Everyone had been against me.

Now that I was older, I knew there were programs in place to help teen mothers. If I'd heard about them back then, maybe things would have turned out differently. For one, I would have known I had the right to keep my baby. Second, those programs would have given me the tools I needed to not only hold on to my child, but to give him a decent life.

It was too late to go back and change things, but I could do better. Since I didn't know Santiago's current situation, or how Atilla planned to get him for me, I wasn't sure it would be safe to check into those sorts of places right now. What if I reached out, and some loophole gave the state the right to take my son away? No, I couldn't risk it.

* * *

Atilla

I saw the determination in her eyes and knew, whatever her thoughts had been just now, she'd decided she'd do whatever it took to make a good life for her boy. I couldn't have been prouder of her. I also knew she couldn't do it all on her own, not without any sort of support system. Going to the government wouldn't be an option right off. Not until I had Wire do some work on his end.

How did I tell her what her little boy had been through? Outlaw might not have spelled things out, but I could read between the lines. If he thought the kid had gotten mixed up in a human trafficking ring, I could imagine the horrors he'd faced. That boy was going to need a lot of help. Mentally and emotionally. What the fuck had her parents been thinking?

I needed to pay a visit to Su and Mark before it was too late. Once Wire had all the dirt he needed on them, the club would most likely make them disappear. I knew all the kids involved would be taken care of because that's just the sort of thing the Reapers lived for. Taking in abused women and children seemed to be their calling. If someone at the club didn't adopt those kids, they'd find others who would. Hell, even their President had adopted a teenager at one point.

I leaned back in the booth and wondered what it would be like to raise a kid. Casey was too mature to need me for much but emotional and financial support at this point. In fact, I'd already spoken with the club officers about adding a few tiny homes to the compound. The first of which would be right across the road from my house and would be given to Casey.

Solena was right about one thing. Once Casey was old enough, one of the guys might make a move on her. I didn't have any right to stand in her way. If she fell in love with one of them, all I could do was give her my support. If whatever guy she ended up with ever hurt her or cheat on her, I didn't give a shit who he was, I'd bury the fucker. I could be both supportive and protective whether or not she liked it.

Not to mention, I didn't see a reason Solena and Santiago couldn't stay in one of the other tiny homes while she got her feet under her. It would allow her to save money, give the kid an extra layer of protection, and Solena would have the support she'd been lacking all her life. It would give the compound a more family-oriented feel as well. Perhaps it would help Meredith in the long run. I had seen little of her lately, but Lynx watched her like a hawk.

I didn't want to say anything to Solena just yet. Spade had checked into the kits for the tiny homes that would match the cabin style of the other houses. We'd still have to wire them, put up sheetrock, get the appliances in, run plumbing and all that fun stuff. It would just save time as far as the basic structure went. The thought was to use one for Casey for however long she needed it and put in at least three others in case we ever needed to put up guests.

It would have been nice to have them when Meredith first arrived. Instead, I'd had her staying at the clubhouse and told her not to come out of her room when a party was going on. It hadn't been ideal, and I wanted to avoid the same situation if at all possible. If another club asked for help again, I wouldn't turn them away. Better to be prepared for anything.

"Let's get the stuff over to your apartment. I need to check in with Spade, say goodnight to Casey, and then I have some work to do at home." I gave her hand a squeeze. "But if you need anything, call me, all right?"

"I feel like I'm getting whiplash," she mumbled.

I couldn't blame her. I'd gone from keeping her at arm's length to paying more attention to her. I knew she had to be confused. Hell, I was too. The thought of allowing myself to have something more still felt foreign. All these years, I'd thought I didn't have room in my life for anyone other than Rebecca. Maybe I'd just needed the right woman to come along. The age difference still bothered me a little. Not because I saw her as a child -- because I didn't -- but I didn't want the people around town to speak poorly of her or make her feel bad when they made comments. I knew someone would at some point. No one ever minded their own business these days.

"Sure. I need to organize the things we bought anyway." She stood and I dropped some cash on the table to cover the meals plus tip. I placed my hand on her lower back as I led her out to the parking lot.

It was a good thing I'd had the SUV. Of course, I'd had to throw out the trash bag and towel I'd put down for Casey, but they'd done their job and the seat remained clean and dry. I helped her into the vehicle then asked for directions to her apartment. I wasn't thrilled to see where she'd been living.

"What about my car?" she asked. "It's still at the hospital."

"I'll ask one of my brothers to come get the keys. They'll bring the car here for you."

She smiled, but it didn't quite reach her eyes. I could still see the worry in them, and she looked more than a little tired. I needed to get home and see what Outlaw had sent so I could start planning the extraction. The sooner I got Santiago back to his mom, the better off they'd both be.

"You have my number?" I asked.

"No. Only Casey's, since we work together. But I think it's a cell phone and not a landline."

"All right. Hand me your phone." She unlocked it and passed it over. I entered my information, then added hers to my phone as well before handing it back. "Remember what I said. You need something, you call me."

"Thank you, Atilla. I know you don't owe me anything. I really appreciate everything you're doing."

I cupped her cheek. "Solena, I will get your son back, no matter what."

With those parting words, I left and went home. I'd keep my word. I had no idea what I'd be walking into, but those fuckers made a big mistake coming to my town. If they thought I'd look the other way, they were wrong. I was going to get Santiago out safely, and then I was going to make them pay.

Should probably ask the law to look the other way. It was time to call my favorite police officer, or rather his kindhearted wife, Peaches. Wouldn't be the first time she'd helped us out, and I doubted it would be the last. Good thing she had that man of hers wrapped tight around her little finger.

Chapter Six

"According to Outlaw, there are four children inside. One of them is Santiago. I'm going to personally deliver him to his mother. The others don't have anywhere to go," I said.

"One of them does," Lynx said. "Meredith is worried about passing her issues onto a kid, so she wants to hold off on having a baby. She also wants a family, so if those kids need a home, we'll take one of them."

I nodded. It hadn't occurred to me to ask Meredith and Lynx since I knew she'd been having a hard time after losing her baby. Everyone else at the club was single. I wasn't sure any of them would want to adopt a kid, especially one who'd been through something traumatic. I was up for it, though. I'd missed out on most of Casey's life. My little girl was all grown up and wouldn't need her dad for much longer. Then I'd be alone. Not really a good reason to adopt a kid, but I wanted to experience all the stuff I'd missed.

"According to the papers Outlaw sent me, there's a set of twins in there. Fraternal ones. They're four years old. Boy's name is Finn and his sister is Amelia. Then there's Santiago, who is eight. He's Solena's child, and I'm going to make sure she gets him back. The fourth one is a girl. Nora. She's seven." I looked at the men who'd come with me. "We get the kids out safe. I don't give a shit if every adult in that place dies a gruesome death and burns in hell for all eternity, but don't let the kids see it happen."

"I'll handle the adults," General said.

"I'll help extract the kids." Lynx said. "I bet Merry would love the twins."

"You clear it with her psychiatrist?" Truth asked. "And that's not being an asshole. It's me being concerned she might lose her shit when you bring two kids home."

"No, we didn't, and how the fuck do we bring that up? I can just see it now. Walk into the office and start off with, 'Hey, Doc! We rescued these two kids from human traffickers and kept them. That's cool, right?'"

General snorted. "Truth, you're with me. I think Lynx and the Pres can handle the kids on their own."

I shook my head. "No. I'm going to put those fuckers in the ground. I need someone to haul Santiago out of there. I'll deliver him to his mom, but first I want to look her in the eye and assure her I've killed the monsters who hurt her boy."

"I'll help Lynx," Stinger said. "He can grab the twins, and I'll get Santiago and Nora."

"How many adults have you confirmed, General?" I asked.

"I see two adults inside the building and three outside. The two inside are together and keeping watch over the kids. The ones outside are scattered. I say we split up to hit the easy ones first, then we can take out the men inside while Lynx and Stinger get the kids out."

I nodded. "Take the children straight to the SUV and get the hell out of here. Just park at the compound and I'll be right behind you."

Lynx tossed me his keys, and I gave him mine. Since I'd driven my SUV here, and I planned to stay until I was certain none of these fuckers were breathing, it would mean someone else had to drive the children out of here.

"Give us time to handle the men outside,"

General said. "Once we're in the building, we'll subdue the two men watching the kids. Then Lynx and Stinger can pull the children out. We'll see what we can get out of them once there aren't little eyes watching us."

"Or ears to hear the screaming," Truth said.

I pulled a large bowie knife, knowing we needed to move fast and keep it silent. We split up, each of us tackling one of the men. I kept low to the ground and crept forward, sticking to the shadows. The guy leaned against the side of the building and pulled out a pack of cigarettes. I watched him light up and waited for him to look in the other direction.

I lunged at him, placing my hand over his mouth as I stabbed him in the gut twice. There wasn't much point in keeping everyone alive. All we needed was one rat out of the five. I dragged my knife up and across his throat, then lowered him to the ground. Since I knew Truth and General wouldn't let their targets slip past them, I didn't need to hide the body.

Lynx and Stinger approached me, keeping their voices low.

"I saw General tying up the guy he went after," Lynx said.

"Truth left a bloody mess." Stinger winced. "Think he has some anger issues to work through?"

"So we've got at least one alive," I said. "Unless the two inside don't give us a choice, we'll keep one or both alive. Two dead isn't so bad. By the end of the night, none of them will breathe anymore."

"Think your woman knows about this side of you?" Lynx asked.

"My what?" My voice came out a little louder than I'd intended, and I glared at him. "Who the fuck are you calling my woman?"

He smirked and simply pointed to the building. I knew what he meant. Solena's kid was in there, and in his eyes, she was mine. Did everyone draw that conclusion when I brought up this mission? Since she worked with Casey, I hadn't thought much of it when I told the club about Santiago.

"We know you had someone at some point since Casey showed up and you said she's your daughter. Was her mother your one true love or something?" Stinger asked. "Because no one seems to know anything about her. Why didn't you introduce her to the club, or talk about her if she was your one and only?"

I didn't like his questions, but I understood why he'd asked them. "First off, it's none of your fucking business, or anyone else's. Except Casey's. If she wants to know, I'll talk to her about Rebecca."

"And second?" Lynx asked. "Because I have to say, he brings up a good point. Even if you loved her more than anything in the world, you know you're allowed to be happy, right? If something happened to me, I wouldn't want Meredith to be alone forever. Would Rebecca have wanted that for you?"

"No," I admitted. "I know she wouldn't have, but I've never found a woman I wanted to hold on to except for her."

Until now.

"Let's head inside," General said coming up behind me.

We entered the building and went up the stairs. If both men weren't still guarding the kids, we'd handle the issue. I didn't think they were expecting trouble, or they'd have been more on guard. I heard the whimpers of the children and the voices of the two men. At least we could pinpoint their exact location since the fuckers were being loud as shit.

"Stinger and I will wait in the hall. Once the three of you have subdued the men, we'll run in to get the kids, but I don't want to scare the hell out of them." Lynx's brow furrowed. "How likely is it they'll come with us without a fight?"

"Don't know," I said. "The fight might have been drained out of them already. I bet they've trained the kids to obey."

And God did it fucking kill me to say those words. The people responsible for the hell those kids had been through all needed to be put through a wood chipper -- while they were still alive.

"Ready?" General asked.

"Yep."

Truth nodded and gripped his knife tighter. With Lynx and Stinger remaining outside the room, we burst through the doors and rushed the men. The kids screamed, and I hated that we'd scared them. Both men went down. General put his knee in the back of one, pinning his wrists behind him. Truth landed blow after blow on the other man's face. I placed my hand on his shoulder.

"Ease up. Don't kill him."

Lynx and Stinger approached the kids, moving slowly and holding their hands up so the children would see they didn't have weapons. I knew Lynx had one hidden somewhere, but Stinger didn't need one. He'd have a syringe on him somewhere, filled with enough drugs to knock out a horse.

I walked over to the kids and caught Santiago's gaze. He stared at me, his little jaw tense and his hands fisted. This one was a fighter, and it looked like he'd been doing his best to protect the other kids. Good. I knew Solena would be proud of him. I was too.

"Santiago, it's time to go home." His nose scrunched, and he didn't say anything. "To your mom. She's been looking for you for a long time."

Some of the tension left him. "You're lying."

"Nope. It's not my story to tell, but I hope you'll give her a chance to explain everything. That woman loves you more than anything, and she's at home right now, waiting for you."

He glanced at Lynx and Stinger, then the other children. "What about them?"

Lynx kneeled down near the twins. "My name is Lynx. You're Finn and Amelia, right?"

The four-year-olds nodded. The girl stuck her thumb in her mouth and watched him with wide eyes while clutching her brother's shirt.

"Lynx, let's get them all to safety. We can figure out where everyone is going once we reach the compound." I eyed the children. "All of you are safe now. No one's going to hurt you again."

"And them?" Santiago asked, pointing to the two men on the ground.

"I'll take care of them."

He seemed to understand what I meant and gave me a nod. And fuck if it didn't hurt that an eight-year-old would know I meant those men were going to die. Even worse, he was more than okay with it. What the hell had these bastards done to the children?

"We'll go with Lynx," Santiago said. "But I'm not meeting my mother until I know the others are going to be okay."

"That's fine. I'm going to finish up here, and when I get to the compound, we'll sort everything out. If any of you are hungry, just tell Lynx. He can stop on the way to the compound and get some food for you."

Stinger cleared this throat. "Um, if any of you

know what size clothes you wear, we passed a Dollar General on the way that should still be open. It won't be anything fancy, but I'd like to get each of you something clean to wear. Shoes too, if they have some in your sizes."

"Lynx, ask Meredith to meet you in the parking lot of the compound. I know she's had a rough time of it, but I think the kids might feel better if she's there. Besides, don't you want her to meet the twins?" I asked.

"Why?" Santiago demanded.

"Because I want to adopt them," Lynx said. "Meredith and I do. She lost our baby and has been hurting. When she found out about all of you, she agreed we'd offer some of you a home if you needed one."

Little Nora approached me. She didn't meet my gaze or look up from the floor. When she reached my side, she wrapped her fingers around the bottom of my cut and held on. I gently patted her on the back.

"It's all right now, Nora. Go with Lynx and Stinger. I promise they won't hurt you."

I didn't know why the little girl had latched onto me. Shouldn't she fear me? What about me made her feel like it was okay to come over like that? I looked over at Santiago again and noticed the soft expression on his face as he observed Nora. It seemed the two were close. Did Nora think I had any say in whether she got to stay with Santiago? Because I didn't. That was Solena's call, and since she was already stressed over being able to properly take care of her son, I doubted she wanted a second kid right now.

She still didn't release me. Santiago had to pry her fingers loose and then took her hand as he followed Lynx and Stinger from the room with the twins. I turned back to Truth and General, only to find both men watching intently. What the hell were those fuckers thinking now?

"Guess we should grab the man from outside and see who wants to talk first," I said.

"I'll get him." Truth cracked his knuckles as he walked out of the room. Something told me the guy would be sporting more bruises when he got here.

"Sit those two upright," I said. General hauled two chairs over, then dumped the men into them. While he secured them to the frames, I found a third chair for our other guest.

"We ain't tellin' you shit," one man said before spitting at me.

I let my fist fly, landing a blow right across his cheek. The chair rocked from the force and almost toppled over. The asshole spit at me again, then had the audacity to smile about it.

"Take off his shoes," I told General.

He kneeled down and did as I said, pulling off the man's socks too. While General held tight to the man's leg, I pulled out my knife and taught the bastard a lesson. I sliced the bottom of his foot with multiple shallow cuts. He cursed and struggled to break free, but no matter how much he thrashed, he couldn't shake off General's grip. When I'd done the same to the other foot, General tied his ankles to the chair legs.

"Next time you spit at me, I'll take my knife to another part of your body. Understood?" The man glared but didn't speak. Good enough. It seemed we understood one another. I looked at the other one. "What about you? You plan to talk?"

"I don't know anything," he mumbled. "Got paid to watch the kids. That's all."

General shrugged. "He may be telling the truth.

This other one clearly knows more."

"Where the fuck is Truth?" I asked.

"Either he's interrogating the man outside, or..."

Or the dipshit pissed off Truth, and he was already dead. Great. We needed information from these men. Although, if I didn't get it, there was a good chance Wire and the other hackers would find what they needed, eventually.

"I say we end it," General said. "I know those kids are ready to get settled for the night. Can't keep them waiting while we screw around with these two."

"Fine." I stepped over to the more compliant one. "Last chance to tell me anything. Give me something useful and maybe I'll just dump you at the police station."

"I swear. I just took the job for the money. I didn't know anyone else here. Got paid half this morning, and they said I'd get the other half once the kids were shipped off elsewhere. None of them talked much around me." Snot and tears ran down his face. "I'm so fucking sorry. Please. I'll do the time, just... don't kill me."

I pinched the bridge of my nose before sighing. "Fine. I'll see if Officer Benson will come pick up this trash. But you listen well... not one word to the cops about my club or any part we played in this. If they ask, you didn't see the men who took out the trash. Got it?"

"Yeah. I won't say a word," he mumbled.

"Stop doing stupid shit before you fuck up your life even more," I said.

"You sure about this, Pres?" General asked. "What if he's lying?"

"Then we'll handle it. For now, I'll give him a chance to prove he's not a complete piece of shit. The other one is another matter. Gut that fucker."

General used his knife to carve the other man like a Christmas goose. When he'd drawn his last breath, I sent a text to Officer Benson and exited the building. I knew he'd have questions, and one hell of a mess to deal with... but when he found out they'd been trafficking children, I knew he'd look the other way.

Truth was outside smoking a cigarette. The body at his feet didn't even look human. I didn't even want to know what the hell he'd done to the man. I had no doubt he'd deserved every bit of pain, and then some.

"Saw a hose around back," Truth said. "We should clean up a little before heading home. Might scare the kids."

He wasn't wrong. We quickly rinsed any blood off our bodies before getting on our bikes and heading out. I probably had blood on my jeans and shirt, but I'd worn black ones so it wouldn't be easy to see blood spatter.

The second I pulled through the gates of the compound, I heard crying and a frantic Santiago trying to calm Nora down. Shit. I hadn't been around kids in... well, ever really. I didn't have a damn clue how to handle this situation. Texting Solena, I told her to drive over so she could meet her son. Maybe she'd be able to console little Nora.

I turned off the engine and got off the bike. The moment both boots were firmly on the ground, Nora ran for me. I braced for impact and held her against me. What the hell was up with this kid?

"Is this normal for her?" I asked Santiago.

"No. But..."

"But what?" I asked.

Nora sniffled and I kneeled down so I'd be at eye

level with her. She blinked at me. A tear rolled down her cheek and her lower lip quivered.

"Daddy."

What. The. Fuck. I opened my mouth to say something, then snapped it shut. I heard a muffled *oh shit* from behind me but couldn't tell who'd said it.

"Nora, do you think I'm your daddy?" I asked.

She nodded and burrowed into me. I hoped like hell I wasn't getting blood on her. What was I supposed to do now? And why did she think I was her dad? From what I'd read on each of the kids, the only one easily traced had been Santiago. The twins were abandoned at a church. As for Nora, I couldn't remember anything that stood out about her, except it said she didn't have any living family.

I needed to ask Wire who her parents were. Had she been a biker's daughter? Even if that was the case, why me and no one else here? I stood, lifting her into my arms. Her tears stopped, and her breathing evened out. The next time I looked at her, I saw she'd fallen asleep.

"We should get them inside and cleaned up," I said.

Lynx started shaking his head. "Can't go in there. Not with them."

"Why the f… Um. Why not?" I asked.

"Someone didn't follow the rules. Had some girls over, and the place is trashed." Lynx looked pissed, and I understood why. This had been an important night for us. These kids didn't need to deal with this shit.

"Fine. Let's take them to my house."

I didn't know if that was the right decision or not. I had Casey there with her new baby. But at the moment, it was the best idea I had.

Chapter Seven

Solena

I didn't know why the plan changed. I'd thought Atilla was bringing Santiago to me. Now he wanted me to go to the compound? Something felt off about this. Had my little boy been hurt? Or perhaps one of the other children? I didn't understand why he couldn't leave long enough to bring my child home.

When I pulled up to the gate, someone waved me through. At least they'd been expecting me. Only one problem. I had no idea where Atilla lived. I rolled down the window to ask the man standing near the gate.

"Excuse me. Can you tell me how to get to Atilla's house?"

He pointed off to the left. "Just head that way and look for his SUV and motorcycle. You'll see some other vehicles as well. Casey is home with the baby, and Meredith is there with Lynx."

Sounded like Atilla had a full house. It only left me more confused. Why had he taken Santiago to his house? The man had been correct about finding the house easily. I parked on the street, grabbed the small tote of Santiago's things, and hurried up to the door. Before I even had a chance to knock, Casey opened it, looking beyond exhausted.

"Should you be up?" I asked.

"Becca is asleep, and Dad said you were on your way here. Figured I could at least open the door for you."

"What's going on?" I asked.

"The kids needed baths. Some idiot brought girls into the clubhouse, so Dad had everyone bring the kids here. Meredith and Lynx are washing the twins right now. Dad let Santiago use his shower."

Casey slowly walked over to the couch and gingerly sat. She winced a little, and I knew she had to be sore from giving birth. Movement caught my eye and my breath caught when I saw Atilla step into the room with a little girl clutched in his arms. She looked like an angel and seemed incredibly at ease with him.

"How many daughters do you have?" I asked, then bit my lip, wishing I could recall the words.

His lips tipped up on one side in a half-smile. "This is Nora. She seems to think I'm her daddy. I've got a call in to Wire and Lavender to see what they can find out about her. Only thing her file said was that she didn't have any living relatives."

"And my son is in the shower?" I asked. "That's what Casey said. What about clothes?"

"The guys stopped at Dollar General and picked up some underwear and something comfortable for all the kids to change into. Got them each a cheap pair of shoes for now, and a package of socks. They were filthy."

"I had to help Nora wash," Casey said. "Dad didn't feel right doing it, but he had to stand in the doorway with his back to us. Nora nearly came unglued when she couldn't see him."

"Wow." I eyed the little girl. "She really thinks you're her dad, huh?"

"I think he should keep her," Casey said. "It's not like I'll be living here much longer."

I blinked and tried to process her words. She was only seventeen. Where was she going? I knew Atilla hadn't kicked her out. He'd never do something like that.

Atilla nodded toward the front door. "Did you see the construction across the street?"

"I didn't pay much attention," I admitted.

"Have some tiny homes going in. Casey is getting a two-bedroom, but both rooms are only large enough for a full bed and small set of drawers. It's not ideal," Atilla said.

"It's a home of my own," Casey said. "And Becca will have her own bedroom. I don't need fancy, Dad. It's safe because it's here at the compound, and you're right across the street if I need you. Not to mention all your brothers are here too. I have plenty of people to reach out to."

He nodded. "And that's why they're being built."

"Why more than one?" I asked.

"Well... I was going to talk to you about that. The one next to Casey is for you. Assuming you want it. Santiago will have a loft bedroom. Your room will be like Casey's, and downstairs. You'll have a kitchen with a fridge, dishwasher, cooktop, and oven. There's counter space for a microwave and coffeepot. In the bathroom, there's a closet for towels and linens, and another for a stackable washer and dryer." Atilla shifted Nora in his arms. "Like I said. It's not huge, or ideal, but it would give you and Santiago a safe place to live. You'd also be able to save some money so you could buy a house or get a larger apartment than you have now."

Why had he done something like that for me? He'd insisted he couldn't offer me anything. Then he'd gone and kissed me while we'd shopped for Santiago's things. I felt so confused right now. What exactly did Atilla want from me?

"I think the two of you need to talk," Casey said. "I'm going to go lie down until Becca wakes up."

Casey struggled to get up and I walked over to

lend her a hand. She gave me a tired smile and a quick thanks. When she reached the doorway, she paused and studied me.

"I know you're not much older than me. If you like my dad, I'm okay with that." My cheeks warmed. Was I that obvious? "That being said... I think you should let Santiago and Nora share the room next to mine today, and you and Dad should talk things out. Sleep beside him. If you can live through the snoring, you have my blessing."

"You little shit," Atilla grumbled, but I saw the laughter in his eyes.

After Casey left, I shifted from foot to foot. Had she really meant all that? Atilla didn't seem bothered by her words. Is that what he wanted to do? We hadn't been able to spend a lot of time together, aside from the one night I'd gotten drunk at the clubhouse.

"Santiago is protective of Nora," he said. "She's right about letting them stay together tonight. While Santiago might go with you willingly, Nora doesn't want me out of her sight. You'll never get her to leave the compound."

"So you want me to sleep with you for the children's sake?" I asked.

He snorted. "All you have to do is sleep, Solena. I'm not asking for more. The house next to Casey's really is being built with you in mind. I want to keep you and your son safe."

A little boy entered the room, and tears filled my eyes. My son. He had my green eyes and dark hair. The rest of him looked like his father. The distrust in his eyes nearly gutted me. Did he think I'd give him up willingly?

"Santiago," I murmured.

"So you're her?" he asked. "The woman who

didn't want me?"

A tear slid down my cheek. Then another. I sniffled, trying to hold back the flood. I couldn't blame him for feeling that way.

"I was fifteen when I had you," I mumbled. "My parents forced me to give you up. I was too stupid to know what rights I had as a teen mother. Your dad had signed the papers already. My parents said I had to leave if I kept you, except I had nowhere else to go. I was scared and felt like they had backed me into a corner."

"Am I supposed to feel sorry for you?" he asked, his eyes narrowing.

He didn't sound eight. He was acting more like a teenager. Then again, depending on what he'd survived, he'd probably had to grow up fast. My heart broke for him.

"No," I said. "I only wanted you to understand I didn't willingly give you up. I wanted you, more than anything."

"But my dad didn't," he muttered.

I glanced at Atilla. I wasn't sure what to tell my son. The last thing I wanted was for him to find out how he'd been conceived. At the same time, I hoped he never went looking for his birth father. He'd seen enough ugliness in the world already.

"Your parents were only seven years older than you are now," Atilla said. "They were still kids. Didn't have a clue what they were doing. Nor did they have the ability to raise a child. Your mom didn't realize what would happen when she signed those papers. Try not to be too hard on her."

"I don't want to go with her," Santiago said. "I want to stay with Nora."

Atilla nodded. "We figured as much. For tonight,

the two of you will sleep in the room next to Casey's. Your mom will stay here tonight."

"And after that?" Santiago asked.

"I have an apartment in town," I said.

"I'm not leaving Nora." He folded his little arms across his chest and glared at me. I bit my lip so I wouldn't smile, but he looked rather cute. I liked that he was protective of the little girl.

"There's some homes being built across the street," Atilla asked. "I was going to offer one to your mom."

"Where's Nora staying?" Santiago asked.

"With my dad," Casey said as she passed by and went through another doorway. I heard the fridge open and close, then a cabinet. When she went back down the hall, she had a glass of juice in her hand.

Atilla looked up at the ceiling, as if he were praying for patience. Although, the fact he hadn't put the little girl down yet meant he might he really be considering it.

"Then I'm staying here too," Santiago said. "Why can't we live here?"

My cheeks warmed and I couldn't meet Atilla's gaze. I certainly wouldn't mind playing house with him, but I didn't think he was ready for that step yet. He'd barely reached the point where he was willing to give me a chance at all.

"Right now, let's get the two of you settled for the night," Atilla said. "We can discuss everything else after we've all had some sleep."

"Fine." Santiago turned around and walked down the hall. Atilla followed with Nora, and I fell in step behind him. Santiago climbed into the empty bed, and Atilla eased Nora down beside him. He pulled the covers over the kids and smoothed Nora's hair back from her face. The tender look on his face nearly made my ovaries explode. If anyone was meant to be a father, it was this man.

"Good night," I said. "Have sweet dreams."

I backed up and Atilla stepped out of the room, pulling the door partially shut. Then he took my hand and led me to his bedroom. Closing the door behind us, he motioned to the bed.

"Have a seat. Unless you want to get comfortable first?"

"I didn't really plan for a sleepover. And don't you have other people in your house?"

"When you weren't looking, Meredith and Lynx slipped out with the twins. Finn and Amelia took to Meredith right away. They should be fine."

I looked around the room. "That still doesn't change the fact I hadn't planned to stay over."

"You can sleep in one of my shirts. Do you want to shower?" He rummaged in his dresser and tossed a blue shirt to me. I caught it, admiring how soft it felt.

"What are we doing, Atilla?" I asked.

"Nothing. Talking." He ran a hand over his beard. "Hell, I don't know, Solena. I haven't had a relationship since Casey's mom. And certainly not with someone so much younger than me. I don't know what the fuck I'm doing."

"Do you even want me to stay?" I asked.

"Yeah, I think I do. The last day or two has been…"

I knew what he was trying to say. His daughter had a baby. He helped me shop for things for Santiago, and it felt like we'd taken a step in the right direction. Now he had a little girl who insisted he was her father. Maybe there was too much going on. Should I take a step back and give him space? I had my own issues to deal with, like a son who clearly didn't like me.

"I should go home," I said.

"I want you to stay," he said, his voice lower than usual. "I have no idea what the future looks like. Not for me, you, Casey… I've never felt so uncertain about anything in my entire life, and it scares the hell out of me, Lena."

Lena? I smiled a little. Did he even realize he'd just give me a nickname? I liked it. No one had ever called me that before.

"Atilla, no one knows what tomorrow will bring. We aren't guaranteed anything in life. The best we can do is take a leap of faith, decide if we can trust each other, and see where things go. I'm not asking you for a ring and forever. I just want the chance to see if we can make a relationship work." I dropped my tote bag on the floor and sighed. "Santiago hates me, but he likes Nora. And that little girl doesn't want to leave your side."

"What are you getting at?" he asked.

"I have a proposal for you. Not the marriage kind." He motioned for me to continue. "You said the tiny homes across the street were already under construction and you intended to offer one to me, right?"

"Yeah. Shouldn't take more than a week or two. Depends on the electrical, plumbing, and getting it through the city's inspection process."

"Would it be okay for me and Santiago to stay here until it's finished? Or at least stay a few nights? I don't want to separate him from Nora. I think it will also be easier to get to know him if he's comfortable, and he clearly feels safe here."

"I don't have a problem with that. You'll need to get some of your things. We can grab them in the morning."

"Thank you, Atilla. I know it was a big ask." I moved closer and put my arms around him, hugging him tight. The moment he hugged me back, I melted into him. He really did give great hugs.

"Go change for bed. I'll let Casey know you'll be here for a few days." He kissed the top of my head before leaving the bedroom.

I had a few days to get to know my son better and find out whether or not there was really something between me and Atilla. I hoped this didn't blow up in my face.

Chapter Eight

Atilla

I knocked on Casey's door and then went inside. She'd leaned back in her bed with a book while little Becca slept in the crib nearby. I was so damn proud of my girl. At seventeen, she was more mature than I'd been even twenty years ago. Hell, some days she was doing better than I was right now.

"You okay with Solena staying here a few days with Santiago? The kid isn't ready to give her a chance, and he doesn't want to be parted from Nora." I leaned against the doorframe. "This is your home too, so I can tell her it won't work if you don't want her here."

Casey set her book down and stared at me. Damn. She reminded me so much of her mother right now. Rebecca used to give me that same look, usually when I was being a dumbass. Guess that meant my daughter thought I was one too.

"Dad, I love you. I really do, but... you're an idiot."

"Don't sugarcoat it," I muttered.

"You like Solena, right?"

I shrugged. I did. The age thing bothered me a little. Not because I didn't see her as a woman, because I certainly did, but I knew people could be harsh when it came to things they didn't understand. Some might consider our relationship disgusting, and I knew they wouldn't necessarily hold back. The last thing I wanted was to cause her more pain than she'd already experienced.

"Dad." She sighed and closed her eyes. "Tell me the truth. Why aren't you willing to give her a chance?"

I glanced at the bedroom door and saw it was

still shut. I didn't hear any noise from the kids' room either. The last thing I needed was anyone hearing this conversation.

"You don't have an issue with her being so much younger than me? She's only six years older than you."

"So what?"

"Things are complicated, Casey."

She held my gaze. "So uncomplicate them. Her age is just a number, Dad. You know that. Mom was younger than you, right? And what about me? If I fell in love with someone here at the club, and they were twenty years older than me, would you stop us from being together?"

"Um…"

She rolled her eyes. "I meant because of the age difference."

"No. I get your point. It's more than just the age thing. She has a son she's meeting for the first time. I've got you and a new grandbaby. Little Nora in there seems to think I'm her dad. And then there's the club… What if Solena can't handle the shit we deal with sometimes? Your mom wouldn't have been able to."

Casey struggled to get out of bed and peeked into the crib before coming closer to me. "Dad, she's not Mom. No one will ever be Mom, and that's okay. You can love more than one person. She'd want you to be happy. It's what I want too. Stop keeping distance between the two of you and coming up with excuses about why things won't work. You haven't even tried yet!"

Seeing my daughter so upset really drove home how badly I was fucking up. I still didn't know if I could make this work. Right now, the house was packed to the gills with my daughter, two kids, a baby, and… the woman I wanted but felt I shouldn't hold onto.

"Can I ask you something?" Casey went back to the bed and leaned against her pillows again, wincing a little as she got situated. "What are you going to do if someone else comes along and sweeps her off her feet?"

Beat the hell out of him. Something must have shown on my face, because she smirked at me. She really was a little shit sometimes. Too much of her mom's attitude.

"You're right, okay? I don't want Solena to slip through my fingers. Right now, she needs to focus on her son, and I need to find out what's going on with Nora. I don't think this is a good time to start a relationship."

"If you wait for the *right* time, you may miss your window of opportunity, Dad. Kind of like with Mom. Except this time, Solena will leave because it's what she wants to do. She'll give up on waiting for you to make up your mind. I love you, and I think she'd be good for you. Besides, those kids deserve two parents. Would it be so wrong to raise Santiago and Nora together? Be one big happy family?"

No, it wouldn't. "Are you saying I take a page out of Lynx's book and just keep her because it's what I want?"

"You're a biker dad. The President of this club. Since when do you ever ask permission for anything? And did Lynx really keep her against her will? Do you think Solena wouldn't be happy if you said she was moving in permanently?" She huffed at me. "Seriously. Stop trying to be someone you aren't. If she can't handle the real you, then none of this matters, anyway. But for what it's worth, I think she'll do just fine."

My daughter had given me a lot to think about. I

kissed her on the forehead and shut her door when I left the room. I checked on the kids before going back to my bedroom. I could hear the shower running in the bathroom, and only hesitated for a moment. Be true to myself, huh? All right. It was time to see if Solena could handle being mine.

I removed my cut and set it on the dresser before toeing off my boots and removing my clothes. She'd fogged the bathroom mirror from the steam pouring out of the shower. Hell, I couldn't even see her through the glass shower door. I pulled it open quietly and shut it without her even noticing I'd joined her. With her eyes closed, and her head tipped back, she looked at peace. The water sluiced over her hair, which seemed even longer now that it was wet.

I stood in front of her, placing my hands on her hips. Solena shrieked and opened her eyes, her body going stiff.

"Atilla?"

"Were you expecting someone else?" I asked.

"You surprised me. Why are you... I mean..." Her gaze dropped to my cock, which was quickly getting hard, before clashing with mine. "Why are you in here?"

"I had a talk with Casey. She's all for the two of us being together. In fact, she called me a dumbass for dragging my feet." I leaned down and pressed my forehead to hers. "What would you say if I told you I'd only shown you a small part of myself so far?"

"I'd ask to see the rest."

"And if you can't handle it?" I asked.

"That's for me to decide, Atilla. And for what it's worth, I don't think I'll have any issues. I've never wanted anyone the way I want you. We might have only had the one night together, but it was a night I'll remember forever."

"Want to add more memories to it?"

She reached up and placed her hand on my cheek. "I'd love to. Are you sure?"

"I'm done running. We're going to figure everything out together. Santiago and Nora are already like siblings. Might as well make it the real deal."

Her eyes widened. "What?"

I grinned and looked in the direction where I'd left my phone. "Hey, Siri! Message Wire."

I cracked the shower door open and listened for her response. It was faint, but I caught it. *What do you want to say?*

"Do whatever it takes to make Solena, Santiago, and Nora mine. Make sure no one can ever question the fact they belong to me." I heard Solena gasp as Siri recited the text back to me. *Send it?* "Yes."

"What did you just do?" she asked.

"I believe I just made you Solena, Santiago, and Nora Cutler. Too late to change it now." She parted her lips, mostly likely about to protest, and I kissed the hell out of her. Casey was right. It was time to show Solena what it meant to be mine.

I backed her against the shower wall. She whimpered and gave in to me. I devoured her, taking what I wanted. It had been so long since I'd wanted someone this badly. The night we'd shared before had been about her. I'd given her what she needed. This time would be different. I wasn't going to hold back. She was mine now, and I'd make damn sure she knew it. I didn't give a shit who heard us. As long as she didn't scream like I was killing her, then it should be fine. Last thing I wanted was for the kids to think I'd hurt her.

"You're mine. Every single inch of you. And I'm

going to make sure you never forget it." I worked my hand between her thighs and stroked her clit with my thumb. Her nipples puckered and her eyes dilated. "That's it. Come for me. Show me how much you want this."

I rubbed the hard bud faster, and she screamed out my name. Before she had a chance to catch her breath, I eased her leg over my hip and thrust into her. She clawed at my shoulders as I fucked her hard and deep. I felt her pussy tighten on me and knew she was about to come again.

"I'm going to fill you so full of cum you'll have a reminder of me for hours. You might still be dripping tomorrow."

The heat of her release hit my cock and I couldn't hold back. It seemed my woman liked it when I talked dirty. I'd remember that for next time. I pounded her pussy, not stopping until I'd emptied my balls and filled her up. She clung to me as I kissed her. My cock started to soften, and I eased out of her.

"Why?" she asked. "Why now and not that night?"

"You mean admitting you're mine?" She nodded. "I didn't think I was what you needed. Decided it didn't matter because you're what I want."

I helped her wash, taking my time to explore her body. I might not be able to have sex again anytime soon, but it didn't mean I couldn't please her some more. I teased her nipples and clit with light pinching and soft strokes until I'd wrung three more orgasms from her. By the time the water cooled, she could barely stand.

I shut off the water and dried her off, then helped her into my T-shirt. While she climbed into the bed, I ran a towel over my body, then pulled on a pair of sweats. Crawling into bed with her was one of the best feelings. She curled against me, and as I held her close, I remembered what it felt like that night at the clubhouse.

It had been hard to let her go. Harder than I'd been able to admit to even myself. Life was too short. I'd lost Rebecca all those years ago because of an accident. If I lost Solena now because I was too damn stupid to hold on to her, then I'd regret it until the day I died.

"What about the house across the street?" she whispered, nearly asleep.

"Casey will still move with Becca. The other one can remain empty until we need it for something. Your place is right here in my arms."

A smile curved her lips, and for the first time in forever, I felt a sense of peace wash over me. This was what I'd been missing. I knew a lot of guys enjoyed the club pussy and didn't look forward to settling down. Hell, some might never keep a woman. For me, it was the one thing I'd wanted for so very long. Not only me, but quite a few men in my club. We weren't the same as a lot of the others. Lynx hadn't hesitated to claim Meredith, and I knew either Rebel or Maui would end up asking for my daughter.

I didn't think either had the balls to outright take her. They could prove me wrong, though. Whatever the case, it was my daughter's decision. If she wanted one of them, I wouldn't stand in her way. But the second they hurt her, all bets were off. Same for little Nora. She was only seven now, but one day she'd want to date or get married.

I only hoped I lived long enough to see it happen. I didn't exactly live a safe lifestyle. A stray bullet could take me out, or a bomb. Shit, a fucking driver on the road not paying attention could kill me. It was possible I'd live another twenty or so years, or I could breathe my last tomorrow. No one ever knew when their time would be up.

I watched Solena sleep for the longest time before finally shutting my eyes. Breathing in her scent, and feeling her soft curves against me, made me smile. I had no idea if heaven and hell really existed. If they did, this was probably the closest I'd ever get to being in heaven.

We'd need to talk to the kids tomorrow. Santiago seemed more concerned about Nora than his own circumstances. He'd already wanted to stay here instead of going to Solena's apartment. I didn't think it would bother him to discover he never had to move out of this house. I wondered how long they'd been together. Had he been watching over her for a while? Or had the two just clicked?

Looked like we'd be shopping too. They'd both need clothes, shoes, and a ton of other shit children should have. I'd get someone to head over to Solena's place and pack up all their belongings. We'd already gotten quite a bit for Santiago, especially when it came to toys. I'd never had the chance to shop for Casey when she'd been little. Oddly enough, I looked forward to helping Nora pick out dolls and stuffed bears, or whatever else she might want.

I wanted those kids to be happy, to know this was their home, and to feel secure. Picking up my phone, I read Wire's response to my message from earlier.

It's done.

I shot back a reply, thanking him, and checking on any progress with Nora's background. The phone rang, and I answered it quickly, so it wouldn't wake

Solena.

"Hello," I said, keeping my voice low.

"Nora's mom was a woman by the name of Wendy Roberts. The woman grew up in the system, and I haven't been able to track down her parents. On Nora's birth certificate, it lists her father as unknown. If she has a family out there, I have no idea who they are, and so far I haven't been able to track anyone down. The mother is currently in prison for a very lengthy sentence."

"Since I'm keeping her, I guess it doesn't matter. I just don't know why she thinks I'm her dad. If the father wasn't listed on the birth certificate, would she have ever met him?"

"Probably not," Wire said. "Doesn't mean the mother didn't show her a picture at some point, though. The guy could have been a biker. Looking at Wendy's past financial records, she liked going to bars and drinking. I have a feeling Nora was the product of a one-night stand."

"In other words, we may never know."

"Right. Not to risk pissing you off, but have you thought of taking a paternity test with her? Wendy has been all over Oklahoma over the last decade. She may very well have been to a party at your clubhouse before."

"Any way you can hack into her phone records while you're at it? You can see any pictures she has, right?"

"If they're stored in the cloud," Wire said. "Give me a few minutes -- I'll see if I can find anything. What am I looking for? Pictures of bikers?"

"I guess so, or anyone you think could be her dad."

"Nora is seven, so adding in the length of a

pregnancy, I'm going to look back eight years. If I find anything interesting, I'll let you know. Assuming there's anything to find at all. She could also have only used burner phones."

"Why would she need one of those?" I asked.

"They're cheap, for one. It also looks like she's had a lot of issues with drugs. She's been to jail twice. In fact, that's how Nora ended up in her current situation. The mom signed her rights over to the same phony adoption people who took Santiago. It was right before she was sent to jail for possession with intent to distribute. Guess she didn't want her daughter in the system like she'd been."

"Thanks, Wire. Keep me posted."

I ended the call, set the phone aside, and finally let sleep pull me under.

Chapter Nine

Solena

I felt like I'd lost my damn mind. I'd given into him so easily, after everything he'd put me through. Maybe it was because I'd been on my own for so long. Even while I'd been living at home, I hadn't really had anyone to rely on. My parents had been distant. Even cold most of the time. I didn't know why they'd had me, but from what I'd overheard once, I thought my mother had gotten pregnant by accident. Since my parents had an unhappy marriage, they apparently wanted to make sure I'd been miserable too.

I didn't want that for Santiago. Now that I had him back, I wanted to give him a good life. The thought of taking care of him on my own had terrified me, but I'd wanted to do it. Knowing I'd now have someone by my side? It made all the difference. Since the moment I'd met Atilla, I'd wanted to be part of his life. To know more about him, see him laugh, share special moments with him. Now I'd get the chance.

I didn't know what had changed. He'd said he'd talked to Casey. Whatever she'd said to him, it was enough to make him stop holding back. For the first time, he'd shown me the real him. I was both excited and scared of what the future would hold for me. Not only me, but the children as well.

"Morning," Atilla said.

I smiled and accepted the cup of coffee he'd handed me. "Good morning. The children still asleep?"

"Yeah. Checked on them when I got up. Nora was clinging to Santiago like he was her personal teddy bear. I heard Casey get up and down with Becca all night. I think they're scheduled for another feeding pretty soon. Wish I could help her, but she's breastfeeding. I'm not exactly equipped for that."

I snickered. No, he certainly wasn't. Even though he didn't have the body of a twenty-year-old athlete, he'd kept in shape. The only sixty-year-old men I'd seen who looked anything like him were on TV.

"You all right this morning?" he asked, sliding a plate of toast with eggs in front of me. "Sorry about the lack of meat. I need to get some stuff from the store."

"I'm fine. Still processing everything, I think. My son is really here, right? You brought him back to me?" I asked.

"I did, and he is. I had a conversation with Wire last night. He's going to look into Nora's past a bit more, or rather, he's seeing what he can dig up on her mother. She's been in and out of jail quite a bit. He's hoping to hack into her phone records to figure out who Nora's father is."

"Does it really matter?" I asked. "She thinks you're her dad. Since you said we all belonged to you now, why do you need to look into it more?"

"I don't. Except what if Nora asks one day? What are we supposed to tell her?"

I reached over and took his hand. "That her dad loves her very much. Her *family* does. Honestly, I don't think she'll ever bring it up. She seemed quite content to latch onto you and never let go. I'm surprised you got her into the bed."

A scream down the hall had him bolting out of his chair. I was right on his heels as he ran to the kids' room. Nora sat in the bed, tears running down her cheeks, and yelling until her face turned red.

"What the hell?" Atilla looked around the room before staring at Santiago. "What happened?"

"She woke up and thought you'd left her," he said.

Atilla picked up Nora and held her close. "It's all right, little angel. I'm right here. No one left you, okay?"

"Daddy." She buried her face against him and clutched at his shirt. I'd noticed he hadn't put on his cut this morning. Then again, he probably didn't wear it all the time. Not when he was at home anyway.

"That's right. Daddy is here. And your momma is here too." He glanced at me. That's when it really hit me. I hadn't only gotten Santiago back, but I'd gained a daughter.

My son gave me a distrustful glare, but I ignored it and went over to Atilla and our new daughter. "Good morning, Nora. Are you hungry?"

She nodded against Atilla, still not looking up. I motioned for Santiago to stand up and follow me. Surprisingly, he did so without complaint. When we got to the kitchen, I started making a fresh batch of toast and took the eggs from the fridge.

"Santiago, do you want to help make the toast?" I asked.

He looked at Atilla before coming closer to me. He seemed fascinated by the four-slice toaster, and I wondered if he'd ever seen one before. What kind of life had he led until now? There was so much I wanted to ask him.

"We missed your birthday. I thought we could have a party in a few days. There are a lot of people here for us to meet." He didn't say anything. "We could bake a cake, and there would be presents. Do you like balloons? I bet we could get some."

"You don't have to try so hard," he mumbled. "I know you didn't want me."

And there was my opening. "Why do you think that?"

He kept staring at the toaster. "Everyone said so. I'm stupid. Ugly. Worthless. None of them wanted to keep me."

"And they told you I didn't want you?" I asked, fisting my hands at my sides. I wanted to strangle all of them! How could they tell my precious boy such awful lies? He might look a lot like his dad, but he wasn't ugly. In fact, his father had been one of the cutest boys in school. I turned Santiago to face me. "Santiago, you were very much wanted. What I told you last night wasn't a lie. I didn't have a choice but to give you up for adoption, but it was the last thing I wanted to do."

"Your mom was a mess," Atilla said. "She missed you. Wondered if you were safe. If you'd found a good home. Not knowing what happened to you was eating her up inside. It's why I promised to bring you home."

"You called her Nora's mom," Santiago said.

"Well, Atilla is her dad." I wasn't sure how he'd take this next part. "And since Atilla and I are together, that means I'm her mom."

"So, he's my dad?" Santiago asked. For the first time since he'd been brought home, I heard hope in his voice.

"Yeah, son. I'm your dad," Atilla said.

"What's my job here?" Santiago asked.

I stopped what I was doing. Job? What the hell did he mean by that? Had the other families made him work? Or did he mean chores? We should probably assign both children something to do, like make their bed and keep their toys picked up. They could help set the table.

"Santi, what kind of jobs have you had before?" Atilla asked.

"Scrubbing floors and toilets, throwing out the

empty bottles around the house, or helping package stuff. If I didn't do a good job, I got punished."

My heart slammed against my ribs as I stared in horror at Atilla. Packaged products? Like... drugs? And what sort of punishment?

"Did they put you in a timeout?" Atilla asked.

Santiago shook his head.

"Did you get a spanking?" I asked.

Santiago refused to speak. What had my poor boy been through? I didn't know if this was something Atilla and I could handle on our own. Would Santiago speak with a stranger? A therapist, for instance. Nora might need one too.

"Atilla," I murmured. He gave me a nod, and I knew he'd look into what the children had been through. "Santiago, how long have you and Nora been together? Was she your foster sister at your last home?"

He wouldn't answer me. It seemed he'd spoken as much as he'd planned to. Having my son back meant everything to me, even if we had a hard road ahead of us. Would he be able to go to school soon? I'd need to register him, but I didn't have any of his records. Same for Nora.

"Atilla, we need their school records," I said.

"I'll talk to Wire. I'm not sure if the kids will even have school records. May have to ask the school to test them before they start classes." He shifted Nora on his lap as I set a plate of eggs and toast down for her. Santiago took his and sat beside Atilla. "You don't have to call me Atilla when only the family is around. If anyone can use my actual name, it's you. Call me James."

"While I appreciate that, you seem more like an Atilla to me." I smiled at him. "James sounds more like someone who sits at a desk or manages a construction crew. It's not very biker-like."

"Call me whatever you want, Lena." Nora continued to sit in his lap while she ate, dropping crumbs all over both of them. He didn't seem to mind. He wiped a few off her mouth and gave her a warm smile. "Don't eat too fast, angel. You might choke."

"We haven't had anything in a few days, except what we were given last night after you found us," Santiago said. "She's worried the food will go away."

"We'll always have plenty for the two of you to eat. Your mom and I would go without before we'd ever let you suffer." Atilla patted Santiago on the back. "I know this is going to be a big adjustment for the two of you. Things are going to be different from before. This is your home. Not just for right now, but for the rest of your lives. You will always have a spot here with me and your mom."

"Is that our room?" Santiago asked.

"For now. Casey and the baby will move across the street once their home is ready. Once they're settled in their new place, one of you can have the room she's in now." Atilla hugged Nora and kissed her cheek. The little girl cuddled against him, not saying a word. Other than *daddy*, she hadn't spoken much. Not around me, anyway.

"Would the two of you like to go shopping today?" I asked. "I have some toys for you already, Santiago, but we don't have anything for Nora. You're both going to need more clothes and shoes too."

"Are all of us going?" he asked.

"Not Casey and Becca," Atilla said. "They need to stay here. It's just going to be me, you, your mom, and Nora. Is that okay?"

Santiago nodded. "I don't think she's been

shopping before. Neither have I."

Another piece of the puzzle. What sort of parents never took their children to the store? Between the jobs Santiago had to do previously, the fact they punished him in a way he didn't want to speak of, and now discovering he'd never been to a store... my mind was reeling. Who the hell had my parents given my baby to? Since Atilla said Santiago had been through many homes since then, it was clear the people hadn't really wanted him. But still... how could so many people have neglected him?

"We'll go to the nearest Target," Atilla said. "It will have everything they need, plus groceries. We should pick up a few meals and some snacks."

"I guess we'd better all put our shoes on so we can head out," I said.

"I need your apartment keys first." Atilla held out his hand. "Going to have someone go pack up everything. It will be here when we get back."

I went to get them from my purse and set them on the table in front of him. It felt surreal knowing I wouldn't be going back to the apartment. It might not be much, but I'd worked hard for the few things I had. Wait.

"Um, does that mean they're going to rifle through my panty drawer?" I whispered.

Atilla snorted. "Not unless they have a death wish. They'll probably just dump everything from the drawers into bags. Only other women here are Casey and Meredith, and both are busy with kids. I'm afraid I can only send a man over there."

"Fine." My cheeks warmed. "But tell them to close their eyes when they open the top dresser drawer. I won't be able to look at any of them ever again if I know they've seen my underwear."

"They won't look," he assured me. "Now go get ready. First thing we're buying at the store are booster seats. These two are probably still small enough to need them."

Santiago puffed up. "I am not!"

Atilla chuckled. "Son, it's the law. I'm not saying you aren't a big boy. You've done a good job watching over your sister. But there are rules we have to follow. One of them is making sure the two of you are safe when we're in the car."

"Fine," Santiago mumbled.

Casey stumbled into the kitchen, yawning widely. The dark circles under her eyes made me wince. Had she gotten any sleep at all? How many times had Becca woken up? I knew Atilla said he'd heard them off and on all night, but my heart broke for her. She looked exhausted.

"Y'all going somewhere?" she asked.

"Taking the kids shopping. If you need anything while I'm out, text me. Or if it's not something I can pick up at Target, ask one of the guys to go fetch it for you. Just not Stinger, Ravager, or Lucas. They're going to be putting your house together." Atilla stood with Nora still in his arms. "I'm going to grab my cut, then I'll meet everyone in the car. I'll take this little one with me."

"I'll bring her shoes out," I said.

"I hope you enjoy your time together," Casey said, giving us a tired smile. "I'm going to grab something to eat, then try to sleep while Becca does."

"Would you like us to pick up a breast pump while we're out?" I asked. "It would give you a break from having to take every single feeding. Your dad or I could feed her from her bottle. It would still be your milk."

Casey nodded. "That sounds great. I'll text you the bottles the hospital recommended. I don't want to switch her to one just yet, though. They said it was an important part of bonding with her, so I'd like to give this a try for another day or two. After that, I may be bawling my eyes out and begging for a break."

"We'd still let you feed her most of the time," Atilla said. "But if Lena and I each took one feeding, that's an extra four hours of sleep for you. Sounded like she was up every two hours last night."

"She was. I don't think I'm producing enough milk to fill her up to go longer than that." Casey yawned again. "I may call the doctor's office today and ask if there's something I should do that might help."

"Just let us know if you need anything," I said.

"I take it Dad pulled his head out of his butt. Welcome to the family." She paused. "Dad, can you check and see what happened to Su and Mark? Since they don't have my new number, they can't reach me, but I'm still uneasy about the entire thing."

"I'll ask Wire for an update later. I need to talk to him about something, anyway. Go get some sleep."

Atilla walked out, my keys in his hand, and I heard him heading for the bedroom -- Nora still clutched in his arms.

"Good thing she knows how to walk already," Casey mumbled. "Otherwise, I don't think Dad would ever let her learn."

I couldn't hold back my laughter. "I'd been thinking the same thing."

Casey stumbled from the room, and I truly hoped she could sleep for a little while. I hadn't been able to raise my baby, so I didn't know a lot about what she was going through. Well, except for what I'd seen on TV or read in books. She looked both happy and miserable at the same time.

"Go brush your teeth, Santi. I'll put your dishes in the sink."

He gave me a long look before leaving the table, and I realized it was the first time I'd shortened his name. I'd heard Atilla say it earlier, and it seemed to suit him. I hoped I hadn't just made a big mistake with him. I wanted us to move forward, not go two steps backward.

Chapter Ten

Atilla

I'd always wondered why parents let their kids run wild in stores. I now understood it was utter exhaustion. Although, our kids weren't bad. They hadn't pitched fits or fussed even a little. If anything, they were too damn quiet. I'd convinced Nora to walk once we reached the store, but she still held onto the bottom of my cut. Santiago stuck close to her, and Lena walked on my other side.

I knew it killed her to be so close yet feel so far away from Santiago. Part of me understood his attitude. It didn't mean I had to like it. When Lena took Nora to the bathroom, I pulled Santiago aside for a moment.

Kneeling down, I made sure I had his attention. "I know you're angry. You may not be ready to share everything you went through, and that's okay, but what I can't condone is the way you're treating your mother. She loves you more than you'll ever know. Can you try a little harder for me? Give her a chance to show you how much she wants to be part of your life?"

"Casey kept her baby."

I nodded. "She did, and that's because she had me standing in her corner. Your mom didn't have anyone. The entire world was against her keeping that baby, or that's how it felt to her at the time. Her parents wanted her to give you up. Your dad signed away his rights. If you want to blame someone for what happened to you, then be angry with them. If they'd given your mother even a little support, she'd have held onto you."

"Are you Nora's real dad?" he asked softly.

"No. Blood doesn't make a family, though, Santi.

The men who helped save you last night are my family. My brothers. We're part of the same club, and we've chosen to live and die for one another. Same as I did with you, your mom, and Nora. As of last night, the three of you are officially mine, and I will never let anyone hurt any of you again."

"What if she decides she likes Nora more?" he asked.

"She won't. She can love you both equally, same as me." I reached out and wrapped my fingers around the back of his neck. "You're my boy, Santi. Don't let anyone ever tell you different, okay? I love you and Nora the same amount. And I love Casey and little Becca the same too. I don't favor one of you over the others. You're all my family."

"I understand," he murmured.

"Do you sometimes need to vent your anger?" I asked.

"Yeah."

"Hmm. Then I guess we'd better find a healthy outlet for it. We'll get some sports equipment today and see if you like one more than another. Kicking a ball, throwing one, going for a run, or hitting a punching bag can all be good ways to let out your frustration and anger without the risk of hurting someone else."

Lena and Nora came out of the bathroom, and I stood. Santiago held up his hand for Lena. For a brief moment, a startled expression crossed her face, but she smiled warmly as she clutched his hand in hers. Nora came back to me, grabbing hold of my hand.

We spent the next two hours buying clothes and shoes for both children, as well as toys for Nora. Even though we'd already picked out things for Santiago, I let him get a few things in the sports section. I'd also texted Spade and asked him to find a basketball net and have it installed by the street in the gap between my house and the one next door. Santiago could use it, or any other kids, as our club expanded.

Neither child seemed to know what foods they liked to eat and were hesitant to select snacks. I tossed in goldfish crackers, pretzel sticks, chocolate chip cookies, fruit cups, Jell-O cups, and fruit gummies. Even if they weren't the healthiest options, I wanted the kids to have things they'd enjoy. I stocked up on frozen chicken breasts to put in my small freezer, and let Lena select fresh meat too.

I knew Casey liked macaroni and cheese, as well as spaghetti, so I made sure we had what we needed to make both. Lena tossed in some canned vegetables and two boxes of rice. I'd stock up more at the grocery store, but once we added bacon, eggs, and biscuits to the cart, we at least had the basics covered for the next few days.

I paid for what ended up being two shopping carts full of items and then loaded everything into the SUV. Lena set up the booster seats and buckled the kids in. I didn't think Lena would feel like cooking when we got home, and it was nearly lunchtime. The kids hadn't eaten a lot at breakfast, and I'd already heard Santiago's stomach growling, even though he hadn't said a word about being hungry.

I swung through the drive-thru of a local chicken place and ordered a bucket of fried chicken, two large containers of mashed potatoes with gravy, and two of mac and cheese, and a box of biscuits. When we got home, I'd let Lena put everything where she wanted it, and I'd make a quick call to Wire. I hadn't heard anything yet, and since I knew he was looking into Nora's past, I found it odd I hadn't received an update of any sort. The man was typically quick when it came to this sort of thing.

"I'm going to get someone to come help you unload. The kids saw General last night, so he might be the safer bet," I said. "I'll be in the bedroom on the phone if you need me."

I kissed Lena's cheek and got out of the car. After a quick text to General, asking him to come help my woman and kids, I hurried into the house. Everything was quiet in Casey's room, and she had the door shut, so I didn't disturb her. I hoped she was sleeping. The bottles she'd requested had been out of stock, but I'd ordered some for a two-day delivery online. The breast pump was in the back of the car. I'd let Lena pick it since I didn't know a damn thing about them. I knew she didn't either, but she'd seemed excited about helping.

After I shut the bedroom door, I took out my phone and dialed Wire's number. The fucker didn't even so much as say hello when the call connected. He answered and hung up. I called again, but the same thing happened. The hairs on my nape stood up, so I checked in with Outlaw to see if he'd heard anything.

"This is Outlaw."

"It's Atilla. Have you heard from Wire? I tried calling. He picked up and immediately hung up. Twice."

"He's busy."

Uh-huh. Now I knew something was up. Outlaw was never this short with me. Not in all the years I'd known him.

"Talk to me. Does this have to do with my kids?" I asked.

"Did you really need to know where Nora came from?" he asked. "Because it's opened a can of worms no one should have touched."

"He said her mom was in and out of jail and the father was unknown. What's the problem?" I asked.

"I've known you a long time, right?" Outlaw asked.

"Yeah."

"And you've always been up front with me. Anything you think we should know? Maybe, like, say, a brother? A fucking identical twin, to be precise?" Outlaw asked, fury in every word.

"My brother is dead," I said. "He died in 1987 while fighting in a war."

"Ever see the body?" Outlaw asked.

"What the fuck kind of question is that? They shot his plane down over Iran. Government told me the Iranians blew it to pieces. There wasn't anything left of him to send home, except his dog tags. What the hell does this have to do with anything?"

"You really don't know?" Outlaw asked, his tone softer than before. "Atilla, I don't know how to say this. Your brother didn't die in 1987. He died three years ago."

What the fuck was he saying? There was no way my brother had been alive all that time and he hadn't reached out to me. As he'd said, we were twins. John wouldn't have left me grieving all these years. He hadn't been gone a year before our parents died in a car crash. I'd been alone ever since until I'd started this club.

"Atilla, your brother was a secret government operative. Wire couldn't take your call because he was getting his ass chewed by some government person he works with sometimes. He poked his nose where it didn't belong, all because you'd asked him to. Thankfully, he's too valuable for them to lock him up."

"Are you telling me that Nora is my brother's kid?" I asked.

"I am. John Cutler met Nora's mother at a bar. They had a one-week fling before he left to go overseas on a mission, and he never got in touch with her again. You can do a DNA test if you want, but it's the only thing Wire could find that would explain why Nora thinks you're her dad."

"Back up because that didn't make sense," I said. "If he never knew about Nora, then…"

"Nora's mom had a picture of him. A few, actually. We think she showed those to Nora, telling her the man was her daddy. Wire sent me everything he could find before the government shut him down."

"And Su and Mark? The trafficking ring? What's happening with that?" I asked.

"The FBI has stepped in. Wire had to turn over all the evidence he'd found so far, and everyone implicated. However, he made sure Nora and Santiago wouldn't be taken from you. Basically, he made a deal with them. He's going to help them with a few cases they haven't been able to crack by using his hacking skills, and they're going to look the other way regarding the four children you took to your compound. He assured them those children would be well taken care of."

Shit. I really owed him. But John had been alive all this time? I wanted to ask for more. How had he died? Where had he been living? Why the fuck hadn't he ever reached out to me?

Since he was gone, I'd probably never know.

So, little Nora was my niece. Knowing she was the last remaining piece of John, it made me love her even more. I only wished he'd known about her. I knew he'd have given her a good life. It didn't matter what path he'd chosen back then. Some things would never change, and I knew my brother had a soft spot for children.

"Can you tell me if Su, Mark, and Solena's parents will be caught up in the FBI's case for the human trafficking ring?" I asked. "My girls need some closure."

"Su and Mark are already in custody. Wire found evidence of them selling children, in addition to the adoption scheme through their church. Solena's parents are still free at the moment, but they are persons of interest. In other words, you can't touch them. If you do, the FBI will come looking for them."

"How likely is it they'll face any prison time?" I asked.

"Their daughter's baby isn't the only one they helped *adopt* through the church's program. Those children were placed in homes that hadn't been vetted. In fact, the church sold them."

"Santiago said they punished him when he didn't do a good job. Not to mention it sounds like they had him bagging drugs as a fucking job."

Outlaw growled. "Yeah, they did. Wire found that while he was digging. You aren't going to like what I'm going to tell you. Santiago's punishment was to stand in the center of the room, undressed, and take a belt across his ass every fifteen minutes. It would last for hours. They took a few videos and some pictures of what happened. Wire already scrubbed them, so no one will ever find those again."

Son of a bitch!

"Before you get too pissed off, they didn't molest him. They didn't force him into anything sexual. Doesn't mean he didn't suffer. He's going to need some help of the professional variety."

"And Nora?" I asked.

"Wire couldn't find anything on the two families she had before being placed in the same home as Santiago. He'd take her punishments at the last place, so no one laid a finger on Nora. But she saw what happened to him. It probably traumatized her."

"Thanks for everything, Outlaw. Tell Wire I'm sorry this landed him in hot water. I'll talk to Solena and Casey so they won't worry about someone coming for the kids."

"Glad we could help," he said.

I ended the call and closed my eyes. I wanted to rip those fuckers to pieces, but I wouldn't risk the FBI knocking on my door. Casey was in the hall when I opened the door. The look on her face told me she'd heard more than just a little of my conversation.

"So it's over?" she asked. "And those people, they…"

"They were essentially selling kids. As to whether it's over, for you, yes. Solena's parents are probably going to be in trouble with the law, which means I can't touch them. And Nora… is my niece." Casey's eyes went wide. "Had a twin brother. Thought he died when we were twenty-nine. Turns out he didn't."

"And now?" she asked.

I shook my head. She wouldn't be meeting her Uncle John. Not in this lifetime. "Don't say anything to her. We were identical twins. She really thinks I'm her dad. We share the same DNA, so there's no reason to tell her otherwise."

"Fine. I'll go sit with the kids so you can talk to Solena."

I waved her off. "I'll tell her later, when everyone has gone to bed. How's Becca?"

"She's awake if you want to see her."

I smiled and went into their room, lifting my granddaughter from her crib. I rocked her in my arms and marveled at how tiny she was. I wondered if Casey had looked like this when she'd been born. Since Casey rarely said anything about the baby's father, I had no idea what he looked like. She'd not once mentioned what he looked like or his name. Of course, that was probably to keep him safe since she knew I was pissed at the little shit. If she ever wanted to talk to me about him, I'd listen. But I couldn't promise I wouldn't go rip his head off right afterward.

"Are you happy, Dad?" Casey asked.

"Yeah, honey. I am. Happiest I've ever been. Not taking away from what I had with your mom. There will always be a part of me that loves her, but you were right. She'd want me to be happy. I now have two daughters, a son, a precious granddaughter, and a woman to stand by me through all the ups and downs life throws our way."

"Good. Then I think Mom can rest in peace."

I hoped so. I thought Rebecca would have liked Solena if they'd had the chance to meet. The emptiness inside me was gone. My family had filled the space, and I couldn't wait to see what the future would hold for all of us.

Chapter Eleven

Solena

I hugged the toilet as I threw up what little I'd managed to eat for breakfast. This was the third morning in a row. Since the feeling always passed after lunch, I was almost certain I was pregnant. I didn't know how Atilla would take the news. It had been a little over three weeks since I'd moved in, and roughly a month since our first night together.

It hadn't happened in front of Atilla yet, so I'd been able to keep this secret. I didn't want to say anything until I knew for certain. Now that I lived with him, and we had two kids to take care of, he'd convinced me to quit my job at the diner. Which meant I was here all day, every day, except for taking the kids to and from school. They'd only started at the elementary school last week.

Both children were seeing a therapist. Nora seemed to open up more and didn't cling to Atilla quite so much. Santiago was actually speaking to me and would often give me a hug or hold my hand. They both had a way to go, but at least they'd improved a lot since coming home.

Someone knocked on the front door and I groaned, dreading the idea of getting up and walking that far. I stood and splashed some water on my face, then rinsed out my mouth. I really needed to brush my teeth, but whoever it was had already knocked twice more. If I didn't answer, someone would tell Atilla something was wrong at home, and he'd rush over here.

"I'm coming," I yelled out.

"I hope not," Casey yelled back. "That's TMI."

I snickered and opened the front door. She had

little Becca in her carrier, and a plastic sack from the pharmacy in her other hand.

"Come on in. I need to go brush my teeth."

"You might want to change your shirt too," Casey said. "You have a little something on the front."

I looked down and winced. It looked like I hadn't managed to get everything into the toilet after all. After I'd cleaned up, I found Casey in the living room. She tossed the sack to me, and I opened it, shaking my head when I saw the two boxes of pregnancy tests inside.

"I didn't know which one you'd prefer, so I got both brands. They're early response tests. I used them when I thought I was pregnant. They were positive and were clearly accurate since Becca is right here in front of us."

"Does anyone else know?" I asked.

"If you mean my dad, then no. Do you really think you'd be alone right now if he did? He'd have already taken you to the doctor, restricted your movements, and had someone watching you every second of the day for fear something bad might happen." She smiled sadly. "My mom died when she was still pregnant with me. They cut me out of her stomach after the accident."

When she put it that way, it made sense that Atilla would be overprotective if I was pregnant. He'd already bought me the top-of-the-line SUV with all the best safety ratings, so I'd have a reliable car for toting the kids around. He'd kept his as well, even though I didn't know why we needed two of them.

I carried the tests to the bathroom and used one stick from each box. Even though the instructions said it was better to take them first thing in the morning, I didn't want to wait. If they both said negative, then I'd use the other sticks in the morning when I first woke up. And if they were positive…

I capped the sticks and set them on the counter, washed my hands, and set a timer. I paced the bathroom while I waited, glancing at the tests every fifteen seconds. One had a digital display, and the other would have colored lines. Two meant pregnant. I squinted as one line formed. Did that mean it was probably negative?

The timer went off and I checked the digital one first. *Pregnant.* My breath caught in my lungs as I stared at that word. Glancing at the other test, I saw the second line had formed. Holy crap!

In a daze, I went back to the living room and sat down, pressing a hand to my belly. Casey reached over and patted my leg.

"If it's any consolation, I think Dad will be thrilled. He missed out on raising me as a baby. Both your kids are already seven and eight. The two of you are going to be great parents for this little one." Casey smiled. "When are you going to tell him?"

"I don't know. We promised the kids pizza after school today. Maybe once they're in bed?"

She nodded. "Good idea. I'm not sure how they'll take the news. They only gained a family three weeks ago. Everything is still so new for them, they may feel threatened by a baby."

"What do we do?" Panic welled inside me. I couldn't lose Santiago and Nora. What if they pulled away? What if Casey was right, and they hated the fact I was having a baby?

"First, I'm going to call my dad. I don't think you need to wait. Talk to him now so the two of you can figure this out together. Second, I'll pick the kids up from school."

I shook my head. "No, Casey. You're still exhausted from getting up all night with Becca. I can't ask you to do that."

"Then let one of the guys use your SUV. I'll ask Maui to pick up the kids and drop them at my house. They can have pizza there."

"Are you sure?" I asked.

"Positive. Now, sit tight. I'll go back home and call Dad and Maui."

"Thanks, Casey."

She leaned in to hug me before standing and picking up Becca's carrier. Casey left, and I stared into space. I didn't know how Atilla would react. We hadn't discussed having more children. He'd used a condom that first time, but since then he hadn't always remembered one. He hadn't gotten me pregnant on purpose, had he? No. That didn't seem like something he'd do. Things had been so hectic we hadn't really sat down to discuss the possibility of having a larger family. Neither of us had brought it up.

The front door opened, and Atilla hurried inside, kneeling in front of me. "Casey said you needed me. Is everything all right? Are you hurt?"

I reached out to cup his cheek. "I'm fine, just… rattled."

"What happened, Lena?"

"Bathroom. Go look on the counter." I couldn't say the words *I'm pregnant*. My brain was still processing it.

"Holy shit!" I would have laughed under other circumstances. I heard his boots bang against the floor as he rushed back to the living room. "You're pregnant?"

I nodded. I couldn't bring myself to look at him. Was he excited? Angry? My heart raced and my hands trembled. Atilla sat beside me, pulling me into his arms.

"I'm so fucking happy right now," he said.

"Really?" I looked up and saw the big smile on his face.

"Of course. Although, I think four kids is my limit. I'm going to go get snipped before this one is born."

"I wasn't sure how you'd react," I admitted. "Since we didn't always use protection, I briefly wondered if you'd done it on purpose. But seeing how shocked you were, I guess not."

"If this had happened a month ago, my reaction would have been different. I was still trying to keep my distance from you. If I'd found out our first night together had resulted in a baby, I'd have been equal parts pissed and scared. Right now, I'm just excited that we get to raise this one together. And no, I didn't do it on purpose. Can't say I'm sorry it happened, though."

"What about the kids?" I asked. "Casey said they might feel threatened."

He nodded. "It's true. They could think we're trying to replace them. I'll talk to the therapist before their next session. For now, I think we should keep this to ourselves. Since you said Casey was worried about the kids, I'm going to assume that means she already knows."

"She's the one who gave me the tests."

"I'll ask her not to tell anyone. After the children know, then we can share the news with everyone else."

I leaned into him. "Casey said she'd have Maui get the kids today and drop them at her place for pizza. So we have a little time together, unless you need to get back to work?"

"You have my undivided attention for the rest of the day," he said. "We can do whatever you want."

"Binge watch TV?" I asked.

"Which show?"

"*Supernatural*? I think it's still on Netflix."

He nodded and released me, standing up to get the remote. He tossed it onto the couch. "Go ahead and load it. I'm going to get you some crackers and ginger ale."

"How did you know I have morning sickness?"

I wiped a hand over my shirt. I hadn't thrown up again, so how had he known? Oh, no! Was my breath still stinky? Part of me dreaded his answer. What had I missed?

"Just a hunch. Unless you'd noticed your missed period, I couldn't think of another reason you'd take those tests."

Huh. I hadn't even thought about my period. Then again, it was never regular. Some months I'd have one three weeks apart. Other times, I could go six to eight weeks without one. It had been that way all my life.

I picked up the remote and found the show, starting at season one episode one, and pressed play when Atilla came back into the room. He handed me the glass of soda and the package of crackers, then toed off his boots and sat down, putting his feet up on the table. I curled into his side and nibbled on the crackers. They really did help.

Since the kids were eating after school, I knew they wouldn't want a big meal for dinner. I'd make some snacks for them later. Maybe grilled cheese sandwiches. Bile rose in my throat at the thought of making them, and I wondered if I could convince Atilla to cook if my stomach was still iffy by then. It hadn't been so far, but I knew that could change.

Atilla laced our fingers together. I knew he didn't particularly love this show, but I did… so he watched it with me. Until him, I'd never known a man could be so supportive or loving. He may not have ever said the words *I love you*, but he showed me how much he cared every single day. It was enough. Maybe for some women it wouldn't be. I knew people would say I was settling. They didn't realize how amazing Atilla was.

At night, when he thought I was asleep, he'd kiss my forehead and I'd hear him whisper to me: *thank you for being mine*. I didn't know why he couldn't say the words when I was awake. I hadn't exactly confessed my feelings for him either. Could he be waiting for me to make the first move? He'd lost Casey's mom. I knew he still had emotional scars from it. Anyone would.

At the risk of scaring him off, I knew I needed to tell him how I felt. It never seemed like the right time. What I knew for certain was that I'd regret not telling him if I lost my chance. If he left the house tomorrow and didn't come home, I'd wish I'd spoken up sooner.

"Atilla…"

"What is it, Lena? Feeling sick?"

"No. There's something I need to tell you." I shifted so I could see his face clearly. "I know we've only been together officially for three weeks, but it feels like I've known you much longer. Being with you makes me so incredibly happy."

"You make me happy too," he said.

"I love you. You don't have to say it back! But I felt like you needed to know."

He leaned in closer and softly brushed his lips against mine. "I love you too, Lena. There's no one more perfect for me. You came into my life, tearing down the walls I'd built around my heart, and before I realized it, you meant the world to me. I can't imagine living without you."

Tears slipped down my cheeks. I never thought I'd hear him say something like that. I threw my arms around him, hugging him tight.

I went from being alone to having this wonderful man by my side, and children I adored. While I didn't consider Casey my daughter because we were so close in age, I did think of her as a friend.

"Let's watch more of your show while the house is still quiet," he said. "Then you can visit with the kids, and I'll make dinner later."

"I was thinking about grilled cheese sandwiches since they're eating pizza right now."

He nodded. "Sounds good. And if you can't eat that, you let me know. Whatever you want, I'll get it for you."

I kissed him. "I'll hold you to that."

I cuddled against him again and we watched another episode of my show. He was right about one thing. The house *was* quiet. We were alone. How often would that happen, especially as our family grew? My nausea hadn't come back, and I thought it was gone until tomorrow.

"You're thinking awfully hard," he murmured. "What's wrong?"

"Nothing. I wondered if we should take advantage of having the house to ourselves," I said.

He shifted to face me. "Are you saying you want to head to the bedroom?"

"Well, I'm not exactly eager to have sex on the couch where our kids will sit to watch TV. Unless you plan to throw a blanket over it."

"I thought you weren't feeling well."

"I wasn't. I'm fine now, though." I ran my finger

down the center of his chest. "We have at least another hour or two before the kids come back."

"All right." He stood and helped me off the couch. Before I could take a single step, he swung me up into his arms and carried me to our bedroom. I loved when he did things like this. I smiled, feeling like a princess in a fairy tale.

Atilla eased me down onto the bed and slowly undressed me. Once I lay bare, he quickly stripped out of his clothes and leaned over me. He stared at me with such hunger it made me shiver. I'd never had anyone look at me the way he did.

"You're so incredibly beautiful," he murmured. "And mine. Every single inch of you belongs to me. Isn't that right?"

I didn't know what brought on this caveman act, but I liked it. I nodded my head, but it seemed he didn't accept my answer.

"Out loud, Lena. Tell me you're mine."

"I'm yours, Atilla. Only yours." I swallowed hard. "You're the only one I've ever belonged to."

"Damn right." He leaned in to kiss me, devouring my lips with his. When he drew back, he slid his hands down my thighs to my knees, then spread me open. Dropping to his knees beside the bed, he gently blew on my pussy.

"Atilla, I..."

"Hush." He tapped my pussy. "This is mine, right? Then let me enjoy it."

My heart raced in my chest. I wasn't sure what he got out of this, but I knew I would certainly be happy. He rubbed my clit and I felt pleasure start to hum inside me. He made me come twice before he put his mouth on me, his tongue lashing my clit before slipping inside me.

I fisted the bedding and fought for control. It felt so amazing I wanted to clamp my thighs around his head and hold him in place. He eased two fingers inside me, pumping them in and out. The next stroke across my clit had me screaming his name as my back arched off the bed. My legs trembled and I couldn't catch my breath.

"Please, Atilla. I need you inside me."

He rose to his feet and flipped me onto my stomach. I got onto my hands and knees as I felt the bed dip from his weight. He gripped my hips and tugged me back toward him. Thrusting against me, he slid his cock along the lips of my pussy, teasing me even more.

"You sure this is what you want?" he asked.

"Yes! Please… I need it."

"It? So any cock will do?" he asked.

"No." I groaned. "Just yours."

"Good answer." He pressed a kiss to the center of my back, then he slowly pushed inside me. His cock stretched me in the most delicious way. The way his shaft slid against my inner walls made me want to beg for more. He shifted his angle and hit just the right spot. With every stroke, I got closer to orgasm.

"Yes! There, right there." He hit the spot over and over, and I felt the gush of my release as I came.

Atilla tightened his hold on my hips and drove into me, taking me fast and hard. It didn't take long before I felt the heat of his cum filling me. He pressed against me, his cock jerking inside me.

"You're going to kill me with sex one day," he said. "But it will be one hell of a way to go."

"Don't even joke about dying." I glared at him over my shoulder. "You said I'm yours, but you're also mine… and I don't give you permission to leave this world anytime soon."

He smirked. "Yes, ma'am."

Oh, God. That did odd things to me. It felt like butterflies rioted in my stomach, and I knew I'd never love anyone as much as I loved him.

He pulled out and helped me stand. We took a shower together, and got dressed, then managed to watch another episode of my show before the kids came home. I helped Nora with her homework, while Atilla took Santiago outside to throw the ball. Our son liked baseball over the other sports so far, and we'd talked about finding him a team to join. We both thought it would be good for him.

I hoped we had many more nights like this one. We'd all found what was missing in our lives -- family.

Epilogue

Atilla
Four Months Later

I could hear the laughter in the living room and couldn't wait to rejoin my family. I'd already popped one bag of kettle corn, and I was waiting for a second one to finish. Once I'd poured both into a bowl, I grabbed the little plastic basket of drinks. On the nights Casey and Becca joined us, I'd found it easier to cart everything around at one time instead of making multiple trips to the kitchen.

Lena's ankles were swollen already, and she'd had a scare two weeks ago with some spotting. The doctor said she needed to take it easy, so I'd taken over most of the cooking and cleaning. Casey pitched in when she could, and even Meredith stopped by now and then with a casserole for dinner.

"Bottled water for everyone except me," I said, setting the basket down.

"Aww." Santiago pouted. "I wanted a soda."

"Not tonight. It's too close to bedtime," I said. "You can have one with lunch tomorrow."

"Yeah! No school tomorrow." Nora grinned. While she'd made a lot of progress, and even had friends at school, she still preferred being home with us. I didn't see that changing anytime soon.

"Dad, can you give Becca her bottle?" Casey asked, shoving her hand into the bowl of popcorn.

I held my hands out for my little granddaughter. At five months, she could roll over, get up on her hands and knees, and babbled at anyone who would listen. She rocked back and forth, and I held my breath, wondering if this would be the time she decided to crawl. Instead, she fell back to her belly.

I scooped Becca off the floor and took the bottle from Casey. Judging by the thickness, I knew this one had cereal mixed in. Little Becca had developed bad reflux, and this was the only way she could keep her food down. Once she'd reached a month old, Casey had switched her to formula at the doctor's recommendation. Since then, Becca had grown rapidly.

I held her in the crook of my arm and fed her while everyone laughed at the cartoon playing on the TV. Lena leaned against me and I smiled down at her. With her stomach starting to round, I found her more and more beautiful with every passing day. I couldn't wait for our family to expand.

"Mom, when can we find out if the baby is a boy or a girl?" Santiago asked.

I smirked, looking at my woman. We hadn't told anyone yet, but it seemed like tonight would be the perfect time.

"Actually, you're not getting a brother or sister," Lena said.

Casey snorted. "What is it? A puppy?"

"No, smartass," I muttered.

"It's one of each." Lena smiled. "We're having twins!"

"Are you kidding?" Casey's eyes went wide. "Where are you going to put them?"

"Nora and I can share a room," Santiago said.

"No. You're both going to be too old for that. You'll want your own space when you're teenagers." I burped Becca and handed her back to Casey, along with the empty bottle. "We're going to move."

"What?" Santiago looked stricken, and Nora reached over to grab his hand.

I'd known he wouldn't handle the news well. Both of them didn't need a lot of changes right now.

This was the first home they'd had that was a truly safe space for them. I could understand why they wouldn't want to give it up. And I knew Casey liked being across the street.

"We're just going to have a new house built down the street. You know the empty spot in the curve of the road?" I asked, nodding my head in the general direction I meant. "We'll put a house there for all of us."

"What about Casey?" Nora asked.

"Well... I thought she might like to move into this house." My oldest daughter's eyes misted with tears and she gave me a smile. A quick nod was all I needed from her. It was the best way I could think of to not only take care of her and Becca, but also ensure Santiago and Nora wouldn't feel like they'd lost this house. At least, not right now. If Casey settled down with someone later on, then things might change.

"I'll even keep a room for you," Casey said. "That way you can come spend the night whenever you want."

"You get to decorate your new rooms however you want," Lena said. "And you can help us decide on the layout of the new home. Your dad has a few sets of plans we can look at tomorrow."

"All right." Nora released Santiago's hand and went back to eating popcorn. It seemed that was good enough for her. Our son, on the other hand...

"You okay, Santi?" I asked.

"Yeah. But what happens if you have more babies?" he asked.

"The doctor said there's only two," Lena assured him.

"Not now. I meant later," he said.

"I'm going to make sure that doesn't happen."

And I would, right after our babies were born safely. I didn't want to get snipped before then, just in case anything went wrong. Especially after the spotting scare. If there was even a chance she could lose the babies, I'd hold off. Even though we hadn't planned for the twins, I didn't want to rob Lena of the opportunity to have more children if that's what she wanted. "The five of you are more than enough for us."

The kids went back to watching the movie. I felt Lena lean into me a little more and realized she'd fallen asleep. She did that frequently these days, just nodded off out of the blue. As for me, I watched Casey and little Becca. I couldn't have been prouder of my family. I had an amazing woman who wrangled the kids like a pro, a daughter who was doing an incredible job raising her baby, and two little kids who surprised me every day with the things they learned.

It was my hope that one day every brother in my club would know this sort of happiness. Even the ones who didn't seem eager to go find a woman would eventually fall for someone. I'd already scaled back on a lot of the shit the club had been involved in over the last few years. We'd also started several legit businesses around town, and I planned to open even more.

The Savage Raptors had been my family for a long time. I loved my brothers and wanted the best for each of them. Just like the family sitting in the living room with me... I only wanted good things for them.

We'd all had a rocky start, but every day was better than the last.

"Love you," I said to all the kids.

Casey smiled. "We love you too, Dad."

Santiago nodded, and little Nora came running.

She climbed onto my lap, and I hugged her tight.

If every night was like this one, then I'd die a happy man... because I'd found exactly what I'd been looking for.

Harley Wylde

Harley Wylde is the International Bestselling Author of MC Romances. When Harley's writing, her motto is the hotter the better -- off-the-charts sex, commanding men, and the women who can't deny them. If you want men who talk dirty, are sexy as hell, and take what they want, then you've come to the right place. She doesn't shy away from the dangers and nastiness in the world, bringing those realities to the pages of her books, but always gives her characters a happily-ever-after and makes sure the bad guys get what they deserve.

The times Harley isn't writing, she's thinking up naughty things to do to her husband, drinking copious amounts of Starbucks, and reading. She loves to read and devours a book a day, sometimes more. She's also fond of TV shows and movies from the 1980s, as well as paranormal shows from the 1990s to today, even though she'd much rather be reading or writing. You can find out more about Harley or enter her monthly giveaway on her website. Be sure to join her newsletter while you're there to learn more about discounts, signing events, and other goodies!

Harley at Changeling: changelingpress.com/harley-wylde-a-196

Changeling Press E-Books

More Sci-Fi, Fantasy, Paranormal, and BDSM adventures available in e-book format for immediate download at ChangelingPress.com -- Werewolves, Vampires, Dragons, Shapeshifters and more -- Erotic Tales from the edge of your imagination.

What are E-Books?

E-books, or electronic books, are books designed to be read in digital format -- on your desktop or laptop computer, notebook, tablet, Smart Phone, or any electronic e-book reader.

Where can I get Changeling Press E-Books?

Changeling Press e-books are available at ChangelingPress.com, Amazon, Apple Books, Barnes & Noble, and Kobo/Walmart.

Changeling Press, LLC

ChangelingPress.com